# MARKED BY THE MOON

## BOUND BY THE VEIL
### BOOK ONE

HELEN SCOTT

Marked by the Moon
Bound by the Veil Book One
Copyright © 2023 by Helen Scott
Cover Design © Moonpress Cover Design

# MAP OF EAORIN

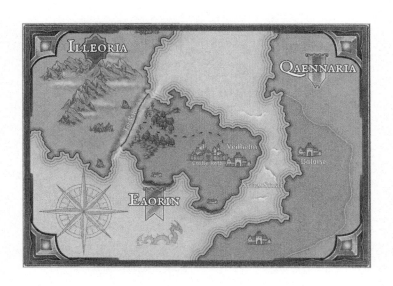

# CHAPTER
# ONE

Senara

I hurried along the rain-slicked cobblestone streets, eager to see my best friend for the first time in years. Letters had gone back and forth over the years I'd been away, but when I found out I was being recalled, we decided to meet at the square in Low Town at sunset. Still, I didn't want to be late and make her worry.

When my gaze caught on a patch of red hair gleaming in the setting sunlight, I knew that she was already there, waiting for me. "Wyn!" I shouted as I barreled toward her.

It had been too long. She looked older, more mature, than the version of the woman I thought of as my sister was in my head. Then she smiled, and the young girl was there again. "Senara!" Wyn squealed with glee.

We ran toward each other, clashing and nearly falling to the ground as we hugged. "Watch it!" someone yelled when we almost toppled into them from overcorrecting.

Wyn giggled, which made me laugh in turn, and the older man we'd almost collided with grumbled under his breath. "Sorry!" I called out as he shuffled away.

"So how are you? How was the trip?" Wyn asked as she pulled back from our hug.

I sighed happily. "I'm good, at least now I'm with my sister. The trip could have been better, you know me and the sea don't get along." I silently wished that had been the only issue.

"You weren't sick the whole time, though, were you?" Her brows pinched, and her dark eyes studied me with worry filling them.

I shrugged and slung my arm around her shoulder, and we started walking. "Come on, let's get to the Kraken."

Wyn paused, making me turn to look at her. When I saw her chewing on her lower lip, I knew she had a favor to ask, it was her tell that something was on her mind. "Actually, since this is the one night I've got off for a while, can we stop by the market?" She looked at me knowingly, and I realized that it wasn't just any market she wanted to go to.

I stepped closer, so no one could overhear us. "I'm a member of the King's Guard as of tomorrow. I can't go to the underground markets!" I muttered.

"Please? I just need two things from one place. It'll be quick. In and out. No one will ever know." She sighed heavily, looking up at me through her lashes like a stray pup as she clasped her hands together in front of her chest. "You know I wouldn't ask if it wasn't urgent." When I still hesitated, she added, "Pleasepleasepleasepleaseplease—"

"Okay, fine!" I shoved my fear of being caught at the underground market to the side. We both knew that if we were caught, I'd be dead. There were no ifs, ands, or buts about it. As soon as they realized I was Moon Marked, I'd be heading to the execution block. "We have to be fast, though. I told Grimsby we would be there for dinner in my letter."

"So fast!" She giggled as she nodded, linking her arm with mine before we set off in the direction of the market. As we wound through the alleys, my gaze darted around, looking for guards or anyone suspicious in general. After a moment, Wyn said, "Tell me about the front."

Her words made me stumble. The front was screams and sacrifice and nothing but the fight and the kill. Rarely, it was relaxing with my fellow soldiers, but for the most part we were always on alert, preparing for the next attack.

I only replied once I caught myself and we were walking again. "I'd rather not. The front was war and death. I'm trying to focus on what's coming with the new job tomorrow. Being a King's Guard is not where I expected my military career to go, but it'll be good. For one thing, it's an increase in pay and there's the food and lodging at the castle, like with you working at the library."

"Except I only get paid a pittance," she grumbled.

"True. The money is for both of us, though. You know that." I bumped my shoulder against hers.

A huff escaped her before she said, "I wish the King valued books as much as he valued swords. Then maybe we wouldn't be at war all the time."

"By the stars, Wyn. Watch what you're saying," I hissed.

The King wasn't known for his tolerance. Magic itself was illegal, as was bearing its mark–it didn't matter that we were born with it. Speaking badly of the King or questioning him was just as deadly as magic. The way he saw it, he was our ruler, one appointed by the new gods, and what he decided was the law of the land was expected to be followed.

She stopped in front of a different door than we used to use, but the knock was similar. Two fast, pause, two slow. Barely a few seconds passed before the door cracked open and a figure inside eyeballed us.

"We're here to see Madam Nightshade, if she's available?" Wyn sounded so normal and carefree that it was hard to believe this was the entrance to a market that traded in magical goods.

The figure on the other side of the door grunted and opened the door wider. The evening light hit them, and I realized that the man was much older than I originally thought, with scraggly hair that hung in limp clumps from his balding head. Too large eyes watched us as we walked in and quickly shut the door behind us.

We stepped further in and were met with a lovely sitting room area that was quite nice for this area of town. It was covered in vases of dried flowers, which I thought was a little odd, but had luxurious seating and velvet drapes covering the windows. Wyn seemed to know exactly where she was going, though, because she didn't pause in the sitting room like I would have. Instead, she carried on through a kitchen and opened another door that led to a cellar of some kind.

At the bottom of the stairs was a set of shelves that Wyn pushed to the side with surprising ease. As soon as she did, the bustle of the market that lay beyond became obvious. Voices carried, and laughter and faint music reached my ears. Oh, yes, the underground magic market in Veilhelm was alive and well. Thriving, in truth.

That didn't mean I was comfortable being there, though.

I meandered behind Wyn as she searched for a specific stall. There were so many options to choose from that it was hard to believe the city guards weren't aware of the place. Spices laced the air along with scents I couldn't name, and the feeling of magic pulsed along my skin, making me jumpy.

"There!" Wyn called over her shoulder before heading off.

By the time I caught up with her through the crowd, she was paying for her items and shoving them in her bag. She hadn't been lying when she said she'd be quick, but it still wasn't fast enough for me to feel comfortable.

As though the fates wanted to prove me right, shouts came

from the other side of the market. The shouts quickly morphed into pained screams, ones that heralded death in an all too familiar way.

"We need to go. Now!" I called to Wyn, grabbing her by the arm and trying to pull her back the way we came.

When she didn't move, I looked over my shoulder and saw her pulling the hood of her cape up before saying, "This way. There's another secret entrance that's closer."

The shouts and screams were getting closer. "By order of the king, stay where you are!" A voice boomed out over the room.

No one listened—why would they? Staying where they were was certain death. At least if they made a run for it, they stood a chance of getting away. Which was exactly what I was doing with Wyn now. Everyone was trying to get to an exit, though, so the walkways were quickly growing congested.

Suddenly, the crowd surged forward and we followed, spilling out into the street as the screams came from right behind us. The city guard cut people down where they stood. We were just fortunate they didn't have any archers with them.

As soon as daylight hit my face, I took off with Wyn, running flat out. I spun us around a corner, dragging her with me, and navigating my way through the city the way I used to when I was a kid on the run for stealing a crust of bread. Taking as many twists and turns as possible had always been my key to avoiding the guards, that and finding somewhere to hide until they gave up searching, which usually didn't take long.

When I saw a few barrels next to a pile of hay that had been set aside for a few pigs, I pulled Wyn after me. "Hide there." She did as I commanded without question, just like always. I was the one who kept us safe when we were growing up.

The two of us crouched silently behind the barrels, using the hay as a shield, well aware that we could be discovered any second. I silently pulled a dagger from my pack, praying to the old gods that I wouldn't have to use it. It didn't matter what I'd been through–that I'd almost met the old gods more times than I cared to count with my battalion–none of the other soldiers I'd fought with would ever know me like Wyn did, and that was exactly why I'd do whatever it took to protect her. Even if that meant taking a life.

Wyn's hand covered her mouth as she tried to breathe quietly and not gasp for breath. I froze as footsteps echoed off the cobblestones coming toward us. My fingers tightened around the hilt of my dagger, waiting to see if I needed to use it.

The snort of a pig from the pen close by was the only sound, and soon enough, the footsteps retreated. My heart finally seemed to start beating again as I relaxed slightly. Wyn started to move, but I shook my head. The guards might be standing closeby to see if they could figure out where we'd gone or something similar.

We squatted behind the barrels until my thighs burned, and then stayed there a little longer. Finally, when I was confident that no one would have waited around that long, I eased to the side to peek around the barrel and make sure the coast was clear.

No one was around, so I pushed to my feet, my knees objecting after being locked in the same position for who knows how long. I offered my hand to Wyn, pulling her to her feet next to me before I sheathed my dagger. Once she was on her feet I spent a moment pulling my leather uniform straight and making sure everything in my pack was still there.

We cautiously made our way out of the back alley we'd huddled in and toward a more main thoroughfare. When I was confident that no one suspected us as being on the run from the underground market, I turned and quietly asked Wyn, "Do raids like that happen often?"

She shook her head. "I've only seen one other since you left. Each time, the market has to move. It'll take months until it's up and running again."

I wished I could say I was sorry to hear it, but at least I knew it would be months before Wyn could put herself in danger like that again. "Come on, let's get to the Kraken. Grimsby is probably waiting and worried."

A grin broke across her face, and I knew she'd thought I was going to scold her for going to the market at all. I still wanted to talk to her about it, but I was too exhausted to process whatever she might tell me. I needed some food first. "I hope he's made stew," she murmured as she absent-mindedly rubbed her stomach.

"Don't you get fed at the castle?" I asked, half joking.

"Of course, but it's not the same. You know I love Grims' cooking." She ran her tongue over her lips in a way that reminded me of her as a young girl looking at a crust of bread as though it was a seven course meal of the highest decadence. To be fair, we often both looked at it that way, but she was much more expressive with her gestures than I was. I wondered if that was because she hadn't grown up with a mark on her skin indicating that she was a magic user.

I never liked having too much attention on me. I was too scared that someone would somehow figure out what I was, even though my mark was on my back and always covered by my clothes. Even though I couldn't actually do anything magical.

"I still feel bad that I can't let you stay with me," she said quietly. "If you were found in my room, it would cause trouble for us both. I'm sorry."

"Wyn," I said as I pulled her to a stop to look at her, hoping my words sunk in. "The last thing I want is to cause you trouble, and you know Grims will give me a room. Besides, I already wrote and asked him to hold one for me." It wasn't like his rooms were in high demand, and there were only a couple of them anyway. Most of the patrons were local and preferred to stumble home after their evening libations rather than pay for a bed that they'd have to climb stairs to get to.

As we rounded the corner, Grimsby's tavern, The Red Kraken, finally came into view. I couldn't help but quicken my step. Grimsby was one of the few people from my past who I could look back on with fondness.

Growing up, most people had treated me like a parasite, a thief, and a beggar, but Grimsby had provided me and Wyn with food on multiple occasions. Of course, he'd make excuses about something or another going bad and preferring that someone eat it than waste it. Plus, if I offered, he always liked to have help around the tavern in return. I never minded putting in the hard work, and I certainly didn't expect handouts from a man like Grimsby—gruff and stern, but fair and kind. He wasn't one for affection, but somehow I'd always felt that he cared.

"Hey, watch it!" A tall, older man snarled in my direction when I accidentally bumped into his side.

The people who lived near the tavern were typically grouchy and willing to vent their unhappiness on whoever or whatever had wronged them in the moment. I couldn't blame them since they worked harder than anyone else in the kingdom, and they did it for less than those the King elevated to his employ at the castle.

These were the bakers and the blacksmiths, the king's people who benefited not at all from being his people. Instead, they were tired and stressed, with duties and responsibilities that offered them no riches or rewards but were expected of them nonetheless.

Wyn and I came to a complete stop, and I nodded to allow

another man to pass in front of us, not wanting to get yelled at yet again and draw more attention to us after the shenanigans at the market. The lull gave me time to take in the old building in front of me.

It definitely wasn't a castle or a tent on the frontlines, but it was something almost like home to me. The stone and timber walls of the tavern looked older and more weathered than I remembered, but that was to be expected. There weren't too many people inside right now, judging by the lack of noise, but night hadn't fully fallen yet, which was when things always picked up.

This place had been as much of a shelter and home as I'd had for a lot of my life. It was strange coming back to it as an adult, one who'd both seen and done things I never would have thought possible as a child.

A warm glow emanated from the windows, beckoning me forward, and I could almost smell the stew that Grimsby always used to make for us. Whether he'd admit it or not, Grimsby worried about Wyn and me. We would go in calmly, like we hadn't almost been captured and killed by the city guard less than an hour ago. Like I wasn't ridiculously excited to see him.

When I pushed the heavy wood door open and walked in, I got a few curious stares from the people already in the tavern, though nothing overly watchful. Grimsby was just as I expected him to be. He'd been the owner and operator of The Red Kraken from its beginning.

He was a proud man, one who had a good heart, even if it took some work to see that sometimes. He wasn't one to talk much, or be expressive in general, yet he seemed to have a soft spot for me. I, in turn, had one for him.

When the door banged shut behind us as we walked in, he looked up from his spot behind a work table laden with plates and bowls waiting to be served and smiled. Actually smiled. Which was a small miracle in and of itself.

His gray hair was thinner than it had been the last time I saw him and was pulled back into a low ponytail. The beard that used to be down to his chest had been trimmed to just a couple of fingers below his chin.

"Well, there she is." His gray-blue eyes twinkled with mirth as he walked toward me, drying his hands on an apron that was tied around his waist and bore the stains of the evening's meals and ale. Once he was close, he stretched his arms out to me as he attempted an awkward hug. We'd never really been huggers, so the gesture meant a lot. He was truly happy to see me and was making an effort to show me just that. As I wrapped my arms around him, he felt so much smaller than when he'd hugged me goodbye. "I'm glad to see you're still alive. Always knew you were too stubborn to die out there. Besides, I've been saving barrels for you to move before you leave in the morning, as promised."

Knowing that Grimsby would have a room for me if I asked, I'd written a letter ahead of my arrival, promising to move all the ale barrels he needed in return for lodging. I didn't exactly get paid outside of the food, clothes, and housing the army provided, so I didn't have much else I could offer him. It didn't hurt that he wasn't one to readily ask for help, so me offering to move things was the best I could do for both of us, and I knew he had a hard time moving the barrels himself these days. He wasn't the young man he'd once been.

A laugh escaped my throat as a smile cracked my face for what felt like the first time in ages. "It's good to see you, as well, Grimsby. Thanks for saving a room for me." I looked around the main area of the tavern. "Where are the barrels, anyway?"

Grimsby pointed to a stack of them in the back corner, close to the rear entrance. "As long as you get them moved before you leave in the morning, we'll be even." He handed me my room key, avoiding eye contact. I suspected if he looked up, there would be a tear in his, and he was too proud to let me see it.

"No problem," I assured him. "I should be able to get them taken care of before then." I certainly would. It didn't matter if I had to get up before dawn to get it done. Nothing would stop me from repaying this man as much as I could for all the kindness he'd shown me over the years.

Grimsby nodded and finally looked past me to Wyn. "How are you doing, little one? It's been a while."

"I'm not so little anymore, Grims, now am I?" Wyn smiled up at him. But then he'd always called her *little girl,* and she'd always had an answer.

"I bet a week's profit"—still not much by any standard—"you two are hungry."

Poor Grimsby. He had such a hard exterior, but he never thought much about himself. Whenever Wyn and I were around, he put our needs before anyone else's. There must've been at least two other tables waiting to place an order, but he focused on the two of us.

"You know me, Grims. I never mind a bite to eat." Wyn grinned at me. "How about you, Senara? You hungry?"

"Of course she is. Got stew today. And pork belly. I'll bring something over in a few minutes." Grimsby interrupted, not much need for me to speak for myself with him around. The man could read me as well as any parent could with a child, even though we weren't related in the slightest. It didn't hurt that I was so ravenous my stomach growled loudly at the idea of food, which made him chuckle.

He turned and made his way back to the bar, leaving me with a feeling of warmth in my chest. There were few people left in the world who would help me as he did, and I would be forever grateful for it. Taking a deep breath, I clutched the room key. "I'm going to go and get cleaned up. I'll be right back down. Will you get us a table?"

Wyn gave me a smile and a firm nod. Tonight was my single night of freedom before I started down a new path, one that might keep me away from this part of town for a long time.

Honestly, I had no idea when I'd be able to see Grimsby again, and it was only a vague hope that I'd still be able to see Wyn since we would both be working at Castle Roth. It wasn't a guarantee. Tonight I was determined to enjoy myself and spend time with my sister, no matter what.

# CHAPTER
# TWO

S enara

My legs ached as I climbed the stairs, the sudden burst of action after not being able to move much while we were at sea left my muscles reeling. I was at the Red Kraken though, I'd made it. Finally. Now all I had to do was clean up so I didn't stink of pig shit anymore.

At the top of the stairs there were two rooms, one was the one I was staying in and the other was more of a storage room, but could be used as a bedroom if needed. With sure movements I inserted the old iron key into the lock and turned, listening to the mechanism clunk as it turned over. The door swung open a moment later revealing the inside.

The room was just as I remembered it with a small bed parallel to the window on the right, a chest for storing personal items at the end of the bed, and a small three-legged wooden table with one wobbly chair that were both pushed up against the wall opposite the window. There wasn't much room to move between the furniture and the walls, especially since the door opened inward. It barely cleared the bed, the material of the blanket catching a little on the rough wood, and it always hit the table if it swung too hard.

This wasn't the height of luxury or anything that could be considered palatial, certainly not something people were lined up to rent, but it was a whole lot better than the tent I'd been sleeping in on the front. Plus, it was warm with a small hearth in the wall opposite the door, and it was a somewhat safe place to sleep. I couldn't have asked for more.

I took a deep breath, and even the smell brought back memories of staying at the Red Kraken when I was younger. The air was musty thanks to a leaky roof, and the scent combined with a splash of stale ale, made me feel like I was a teenager again, grateful for a roof over my head and food in my belly.

Grimsby let Wyn and I stay for free on a couple of occasions where we probably would have frozen to death otherwise. I couldn't help but smile at the ridiculousness of it. Most people felt nostalgia when they smelled fresh bread baking or the scent of their mother's hair. Me? I found solace in the gritty aroma of a lower-class tavern..

As much as I might hate to admit it, this was the only place I'd ever felt safe.

I quickly stripped off my leather armor and spotted a pitcher of water and an empty bowl Grimsby must've left for me on the table. I dipped a finger into the liquid. The water was ice cold, but I didn't dare complain, especially when I saw the small bar of soap sitting next to it as well. Grimsby had gone to an unexpected length for me and I was grateful. Cold or not.

After a brief mental pep talk, I scooped up a handful of the frigid water from the bowl and washed my face, followed by my underarms and other hard-to-reach areas. It wasn't rose scented water like the women who lived in the castle, and it certainly wasn't perfect, but it made me cleaner than I was, so it would have to do.

I eyed the chest. There was nothing special about it. I was just a simple wooden box with a lock, small and probably easily broken if the intent was strong enough, and by that I meant, moderately strong. It certainly wouldn't do to protect my belongings. The last thing I wanted was someone stealing my armor and having to turn up at the barracks with nothing except what I'd worn the night before.

I couldn't help but feel a little bubble of excitement as I thought about my new job. Being one of the king's greatest warriors, protecting the innocent...It had been one of the dreams that kept me alive on the nights where I wanted to give up, where I was ready to let anyone find out the truth about me just so I didn't have to struggle anymore.

Now though? I was getting recognized as one of the most talented warriors the king had, I just hadn't expected that to mean coming back to Veilhelm and the castle. The anticipation of what being a king's guard might entail was enough to make me giddy in a way I didn't usually get.

Imagining long days patrolling the city, protecting its citizens from danger and injustice kicked up my strong sense of pride. I could be useful. Actually help people.

From what little I could remember about the King's Guard, I'd have a shiny, gold uniform waiting for me and maybe a sword, but that was about it. When I was a starving child, the King's Guard and by extension the City Guard had meant death, so I was always more concerned about running away from them as a kid. As far as I could remember, though, I'd never gotten a good look at their armor.

Being trained as a soldier rather than one of the king's personal guards had kept me separated from the castle, so I wasn't exactly sure what I was in for. I certainly had no idea what it looked like inside the walls.

Remembering the men who'd eyed me as I'd made my way upstairs gave me pause. It was possible that they were staring at me because I was a young woman in a tavern like this. Also as likely that they had spotted my valuable weaponry and were plotting and planning their means of theft.

No matter their true reasons for staring, I couldn't take any chances. I quickly placed my less expensive items—a dagger, a pouch with two coins and a button in the chest and locked it, then shoved my armor and weapons under the bed and wedged them up to the frame so if someone simply looked, my things couldn't be easily seen.

I pulled the only other clothes I had out of my pack, ones I'd refused to wear on the ship so they didn't end up stinking. A chemise and corset-like top were combined with my other pair of leggings and boots.

The sleeves of my outer top came to a point over my middle knuckle with a loop that slipped over my finger and allowed me to hold a sword without the flappy material getting in the way. Although the corset looked feminine enough, the boning within and leather belt I put on top provided an extra layer of protection over my stomach. It wasn't chainmail or a breastplate, but if I couldn't fend off one of the drunken tavern goers then I deserved any injuries I got. At least my boots, which were tall enough to come to my knees, looked feminine without the armor that usually accompanied them.

Pulling one side of my long, brown hair back into its typical side braid, I left the rest loose, letting the waves fall down over my back. Wearing my hair like that helped me feel like I had an extra layer of protection over my back. My long braids and waves helped me hide what felt like it was always on display, even though I was paranoid about my back and neck being covered. It was partially why I liked this top. Even though it had a corset-like bodice, the material came up and became sleeves, and there was even a high, ruffled collar at the back of my neck. I never liked wearing my hair up completely since it felt like my mark could be discovered at any moment, but I needed the hair out of my face in the event of a fight.

Not that I expected one, but if the army taught me anything, it was to always be ready to fight.

I looked down at my full body and wondered if I was what a man might consider attractive at all. I'd spent my adult life as though consumed by the idea of being strong, resilient, and independent. Looking fierce had kept me safe up to this point.

But even in my armor, I stood out against the many uniformed guards as being somewhat feminine. My height was one of the main reasons and my curves were another. I couldn't help it. There was only so much I could do to hide who I was.

I would never be viewed like the others, and it wasn't that I cared. But suddenly, the thought of meeting a whole slew of new people who knew next to nothing about me made me want to know. Before, I'd never seen myself as an attractive female. I had gone from a skinny runt, just trying to survive on the streets, to a strong warrior who scared children when they passed me. Not much feminine was left about me. Not that I took advantage of, anyway.

Without letting myself dwell anymore I turned and left the room, locking up before I raced down the stairs. I couldn't wait to actually talk to Wyn for more than a few minutes, plus I wanted to find out what she'd needed at the market so badly that she was willing to risk her life. I was busy imagining how much fun she and I would have catching up on each other's lives. I was so lost in thought that I didn't see a large object in front of me and slammed right into it.

I was never caught unaware like that, even if I was lost in thought, so who was this that they snuck past my senses?

# THREE

S enara
My free hand clenched against the chest of the massive person I'd slammed into and a jolt of... something ran through my body. Maybe awareness. Maybe...attraction? Either way it was shocking in the intensity of it.

Every inch of my body raged with a desire to stay close, an urge I knew I should fight off, but reveled in for a moment instead. Finally, I shook my head, the sudden realization of what I was doing burning through me.

Stepping backward, I looked up into the eye and eye patch of a man who stared down at me with an equal amount of amusement and curiosity. At least I thought so. *Hoped* so. I blinked, forcing my gaze away, not wanting him to think I was staring at the burn mark that peeked out from around the edge of the eye patch. I wondered at my reaction to him and how I was supposed to react to such a large man whose arms hadn't yet released me. One hand still wrapped around my wrist holding me there almost like a child with a doll.

I opened my mouth to speak then snapped it shut because I had no words. And had no idea what to do. My body was sending every signal it could all at once. Run away. Get closer. Smell him. Scream at him. Cower from him like a mouse. The list went on.

He waited for me to make up my mind as to which direction I wanted to go, releasing me in the process. My glance was brief, but it hadn't taken me long to realize how handsome he was, despite the painful looking scar over his eye and the large hood of his cloak which was covering his head so I couldn't see more over his eyes than forehead and fabric.

The patch covering his bad eye only drew attention to his sharp facial features. A strong jawline was dusted with scruff that was a day or two old, highlighting full lips. When he tilted his head, strands of long, wavy black hair shifted free from the material surrounding him, reminding me that he was watching me as I just stared at him. As though that wasn't enough he was also muscular and extremely tall, the type of man who possessed the immediate power to intimidate anyone who met him.

"I-I, I'm so sorry." I tripped over my words. "Please excuse me."

Then, like I'd caught fire and needed to find a pail of water with some speed, I darted clumsily away from the man. I could feel his gaze, staring a hole through the back of my head. I had no idea who he was or why he'd had such a strong effect on me, and I was curious, but not so much that I would delay dinner with Wyn. Not any more than I already had, anyway.

As I moved between tables, trying to put as much distance between myself and the stranger as possible, someone grabbed me from behind, interrupting my inner thoughts. I jerked away, twisting out of the attacker's grasp, reaching for a tiny but razor sharp dagger I hid in my boots.

"Whoa, there, sister." Wyn smiled and hugged my neck. "No need in fighting just yet. I just wanted to show you the table I got."

Relief washed over me as I embraced Wyn. I must have still been a little wound up from everything that happened at the market, but then why didn't I sense the stranger before I ran into him?

"Come on." Wyn smiled and jerked her head in the direction of the table. As she wove through the other tables she smoothed her long, red hair which was currently tied in a knot on the top of her head. She preferred to keep it up so that it didn't get in the way of the books she sorted and cataloged for the Royal Library. Some of it had come loose while we were running away so she must have retied it while I was upstairs.

I waved my hand through the air, letting Grimsby know that we were ready for our ale. He nodded and as he turned away I saw a smile quirk his lips once more. The man was going soft in his old age.

Wyn laughed. "For someone who ran a few miles, you certainly look well put together. Is there anyone you're trying to impress? Perhaps that brooding gentleman in the corner?"

"We hardly ran miles, but I did have to run from the harbor to meet you. And who would I have to impress when I haven't been in the city for longer than a couple of hours?" I arched an eyebrow at her as we both relaxed into our seats.

"I don't know, but I don't think I've ever seen you blush as hard as you were when you were running away from your friend in the corner." Wyn chuckled.

I carefully glanced over my shoulder to see the dark, tall stranger I'd run into. Once again I was struck by how handsome he was. Even with an eye patch. I wrenched my gaze away from him, not wanting to get caught staring any longer than I already had.

He sat alone in a dark alcove of the tavern, staring in my direction, a grin twisting his lips. How odd. It wasn't the staring that bothered me though since he was probably still as confused about what happened as I was. What bothered me was that he was alone when most people came to a tavern for company. The man seemed completely unaffected by his solitude. Possibly, it was more smirk than smile on his face, but the candle glow was too dim for me to be able to decide.

I wondered if perhaps he'd come looking for a companion for the night. My mind began to wander off into a daydream where I imagined what he might want to do with a temporary lover and if I could be such a partner. It had been a long time since I'd scratched that particular itch, and I couldn't deny that the idea was appealing.

Shaking my head, I focused my attention back on Wyn. "How's your post at the library coming along?"

Before she could answer, Grimbsy appeared with two large wood mugs of ale. "She already had a pint of ale while you were primping yourself," he grumbled as he watched Wyn. For a second he frowned as though he was actually concerned that she'd already downed one pint, but he couldn't keep the act up and a smile spread across his face. He was a gruff, old codger but he had a heart of gold.

He placed our drinks on the table and patted Wyn gently on the shoulder. "Forgot how much you can drink, little girl."

"I'm not so little anymore, Grims, now am I? And I can still hold my ale just fine, thank you." Wyn took a sip of her ale and smiled up at him. But then he'd always called her *little girl* and she'd always had an answer.

"Let me get the food for you," he said before turning and snaking his way back between the tables. Surprisingly agile for an old man.

The motion of the sea had left me in such a horrible state that I'd barely eaten anything for days. Now that I was back on solid ground, my stomach had settled, and sitting here, I could smell something divine, making me realize how much my body desired food and I couldn't wait to dive in to whatever Grimsby brought us.

21

"Now," I continued and smiled at her because I'd missed her so much, "tell me about that fancy job of yours."

Wyn smiled and leaned forward, her eyes bright and twinkling, obviously excited to tell me all about her position at the castle. "If I don't think about the lack of pay, then I love it. I still have to pinch myself every morning. I wake up in a warm room and then spend my days surrounded by manuscript after manuscript. If I want to read ancient scrolls, they're right at my fingertips." She was positively gushing. "It's like a dream." Wyn paused and took another sip of ale. "And to think that I used to steal books to have access to them."

"How times have changed." I reached across the table and squeezed her hand. "You look well. By the stars I'm glad to know that you're enjoying your work. I know we didn't write each other much, but I was worried about you."

Even though we were no longer kids, I still fretted over Wyn. She was so passionate about her work, and I wanted to make sure she stayed safe and healthy. The job at the castle library was a step in that direction. Was it dangerous? Of course. She was a magic user, and as such was considered an enemy of the Eaorin Kingdom. When I'd left for the front she'd promised me she'd only use it when absolutely necessary, but I also knew her and the more comfortable she got the more magic she was going to use.

I knew she'd gone through a lot of hardships as a child, and it made me anxious that all of that might repeat itself in one form or another. It was why I'd worked so hard to get her considered for a library apprenticeship. As dangerous as it was, it got her out of the streets and kept her relatively safe. Even after all these years, I still felt a duty to protect her.

"Let's just hope the good fortune lasts." Wyn grinned before finishing off her ale, but it was tinged with sadness, one that made me uneasy. This wasn't the time or place to ask about such things though, not with so many ears potentially listening. "But for now, we should enjoy this moment and celebrate the two of us finally getting all the things we deserve."

Grimsby returned sooner than we expected and plopped two plates onto the table. My mouth watered as I breathed in the aroma of smoked chicken and roasted potatoes. "Thought you had pork belly and stew."

He gave me a quick wink. "I do." He was a masterful cook. When Wyn and I were much younger, we'd ask him for specific foods and he would refuse to cook them. "You need meat and potatoes to stick to your scrawny bones." And so, many years later, he still insisted on us eating the same type of meal, using the same line as well.

"This smells delicious." I smiled up at Grimsby. "Thank you."

He huffed, probably not wanting to show too much emotion and get labeled as a softie by the regulars. "You can thank me by getting those barrels moved before you leave tomorrow. There's more of them there than you think."

I saluted him with two fingers. "You've got it, sir."

Grimsby turned, slid away from the table, but not before I caught a twinkle in his eyes. I knew he'd made this just for us. No one else was getting chicken tonight, just the stew.

We both dug into our food, hardly coming up for air. There was something about growing up, not knowing when you'd eat again, that made a person eat quickly. There wasn't time to savor. Sometimes, not even time to taste.

I was typically the first soldier to finish eating when on assignment, which always left the other soldiers staring in disbelief. The skill came in handy when we were in the middle of a conflict and had only a minute or two to eat.

"So, Senara, how was the front?" Wyn wiped her mouth with the back of her hand and took a long gulp of the fresh ale Grimsby had dropped off at the table shortly after the food.

She smiled a little drunkenly. "I'm sure you're glad to be back at the capitol. I can't believe you're going to be a King's Guard as of tomorrow. Are you excited?"

I shook my head, twirling my fork around before I licked it clean. "I am. It's a high honor, especially for a female, but I don't want to talk about the front or where I'm going tomorrow. I just want to be free for one night." Was that too much to ask? I knew she was curious but I really hoped she'd let it go for the rest of the night.

With starting my new post the next day I had no idea when I'd be able to relax like this again. The idea made me want to be reckless, act as though my new job was never going to start, but I couldn't afford to do that, at least not as much as I wanted to. I could have a good night with Wyn though, I just hoped that I didn't bring her down in the process. She seemed so happy and there I was just a ball of nerves.

What would being a member of the King's Guard mean and would I even enjoy it? I had no idea and I didn't want to think about those questions. All I wanted was to drink ale with my favorite person in my favorite place. Everything else could wait.

CHAPTER

# FOUR

S enara
As the night wore on, the crowd grew larger and some of the men became a little too rowdy–friendlier than I liked. Sloppier, too. The table behind us was so loud I couldn't hold a conversation with Wyn. We couldn't hear our own voices over them, much less each other. But we could hear theirs. The laughter. The bawdy jokes and snide comments. Of course we heard all of that.

Finally, after I'd had to shout the same question to Wyn for the fourth time, I'd had enough. Just as I turned to tell them to lower their voices, one of the men stood up too quickly and lost his balance, spilling his drink all over me as he lurched to the side, pushing me backward into the table so the edge pressed into my back. He reached an arm out to brace himself, knocking my ale over in the process. When he pulled himself upright once more, he simply shook his hand, spraying drops of ale everywhere.

Irritation flared through me, hot and bright. As though I hadn't been dealing with enough crap since I got on that damn ship, and now I had to deal with this guy too? It made me miss the simplicity of the frontlines, where fighting and not dying were the only things I had to worry about.

Of course, he had to soil my clothing too, the one thing I had planned to show Wyn in hopes of proving to her that I was doing well for myself. I wanted her to know I was okay and we each had our places we belonged now. I certainly didn't want her to worry about me as much as I worried about her.

And now, this huge ass of a man had tarnished the only free night I was probably going to have for a very long time. He was just like all of the other men I had to deal with daily. Completely consumed with his own desires with little to no care about those around him.

I jumped up and shoved the burly man. "Hey! What do you think you're doing?"

He bent forward, his own wood tankard slamming down on the table as he staggered then stood straight before turning, ready to fight the person who'd shoved him. He looked over my head first, as if he was expecting someone taller. Then he glanced down, chuckled, and rubbed his beard, which was a disgusting mass of knots with bits of stew stuck in it. "I'm sorry, little girl. Did a drop or two spill on your pretty clothes?"

Oh. Stars no. I stared at him in disbelief with my mouth hanging open, my irritation giving way to rage.

"If you could control yourself for two seconds, knowing when enough is enough, you might not be so drunk that you can't even stand properly." Obviously, we were beyond that. Maybe that was why I reacted so badly, so swiftly, so ready to show him that size mattered—brain size. Before I realized what I was doing, I poked the man in the chest for emphasis. "The least you could do is buy me a new drink since you knocked mine off of the table."

I noticed Grimsby over the man's shoulder, watching from the bar. His glare was a reminder to tone it down.

"Sorry, honey." The man swayed and slurred his words. "I won't be buying you a new drink, so you need to just sit your puny little self down and leave me alone."

The men at his table whooped and snorted as if he'd cracked the funniest joke in all of the kingdom.

My temper was getting the best of me, so I took a deep breath and tried to think of a quick solution. The last thing I needed was to get kicked out of the tavern for violence. And Grimsby wouldn't think twice. If I was the one fighting, out on my ass I'd go, tossed by the bar owner.

"How about this?" I crossed my arms and glared at the man. "I challenge you to an arm wrestling contest. If I win, you buy me and my friend another round. If you win, I'll buy your drink." Not that he needed one, but also not that I would be buying one. He was too busy underestimating me, already tasting an ale I hadn't bought.

The man and his motley crew laughed at me, and I knew this would be one of the sweetest of my most recent victories.

Once he caught his breath, he nodded his head. "Sounds like you've got yourself a good deal to me, sweetheart." He laughed again. "Or I should say, I'm getting a good deal."

Out of the corner of my eye, I caught Grimsby grinning and shaking his head. I clamped my lips shut and fought to keep a smile off of my face. This poor guy had no clue what he'd just agreed to. I was going to deliver a humiliation he wouldn't likely recover from.

One of the man's companions stood and gestured to his chair, allowing me to sit opposite my opponent. If the table had been any wider it wouldn't have worked. We both placed our right elbows on the table and grasped one another's hands. He was squeezing tighter than necessary, but it would be his downfall.

The man leaned in so close that I could smell his sour breath. "Don't expect me to take it easy on you, sweetheart."

His friend counted us down as Wyn watched on sipping her ale, well aware of the dish of humiliation I was about to serve this guy.

He was as big as a mountain, but that didn't mean he was strong. Likely, it meant he was slow. I gave it a few seconds, allowed him to believe that he was winning the contest at first, keeping my strength hidden and making subtle motions that allowed him to believe he was in control. In truth, I was making adjustments, gradually beginning to increase my pressure on his arm, slowly yet surely gaining momentum until finally, the back of his hand slammed flat onto the table, and I had won the contest.

The small crowd that gathered around us roared in approval, and some of the men patted me on the back as I stood up, beaming with pride. Even Wyn was cheering for me from where she waited in safety on the other side of our table.

The man who challenged me pushed to his feet and stumbled backward, embarrassed to be beaten by my strength. "You scrawny little broad. You cheated. There's no other explanation. I demand a rematch." I came around the table, intending to rejoin Wyn, but his hands landed on my shoulders and pushed, making me stumble forward. On instinct I spun and pushed him back, almost reaching for my dagger, but stopping myself when Wyn's voice sounded in my ear. "Teach them a lesson, Senara." He shoved me once more and I knew if I didn't change things then it would spiral out of control into a full on brawl.

And now he had a few of his friends backing him up, insisting that I was a cheater.

I stepped back and lifted my hands into the air, glancing over at Wyn, who just nodded in encouragement. "I'll wrestle all of you if you insist." Big words were my specialty. "But I'll win, and when I do, each of you will owe us another round."

The men were long past caring what the terms of the

contest were and how much they might have to spend on beer, each one sat down heavily in front of me, glaring at me as they did so. One after the other, they all seemed focused on proving that they were stronger than a tiny little female.

They each stepped up and tried to beat me in a match of strength. And one by one, they lost. After the last man was defeated, Grimsby stepped forward and handed us each a full mug of ale. All around us, the patrons were quiet, mouths hanging open. They were in shock.

"Well done," he said with a smile, his voice practically the only noise in the tavern. "Just the beginning, my girls." He clapped his hands together. "It looks like tonight is on you," he said to the men.

The first man I'd wrestled, the drink spiller, started to protest, but one strong glare from Grimsby shut him up. My opponents held to their word, each paying Grimsby for a round of drinks for us. They quickly moved to another table on the opposite side of the tavern like puppies retreating with their tails between their legs.

I took my seat at the table with Wyn and dabbed at the newly formed stains on my still-damp garments. I'd rinse them when I went back to my room and hope that they were dry by morning, so I could pack them up.

"You should've just knocked them all out," Wyn said with a sly grin. Obviously, she knew I would win. This was an old game that had won us more than a few drinks over the years. When we were barely old enough to fill out corsets we tricked men, and sometimes women for that matter, into buying us drinks. It kept the darkness away from us, at least for a few hours.

As I grew I realized that I was stronger than most, which was funny considering how weak I felt most of the time. It gave us an unexpected advantage in the tavern scene, though. I would arm wrestle a person, and then Wyn would follow it up with a sympathetic shoulder to cry on while deftly relieving them of their coin purse, which was usually discreetly passed off to me so she could make a clean getaway.

Right up until I'd joined the army, it was our go to move if we wanted a decent meal. The only trick was keeping it spread out enough so no one recognized us or caught on.

"Oh, yeah?" I asked. "And why is that?"

"It would've lowered the volume, so we could have a decent conversation." Wyn winked. "And, we could've just grabbed their money bags and had a fine celebration." There she was, the troublemaker I knew and loved.

For as shy as Wyn was, she certainly knew how to walk the line of what would get us into just enough trouble to be thrilling without being too dangerous. Or at least, no more dangerous than normal.

I laughed and rolled my eyes. Even though we'd both lived a life of poverty and had been forced to steal all the things we needed to survive, I liked to think that we'd made it to the other side and would never have to go back. "Nah, we're past that," I said, shaking my head and willing it into existence that we would never have to steal to survive again.

"Oh, come on. It was a good plan," Wyn said with a shrug, as serious as I'd ever seen her, but only for a second. Then a smile spread slowly across her face. "Might have made for a grumpy Grims, though, and no one likes that."

We both laughed, enjoying the moment of peace and freedom that the tavern provided us. Tonight, I was free. Once more, though, before I could stop it, my mind drifted to thoughts of what tomorrow held for me as a new member of the King's Guard, but I pushed them aside and focused on the present. I didn't know how much time I would have with Wyn as we grew older, especially with how different our jobs were, so I didn't want to waste it now.

Already, I had proven to myself that I could take on any

challenge with a steady hand and a fighting spirit. And, no matter what the future held for me, at least for this one night, I was victorious.

My cool, calm, and collected attitude quickly went out the door as I realized the dark stranger had come to stand over our table.

# CHAPTER
# FIVE

## Senara

With the light behind him, the stranger cast a long and wide shadow across the table and onto me. For reasons I couldn't begin to guess or understand, I was strangely drawn to him. He was dark—dark eyed, dark-haired, dressed in black and dark brown—which added to the air of mystery, but it only intrigued me more. I sat my ale on the table and stared, unable to form words. I'd never been so captivated by anyone as I was by him.

Without his cloak, I was better able to see the dark hair that was partially tied back and the scar that stretched out from behind his eye patch. When the lantern light hit the side of his face, all I could see was planes and shadows, the stark contrast given by his angular brows and cheekbones.

"How did you become so good at arm wrestling?" he asked, his voice low and deep, rolling over my skin like thunder before a storm.

I didn't want to admit that I had grown up in taverns and used to bet the older men that I could beat them in return for food, or that Wyn and I used to steal from them. The thought of speaking the truth out loud left me with feelings of inadequacy, and some part of me wanted to impress this random stranger. It frustrated me.

"Oh, well, I, um, used to spend a lot of time chopping wood for my parents," I lied. "I suppose I built up a good amount of tolerance and strength over the years."

Wyn snorted into her ale, sputtering and coughing when she set it down. "Sorry, fly," she mumbled, not looking up at either of us.

The dark stranger nodded his head as if he accepted my lie and the one Wyn had told him, though I doubted he bought either of them.

He gestured, as if asking if he could take the seat opposite mine. When I nodded, Wyn's eyebrows shot to her hairline while the stranger said, "I'd like to challenge you to a no-stakes round. Just so I can test your strength."

His voice was thick with curiosity and something else I couldn't quite place.

This was a man with an intensity that made my heart race and my palms sweat. I had a feeling that this could be more than just two people arm wrestling for fun; it felt like a test of strength between us.

"Sure," I replied, my voice coming out breathier than I intended.

He smiled, as if he'd just had a funny thought, and casually rolled up the sleeves of his tunic, revealing strong arms with defined muscles. His hands were slightly calloused, but mine weren't as smooth as if I spent my day sitting in a drawing room practicing my needlepoint.

I glanced up at him once more, our gazes locking, and I shivered under his stare. I'd been wrong before. His eye wasn't dark, or at least not a dark brown like I'd thought. Instead, I found myself staring into an eye that looked like cracked amber.

There was something about his presence, about *him,* that made me feel safe and secure. His gaze shifted from mine, breaking the spell between us, as he readied himself for our match. He clenched and unclenched his fingers, took a slow deep breath and blew it out, and captured my gaze again, almost as if he were preparing for battle.

I was having a moment, the kind that felt familiar, as though I had done this before. It wasn't in a bad way, but more in a comfortable sense that left me feeling at ease despite the pressure of this unexpected encounter. Mustering up the bravery I needed, I placed my elbow on the table and we clasped our hands together.

As soon as our hands touched, a jolt of awareness powered through me, knocking me backward as an uneasy sensation rushed through my body. I yanked my hand free and shoved it under the table, examining it for anything that might explain the strange sensations I'd just felt.

When I looked up, I found him, and to a lesser extent Wyn, watching me intently. I couldn't tell whether or not he thought I was a crazy person—Wyn already knew I had a few screws loose, and loved me for it. Maybe he was thinking that he'd misjudged me? At the very least, I was sure he wondered what my problem was.

"Sorry." I waved my hand in the air, looking at it with a cocked brow and pinched lips. Then I looked at him and wagged my fingers. "I need to shake my hand out after those last few rounds of arm wrestling. I want to give you my best shot." I grinned at him, hoping he'd buy yet another lie from me.

He nodded as if my explanation made perfect sense, but I had the impression he knew I was hiding something.

Against my better judgment, I took his hand again. Our breathing slowed in unison, and before long, we were completely focused on each other, with all other distractions fading away until only our duel remained. At least, that was how it was for me. And when I stared hard enough, I could believe it was so for him, too.

We went back and forth for what felt like an eternity, earning some onlookers who were intrigued by the lengthy match. Though most didn't attempt to approach us, instead watching quietly from a distance. It was interesting that no one approached, as though they sensed the danger this stranger posed just as much as I did. The difference was that they were smart enough to stay away, whereas I was trying to pet a wild cat.

The battle stretched on for minutes as we stared into each other's eyes, neither one of us willing to back down. The intensity of our duel caused some of the onlookers who had dared to approach to take a step back.

His bicep bunched under his sleeve, and I knew that he wasn't trying his hardest. Unlike me. I wondered why he wasn't giving this battle his all, feeling sure that if he did, I would be unable to win.

His expression was stoic, but I could sense some kind of emotion behind it that I couldn't quite place. I felt a wave of heat pass through my body as my grip tightened on his hand, and he responded in kind.

Despite my determination to keep up in the fight, it wasn't long before I had to concede defeat. My arm muscles quivered and quaked with effort, and I just didn't have the will to win this one. Whether that had to do with the man, or his muscles, or whatever was happening between us didn't matter.

I relaxed my arm and let him push my hand to the table in one fell swoop. And just like that, the match was over.

The stranger quirked an eyebrow at me as I let go of his hand, and this time I noticed something different in his face. A hint of an amused smile, eyes glimmering with admiration, as if he appreciated my attempt despite the inevitable outcome.

I sat there for a moment taking it all in, admiring how much one simple smile could change his entire demeanor. He was handsome before, but the smile was... beautiful. He stood and turned to walk away, which made a strange feeling leap in my chest. The only thing I knew was that I didn't want that.

Taking a deep breath, I summoned my courage and looked up at him. "Would you like to join us?"

The stranger's smile broadened. "Sure."

He sat back down on the chair he'd pulled up to wrestle with me, never taking his eyes off me. My face flushed, and I looked around the room, hoping no one noticed. My gaze landed on Wyn, who had a devilish grin across her face.

The stranger chuckled, breaking the silence. "Not a bad match. You almost had me there." He was lying. There wasn't a chance I was ever close to winning.

I felt my cheeks heat up even more, and I shifted in my seat, trying to appear more confident than I actually felt. "Well, it was good practice," I said with a shrug. With nothing else to occupy me, I grabbed my tankard and took a healthy swallow of the remaining ale inside.

"Indeed," he replied, his voice drawing my eyes as his gaze felt as if it pierced into my soul. A chip of brilliant amber shining in the sun, that's what his eye reminded me of. In some ways, I was glad he had the eye patch and the scar, he'd just be too much without it.

He reached for my hand, the one not gripping the tankard for dear life, and brought it to his lips, kissing my skin so softly I wasn't sure if he'd actually made contact, although he continued to hold my fingers in his after. "Thank you for the match, Miss..."

"Oh. Senara." I pulled my hand back, hoping the wiggling sensation inside of me would stop if I ended the contact. It didn't. "Just call me Senara." My voice was thin and high-pitched and hurt my ears, but I couldn't fix it because I didn't know why or how it had become so unrecognizable.

"It's nice to formally meet you, Senara."

Hearing him say my name sent chills down my spine. What was wrong with me? Maybe the sea sickness had spread to my head.

"And I'm Wyn, her best friend," Wyn said from off to the side. I was an ass. Tonight was supposed to be about the two of us spending time together, and I'd become so captivated by an amber eye and a mouth that silently promised wicked things that I'd invited someone else to join us without even checking with her.

"My pleasure, Wyn," the stranger said as he very briefly dropped a kiss on her hand as well. It was a shadow of the one he'd given me, and the action seemed more perfunctory than anything else.

Before I was ready, he turned all of his intense attention back to me. "I think I've figured out your main strategy." He leaned back and crossed his arms, grinning mischievously from ear to ear. His amber eye sparkled, and I found myself leaning forward, hanging on his every word.

"Oh, yeah?" I asked. "What's that?" I didn't have a strategy. I'd been training for years. Learned to win because I needed to eat.

"You mesmerize the men with those pale blue eyes of yours." He held my gaze with his. "They become powerless, unable to beat you in the arm wrestling match."

Okay. So we were flirting now?

That was flirting, right?

It had been a while since I'd experienced it, but judging from the way Wyn leaned back and fanned herself while nodding in encouragement, that was definitely what was happening.

I shifted in my seat, suddenly feeling uncomfortable with the attention he was giving me. "I wish I could wield that type of power over men." Actually, until this moment, I'd never had a thought about the potential of me being able to wield any power over anyone, much less a thought about power over a man. I wasn't the type of woman who could command a situation like that. "But, alas, my eyes aren't part of any type of strategy. I'm just that good with my hands."

Wyn barked a laugh at my expense before smothering her amusement in her tankard.

It sounded a lot different than I'd meant it. It sounded tawdry, and I'd certainly not meant to give myself away like that. Oh well. I suddenly didn't mind the stranger knowing that I was attracted to him.

He leaned back in his chair and let out a hearty laugh, holding his stomach and eventually wiping moisture from his eyes. I was thankful that he found it as amusing as Wyn had.

His laugh was contagious and before long, Wyn and I leaned over the table, chuckling and gasping for air, our ales abandoned. Perhaps we'd had a little too much to drink, but it felt so good to be carefree... if only for a small amount of time.

"Well, can I at least buy you another round since you won?" I asked.

He nodded, and his hair looked like silk against his shoulder as he bobbed his head. "That's a wonderful idea."

As I stood to walk away from the table, Wyn pulled me down and whispered in my ear, "Maybe you should invite the man back to your room before you have to marry the Crown." The problem was her whisper was no whisper at all and more a loud encouragement.

"Hush!" I giggled, refusing to look at the stranger, and

gave Wyn a gentle shove as I made my way past her to the bar to order our drinks.

I had to admit it wasn't a bad idea. Sure, I'd had the thought earlier, but I'd never expected it to actually be a possibility. But after what just happened? I knew my night could get a lot more interesting.

# CHAPTER
# SIX

S enara

Once the tavern got busy, I knew Grimsby wouldn't have time to tend to us like he had earlier in the evening, which was why I'd gone to the bar myself. Plus, I didn't want to know what kind of looks or questions he might have for our new friend. It wasn't that Grims was overprotective, but he liked to keep an eye on things.

I didn't want to admit it, but going and ordering our drinks also gave me a breather from the strange feelings that were conjured in me by this man. Just being near him confused my body. Getting some space while I got drinks was a good thing.

With my hands full of mugs, the froth of the ale sloshing over the sides while I tried to step carefully and also avoid the drunks, I made my way back to the table just in time to overhear Wyn's conversation with the handsome stranger. I stopped near but not quite at the table. I wanted to hear what Wyn had to say.

"You know, I'm sure Senara could satisfy you if you gave her the chance." Wyn leaned toward the man as she tried to convince him of my sexual abilities. "You look like the kind of guy who could use a woman's touch."

It wasn't often that I blushed, but for at least the second time that night, I felt heat climbing my neck and into my cheeks. What in hell was she doing? I didn't need her trying to convince him for me. If I wanted him I could ask him myself... But I wasn't even sure what I wanted, or what I would or could do...

I pushed the thoughts away, pasted on an enthusiastic smile, and tried to appear unphased as I set the mugs on the table. My skin prickled as his attention turned back to me.

"What did you mean by marrying the Crown?" the man asked.

I wasn't sure if he was talking to Wyn or me since I was busy focusing on wiping the ale that had spilled from the table, but I wasn't about to let her tell him everything there was to know about me. The last thing I needed was her using my history to try to convince him to come to my room tonight. Not when all the truth would do was drive him away, convincing him once and for all that I wasn't the type of woman a man could find attractive. Not that I cared. I wasn't even sure I wanted him to find me attractive.

"I'm going to be working in the kitchens at the castle, and I've heard that the head cook isn't fond of giving any time off." I cracked my knuckles nervously. I'd spent years lying to save myself or Wyn, and even for reasons not so noble, but now I sounded like an amateur. Time off? I would've rolled my eyes at myself, but I knew enough not to give myself away completely. "Might as well be married to the job, in my opinion."

People acted strange when they found out a woman was in the military. It wasn't exactly a commonplace occurrence, so I didn't feel comfortable explaining my role. Not to him and not to anyone else. It was no one's business but mine and people I patrolled and fought beside.

Not to mention the fact that I was about to become a member of the *Royal Guard*, which could be even more intimidating than just a normal soldier. So I preferred to keep that information to myself.

I glanced at Wyn, and she gave a slight nod in approval of my explanation. Not that I needed her approval, but it was always nice to know I had it. I offered a weak smile and pushed a loose strand of hair behind my ear, eager to change the subject.

"So, you never told me your name." I took a sip of ale and shifted my gaze to the stranger. "Do you have one?" Everyone had one, but I'd used all my ability to flirt smoothly a few minutes ago, not that there was much of it to begin with. Now I was winging it.

He chugged his ale before wiping his mouth with the back of his hand. "My name's Branok Thorn." He cleared his throat and looked down into his nearly empty mug. "Everyone just calls me Thorn, though."

*Thorn.* The name suited him. And it somehow sounded familiar to me, though I couldn't quite put my finger on why. The thought continued to plague me until it finally disappeared in a haze of ale as the night went on.

The two of us flirted with each other, and with each passing remark it felt like the atmosphere of the bar became more charged. Thorn looked at me with a smoldering intensity, his amber-colored eye searching my body in a way that felt almost intrusive. But I liked it enough that the shivers were welcomed and I smiled more readily. Smiles that he returned more frequently as well.

My heart fluttered in response, and I quickly looked away. While I tried to focus on my mug of ale, it became increasingly evident that Thorn was more interested in me than Wyn.

Though she didn't seem to mind and even encouraged the connection.

"You know, Thorn, Serana has more tricks up her sleeve than winning arm wrestling competitions." Wyn smiled and finished off her last mug of ale.

Thorn scratched his cheek with the fingertips of his opposite hand and smiled. "Is that right?"

I looked up at him, my eyes searching his, trying for the tenth time to remember why his name sounded familiar. I ran my fingers along the rim of my mug before taking another sip, buying myself time to think of something witty to say. "It's true. I do have more talents than just arm wrestling. For example, I'm really good at... cooking eggs." Oh. Now it sounded as though I was offering him breakfast. And I was a liar. I couldn't cook an egg to save my life.

Thorn's eyebrows rose in surprise. He leaned back in his chair and laughed. The sound rolled through me, making me smile in spite of myself. "An egg-cooker? Wow, now that is impressive!"

Did I feel a little silly for claiming to be an expert cook and wishing I had thought of something more exciting? Definitely, but I wasn't going to back down now. "Well, it's not exactly a talent, but no one's ever complained about my flavor." Probably because I was a trained fighter and I'd only made eggs one time in all of my years.

Thorn cleared his throat and shifted in his seat, clearly taken off guard by my flirtatious comment.

"Have I embarrassed you?" I raised an eyebrow at him. "Are you thinking about my eggs right now?" I asked as I leaned across the table, letting my breasts push against the edge of the corset top.

"Oh, no, absolutely not." Thorn sat up straight. He looked down into his mug again, and I could swear his cheeks were flushed. I made him excited? Nervous? I wasn't sure what, but the power felt fantastic. It was nice to have a man like Thorn practically falling over me, hanging on my every word.

Being one of the few women in the military left me feeling inadequate in comparison to other, more feminine, women. It was reassuring to know that someone like him could find me attractive, even if we were strangers.

It didn't hurt that I wasn't just a curiosity, as I was for so many of the men in the army. The men in my previous regiment had quickly got over that once they saw me fight, but the men on the ship? The ones who would be in the King's Guard with me? They hadn't. They thought because I was seasick that I was an easy target, so I put them on the floor. Something that they hadn't forgiven me for, judging from the scowls I received as we got off the ship.

I refused to let that seep in and ruin the wonderful night I was having, though. When I looked over at Wyn, she raised an eyebrow at me and I shook my head. We had known each other long enough for her to pick up on the subtlest shifts in my mood, even now after all the years apart.

"So you may be a talented egg cook, but tell me, have you ever worked with sausage?" Thorn asked, his eyes twinkling with mirth as I choked on the sip of ale I was taking.

The flirtatious conversation went on for a while, the double entendres seemingly never ending, but it wasn't long before I felt exhaustion seeping into my bones. The food, drink, and warmth worked their magic, and I could no longer keep my head up. Plus, I still wanted to try and rinse the spilled beer off of my top before bed.

"Well, I hate to break up such a fun evening, but I'm exhausted after a long trip here. I'm heading up to my room." I paused and glanced at Thorn, and we studied each other for a moment, those same prickles breaking out over my skin like I was standing too close to a fire. "Feel free to join me if you want."

I stood and pushed my chair under the table. Wyn popped to her feet as well and came around the table to give me a hug. I held on an extra few seconds because I didn't know when I could get to see her again, and I wanted to savor her friendship for a few more seconds. "Good night, dear friend. It was so good to catch up. We'll talk soon."

Wyn kissed my cheek. "Take care of yourself, Senara. If the, uh, head chef lets you have some free time, come find me."

"Promise," I said quietly to Wyn before I stole one more glance at Thorn, who hadn't responded to my offer in any way and still remained seated, his hand curled around his mug with his eyes down. I took that as a lack of interest. He wouldn't be joining me upstairs.

Part of me was let down and another part relieved. I wouldn't know what to do with him if he came upstairs anyway. It had been a while. Longer than I cared to admit, but that's what happened when you couldn't trust anyone other than your best friend.

As I walked through the crowded tavern, I could still pick out Wyn's voice among the others as she talked to Thorn. "You're missing out on a good night."

I chuckled to myself. Wyn always had my back, which was encouraging. I couldn't deny that I was a little disappointed that Thorn had chosen not to join me. Maybe he was more interested in Wyn after all, or maybe it had all been a game to see how far it could go.

There were no answers to my questions in this situation, nor did I expect there to be any. As my feet carried me upstairs, I realized that at least I stood a chance of getting a few hours of sleep since I wouldn't have company.

I shook my head and pushed open the door to my room. It was just as I'd left it, and there was some comfort in that, even if I was going to bed alone. I had a big day ahead of me, so it was probably for the best.

Still, I couldn't help but wonder what might have happened if he had said yes. The nervous energy that ran through me all night was still there, so I quickly stripped out of the clothes I'd been wearing and changed into my oversized bed shirt, not wanting to be exposed for any longer than necessary, even in a private room. I took a little of the water from the pitcher and doused the ale stained areas of my top before setting the fabric on the floor in front of the fire, close enough to dry but not burn.

I took a moment to confirm that my armor and weapons were where I'd left them. I untied them from their hiding spots but left them under the bed, just in case. No one would break in without me knowing, but I felt better having a sword or chakram within reach instead of tied up under the bed.

After sitting on the floor in front of the fire for a moment while I unbraided my hair, I realized that while I was tired, my body had other ideas. It had apparently been expecting activity, and getting ready for bed and cleaning my clothes wasn't enough, so I did push ups until my arms were ready to give out, which was, of course, when a knock sounded on the door.

# CHAPTER
# SEVEN

S enara
The fire was bright as I stared at the door, giving
out more warmth than this tiny room could handle.
"Just a second," I called to whoever was on the other side of
the door. If it had been Wyn, she would have replied, but the
silence told me everything I needed to know. I honestly wasn't
sure if I hoped it was Thorn or not.

My sleeping shirt was thin, thin enough that if I turned the
wrong way the fire would highlight the exact thing I wanted to
hide. Plus, I preferred sleeping in the dark, so I poked at the
logs with the tool Grimsby left for me, almost guttering the
fire and only allowing embers to remain burning as I hoped it
would emit enough heat to aid in the drying of my clothes.
When I was satisfied, I straightened before going to the door.

Before I could second guess my instincts, I snatched a
dagger from the boots I'd just taken off, the one I'd almost
pulled on Wyn earlier, and held it behind the door. I took a
deep breath and opened the door, just enough to see who was
on the other side. To my surprise, Thorn's face filled my view.

He stood with his arm resting on the doorframe, leaning

down and invading my personal space as he asked, "May I come in?"

The prickling sensation swept over me once more, and it felt like the air between us became charged as I hesitated for a moment before backing up and opening the door for him. What I was doing was stupid. I should have sent him away.

The idea was fine when I was in my corset and it would have been a quick fuck, but now I was almost naked, almost entirely exposed, and tension sang through my body. Yet I couldn't find it in myself to say no and turn him away.

I stepped backward, not sure what to say, and tried to discreetly place the dagger on the table with the pitcher and bowl. My heart raced as Thorn stepped into the room, his gaze landing on the dagger a moment before he reached for me, a grin quirking his lips as though he found the dagger amusing.

His hands wrapped around my waist as he leaned down, pressing his lips against mine briefly. The few seconds of contact made my heart thunder in my chest, and a gasp escaped me. Without taking his eye off of me, he kicked the door shut.

I took a step back and Thorn followed me, never looking away. I bent down to the table and blew out the candle I lit when I first came back to the room. Only the soft glow of the diminishing embers lit the room, but that didn't halt Thorn. When I straightened, a rumble of what might have been approval, or maybe need, escaped him before he pounced, his mouth demanding control over mine once again.

Falling into his embrace, I claimed his mouth just as thoroughly. He caressed his hands over my body, and when he pushed to roam over my back, I gently halted his hands with mine and redirected them to my breasts.

I couldn't deny the chokehold my fear had on me at that moment, that he would somehow discover I was Moon Marked–that I supposedly had magic, not that I'd ever seen any evidence of it other than the mark on my skin. All he needed was see it or touch it, anything that would lead him to make an accusation, and my life could be over. Literally.

The King wasn't shy about executing people who had magic in their blood.

As Thorn's tongue explored my mouth and tangled with my own, I couldn't bear the thought of turning down this opportunity, even if it was stupid and reckless.

We both took deep breaths when our mouths parted to remove my sleep shirt. My hands went to his thick leather belt while he lifted his own tunic over his head.

The soft chill in the room made me shiver, and my skin erupting into goosebumps, my nipples hardening into pointed buds. I was still trying to get his pants undone when Thorn leaned down, engulfing one of my nipples in his mouth, and I quaked in his hold. I threw my head back, my hair tickling my back, and I was vaguely aware that he had dropped to his knees to better reach me.

His hands stayed on my hips, holding me in place, not that I was going to try to go anywhere. Why would anyone ever want to stop such an overwhelming feeling of pleasure?

Every inch of my body was brought to life by him. He grazed his teeth over the delicate flesh, and my hands clenched over his broad shoulders, my nails digging into his skin. He bit down in retaliation. I hissed, and his tongue stroked to ease the sting. His hands slid from my hips to my breasts, kneading them as he lifted his head, watching me in the firelight as he took in the other nipple and lavished it with the same attention.

I wound my fingers through his hair and pulled, removing his head from my breast, so I could encourage him to stand once more. The last thing I wanted was to be the only naked one in the room. He growled at me but did as I silently requested.

Roaming my hands over his body, I skimmed my fingers across the dark fabric of his breeches and flicked the buttons undone before loosening the ties and finally pushing them down his hips. The thick length of him hit my stomach.

I stared down, mouth slightly agape. He was bigger than any I'd had before. I wrapped my fingers around him, or tried to, and slowly stroked him up and down.

A groan escaped him as I began to work him steadily. As I worked, he somehow got his boots and pants the rest of the way off as well.

His head fell forward, and he attacked the side of my neck, sucking and nibbling at the delicate skin and eliciting a moan from me as I tried to keep some level of clearheadedness about me.

The sucking and nibbling ended, and he lifted his head and attacked my lips again. I wrapped one arm around him then he loosened my hand on his cock, removing it from between us, and pulled me closer. He wrapped his hands around my ass and thighs before he lifted me.

I jolted with the sudden movement, and he chuckled into my mouth, a deep seductive sound. Tightening my legs around him, I leaned down and kissed him once more. I couldn't get enough of the taste of him, the smell of him, or even the feel of him. My hair cocooned us and made the world disappear.

Slowly, he lowered me onto the bed, settling me into the middle. The embers from the fire glowed from behind and made him seem ethereal, a dark warlord staking his claim as he crawled up and over me. My chest heaved with my harsh inhale. Everything about me in that moment was unsteady, as though the whole world was tilting, and I knew that somehow it was thanks to him.

I reached to pull him down to my lips.

"No." He smirked and held his penetrating gaze with mine

as he licked his lips and moved down the bed until he was directly above my core of need. "I've been dying to taste you ever since you mentioned it. I've craved you for too long. Will you let me?"

If I was honest, I was surprised that he was asking, but I liked it. I gripped the blankets as he blew over my heated flesh, teasing me to the point that my entire being was vibrating with need.

I nodded, anything to make the ache vanish from my body.

He grinned, looking decidedly roguish before dropping his head, and those magical kisses that had happened on my lips moments ago now took place between my legs. Long hot strokes stole my breath.

"Yes. Oh, yes." I quivered and shook as his tongue licked and swirled around the bundle of nerves in a way that made my body buck before he plunged inside of me, lapping me up.

Suddenly, he threw my legs wider apart as his broad shoulders made more room for himself. He held my thighs down, tilting me up to him like a starving man diving into a feast.

The soft crackling in the fireplace didn't do much to drown out the sounds of my pleasure, or his groans, or the gentle sucking sound of his mouth. All of it only added to the sensations.

Heat pooled deeper in my core. My skin prickled. I buried my hands in my hair, needing some kind of stimulation elsewhere to make what he was doing less overwhelming. It wasn't enough though, no matter how silky his hair was, so instead I let my hands drift upward.

When I stroked my hands up and down my collarbone, I caught Thorn watching me, and I bit my bottom lip.

He lifted his head, and the small amount of light showed my juices sliding down his chin.

"Don't stop. Touch yourself, play with your nipples, whatever you want. I want to see you come."

I groaned at his words and took my breasts in my hands, tweaking the nipples and twirling the buds enough that an intense shiver shot down to my center. My legs shook in his firm hold.

Thorn growled around my bundle of nerves, and the vibration made me pant. My eyes crossed at the pleasurable sensation.

"Thorn?" His name was a gasp on my lips. I shook my head back and forth on the bed. "I'm so close. So close."

He dived in and ravaged me with his mouth, thrusting a finger into me, then two, and making me shake with how close I was to toppling over the edge into my orgasm. He roughly rocked his fingers in and out as he took my clit into his mouth.

I pinched my nipples hard and screamed out with my massive release.

Thorn lifted his head, wiped the essence off his face but kept thrusting his fingers into me as the aftershocks of my pleasure rolled through me. "That's a good girl. Let it out," he growled, his words twisting my insides even further. "Give me everything you've got, Senara."

When I was limp and panting on the bed he fisted his cock and slicked himself with me before lining himself and pushing in. He went so deep that I gasped at the fullness within me.

A whole other round of aftershocks was triggered, thundering through my system at his thick invasion. Something akin to lightning shot down to my toes and up to my hair. Every part of my being felt alive and altered, as though whatever we'd just done was irrevocable.

Thorn grabbed my thighs, sliding his hands around until he held me up by my ass. I planted my feet on either side of him on the bed, and he pulled himself out to the very tip and thrust into me again. I knew he was big. I'd seen it with my own eyes, but feeling him inside me was a whole different thing.

I screamed again as another orgasm started building while I was still coming down from the first one.

"Do you want more?" he asked.

My brain stuttered, and I pushed up onto my elbows to watch as he slowly slid out of me before pushing in again. He wasn't going all the way, allowing me to adjust, seeing how much of him I could take, which made me realize that he must not have been completely hard when I was handling him earlier.

"More," I whispered, unsure if I could actually take it.

We both watched as with each thrust he pushed further and further into me until I felt like his cock would poke a hole in my stomach. When his hips finally ground against me, my pussy clenched at the sight and the feel of him.

"Fuck, Senara, squeeze me like that." He hissed the words through teeth, as though he was doing his best not to come right then and there.

I wasn't doing anything my body didn't do naturally, but I squeezed my inner muscles around his cock as he moved, and fireworks licked up and down my skin.

Thorn growled, and he faltered in his thrust. A bead of sweat rolled down the side of his forehead, glistening in the low light.

My bones were useless, my energy sapped, but seeing how I affected him made me roll my hips, fucking him from below as his brow crumpled with concentration and his hips struggled to keep any rhythm to his movements.

"Fuck."

He fell and slammed his hands on either side of me as my hips dropped to the bed and jackhammered me into the soft material. The bed creaked under us, and I spared a thought to hope we didn't break it.

At first, I tried to meet him thrust for thrust, but I couldn't keep up, not with the way he was moving. Instead, I curled my hips, hooking my arms around my legs so I could play with my nipples as I chased another release. One that was sure to be epic.

It didn't matter that I was drained. I wanted more of him. I wanted everything.

"Come for me, Thorn." I rasped. I needed to see him lose control. I craved it.

"You first." He moved in and out at a ferocious pace, growing larger inside of me. He had to be ready to explode.

Between thrusts, I panted, "I already did."

He snarled. "That was with my tongue and fingers, not my cock. I need to feel you come undone on my dick. I want your pussy clenching around me. I want you screaming my name as I fuck you into oblivion."

His dirty words were my undoing, and my walls clenched hard on his shaft as a new galaxy burst into existence before my eyes. I screamed Thorn's name.

Thorn roared as he pushed his way deep inside of me, pinning me to the bed with his hips while his cock jerked with release inside of me. He followed up with several jerky pumps before holding himself there once more. "Fuck, Senara. Are you okay?" he gasped as his body worked to try and get more air.

I nodded, grinning up at him like a fool. I didn't trust myself to say anything since it felt like my soul had drifted from my body for a moment before reality set back in, and I melted into the bed.

"You're not hurt?" he asked.

"No, I'm fine. I mean you're big, but I'm okay." I laughed, the sound raspy from all the screaming and moaning I'd done.

He nodded, seeming satisfied with my answer, and eased himself to the side of me, just enough to not smother me but still remain inside me. His hand drifted to my hip and pulled me so I was on my side as well. I hooked a leg over him, keeping him close, not ready for this to end.

A rumble of approval left him, and though I wanted to snuggle closer, I didn't dare to. As much as I craved it, it was still too dangerous. I didn't even realize that he'd fallen asleep until I heard his breathing even out. Usually I asked guys to leave after, if I ever had them come back to my rooms that is, but the idea of waking Thorn and feeling him leave made me go cold, so I didn't say anything when he rolled over onto his back. Instead, I let the darkness and complete relaxation claim me.

Tomorrow would come all too soon, and no matter what happened, I was sure my life would never be the same.

# CHAPTER
# EIGHT

S enara
Birds beginning their morning serenade outside the window woke me, although the morning sun was barely a thought over the horizon. I was typically an early riser and today was no different despite the fact I'd been awake long into the night.

The thought jolted me. I had actually fallen asleep next to another person.

Naked.

He could have seen everything.

I opened my eyes and was surprised to find Thorn still sound asleep in my bed. We weren't cuddling or even touching, really, which I was grateful for. He was relaxed and peaceful, and I stared at him for a moment, taking it all in.

The man was a work of art, even more so now that I could take my time and peruse. His body was like mountainous terrain, all peaks and valleys where the muscles ended and began. Sharp lines and planes seemed to make up his body as though he was carved or sculpted rather than born.

Typically, I would ask my one-night stands to leave as

soon as we were done, but the sex I'd had with Thorn last night was unlike anything I'd ever experienced. It was so intense that I found myself struggling to think clearly. Even now.

My brain was still trying to comprehend what happened the night before.

Quietly untangling myself from the warmth of the bedding, I stood up and pulled my shirt over my head, just in case he woke up, before tiptoeing over to the opposite side of the bed and opening the trunk that held my belongings. I had to get ready. It was a big day.

Quickly dressing for the day, I took a look at myself in the reflection of the window. There was just barely enough light in the room for me to see, and I almost wished I hadn't. My hair was tangled and matted, looking more like a rat had made a nest in it than anything else. I brushed it as best I could with my fingers and pulled it back into my typical style. The hair flowed down my back, loose for the most part, while one side sported a braid that helped keep it out of my face and rested against my shoulder.

Part of me felt like I should try to do something more, after all this was a momentous occasion. I would be presented to the King and accepted as part of his Royal Guard. I couldn't show up looking like I'd just had the best sex of my life, regardless of the fact that it was true. The problem was I didn't have any real bathing facilities or a mirror in which to try and do something fancier. Not that I really had any idea how to do anything other than a couple braids.

It felt like the royal assembly would expect nothing but the best, especially since we'd been summoned specifically. It wasn't only for our warrior mentality either, but also our obedience when it came to the multitude of military rules and regulations. Surely they would laugh if I showed up like this. I didn't really have any other option, though.

Once I looked presentable, fit to be in the company of a king or at least swear my allegiance to him, I bent down and started to pull my armor, one piece at a time, from its hiding place under the bed as quietly as possible. Each time I moved a piece of metal and it made a sound, my chest froze as I waited for Thorn to wake up. There was no way for me to do it silently, though.

Each time he stirred, I thought for sure I was going to have to do the awkward morning after conversation. I didn't want that to tarnish the memory of the amazing sex, so I didn't want him to wake up.

Knowing that putting the armor on would be a loud process, I chose to finish getting dressed in the hallway. As quietly as I could, I took all of my belongings with me and gently shut the door. Putting on all the pieces of metal and buckling them together had become second nature, so it barely took me any time. I could have gone in my leather armor, but I felt more comfortable in the metal plate. Plus, it was less awkward to carry it when it was on my body versus in my pack.

The tavern was quiet, which was a stark contrast to the night before. The lights were out, as always, and I knew Grimsby wouldn't be up yet. It was fairly safe for me to wander around.

I repacked the few things I owned with a sense of urgency, careful to squeeze everything tightly into my traveling bag so it would close completely. Being late in the military was unacceptable, and I hated to imagine what type of punishment I'd receive if I showed up late on my first day as a royal guard.

Finally, I was ready, so I made my way downstairs and placed my pack and my weapons on the bar, not wanting them to get in the way of moving the barrels that I'd promised Grimsby I'd relocate. Picking up the pace, I made my way to the stack of barrels that Grimsby pointed out to me the night before. They were heavy, and I could see why he needed help with them, but I was strong.

I hadn't expected there to be quite so many, even though he did warn me, but I completed the job much faster than old Grimsby could have. He probably would have put his back out as well. The man needed to suck it up and hire some younger help, someone to take over the Kraken when he wasn't able to run it anymore.

The thought gave me pause. I'd never thought about Grimsby not being around. A coldness spread through my chest as I finished moving the barrels, and the feeling almost made me want to go and wake him up. He was definitely not a morning person, though, and I knew if I did, it would be because I was being selfish, not because I needed to. The man needed his sleep if he was going to be up all night, every night. Somehow or another, I would find some time to come back here and thank him again for everything he'd done for me and Wyn while we were growing up.

After strapping my weapons on and slinging my pack over my back, I headed out, leaving through the back door of The Red Kraken so I didn't have to leave the front door unlocked and risk Grimsby getting robbed or something. My pace was far slower this morning than it had been when I first got back in town, but I still covered ground quickly enough.

The sun was well on its way when I saw a baker opening up for the day. I was almost to the nicer sections of the city, and I knew once I crossed over, the prices of food would be much higher. I needed to eat, so I stopped at the bakery on the corner of a street.

The man opening the bakery was one of the one's I'd seen at The Red Kraken the night before. Not one of the assholes, but one of the ones who had watched all the arm wrestling contests. "Can I help you, ma'am?" the baker asked. I was surprised at how awake and alert he appeared. If I hadn't seen him the night before, I never would have guessed he'd been out until all hours of the morning. Maybe he hadn't even gone to bed and that was how he liked to start his day. Who was I to judge?

"Yes, I'd like a roll, please." I pointed to the tray of freshly baked bread. The golden brown rolls were coated with something, honey would be my guess, that made them gleam in the weak morning light.

The baker handed me one and took the coin from my outstretched hand. "You're early, even for me."

I nodded my head and smiled. "The early bird gets the worm. Or roll. Or something like that." He just chuckled and shook his head as I turned away.

The walk to the castle was refreshing. The sun had just peaked over the countryside and hardly anyone was out on the streets, yet.

A mother walked hand-in-hand with a small boy who couldn't have been older than three. He had dark curly hair that framed cherub cheeks and ears that stuck out a little further than was normal. He smiled up at her as she led him to the bakery. "Roll, mama?"

The woman beamed at him as if he was her pride and joy. "Yes, dear. You can have a roll."

"Sweet roll?" the boy asked, his smile turning mischievous.

She shook her head, but a smile curled the corners of her mouth as she reached out and ruffled the boy's hair. "Okay, but only because it's a special day."

A sharp pain drove deep into my stomach. It was always the same. My body had that same type of reaction whenever I saw a family functioning normally. A mother who loved her child. A father who taught life lessons that didn't involve theft and cheating.

I hardly remembered my own parents. And they certainly didn't love me enough to keep me safe from the violent streets, nor did they speak lovingly to me, offering to purchase baked goods as a special treat.

I quickened my pace, trying to outrun the emotions that had suddenly surfaced. But no matter how fast I walked, I couldn't beat them. They were at the surface now, so I distracted myself by taking a bite of the fluffy goodness in my hand. I was pleasantly surprised to find it wasn't just honey that coated the top, but there was a tartness to it as well, lemon maybe? It made the roll sweet and refreshing. Exactly what I needed.

Not quite the icing coated confection that the little boy was after, but it was enough for me.

As I walked, my legs rubbed together and my muscles ached in a pleasant soreness from the escapades the night prior. As the child's giggle echoed down the streets, I chose to focus my attention on my glorious discomfort.

What kind of magical cock was Thorn wielding? He'd certainly made a lasting impression on me.

Maybe I should have stayed a little longer, or at least woken him up before I left. Maybe he would have been up for scheduling a second round. I had no way to contact him, although he probably preferred not to be bothered. He seemed like the kind of man who enjoyed his one-night stands. After all, he'd been sitting in the shadows of the tavern alone, just waiting for the right girl to come along. My arm wrestling show had piqued his interest, that was for sure. And thank goodness for it. I didn't know when I would have another such opportunity.

I had to admit, though, that sex like that didn't come around very often. I rubbed my neck as I remembered the sensation of his breath on my body and the way we'd fit together so perfectly, at least in one specific way. Our height difference certainly made things interesting.

The way he'd shown up at my door, asked no questions,

and claimed me right then and there was enough to drive me crazy. I wasn't the kind of woman who wanted to waste my time on men who didn't know what they wanted or on those who were overly polite and gentle.

No, the men I preferred in my bed were just as rough as me, scarred from the harshness of life. Ready to take what they wanted with an animalistic desire. Thorn had been everything I wanted and desired, and he'd been so much more, too.

I wasn't usually the type to daydream, but it was clear now that I'd been missing out on something good, perhaps a quality that Thorn possessed. I wondered if I would ever find a way to get in touch with him again. The thought was so overwhelming that I actually considered turning around and walking all the way across town again just hoping that he was where I'd left him.

My feet came to a stop, as if to physically call a halt to those thoughts. There was a reason I only ever had one-night stands and tried to keep it to people I was unlikely to see again. That reason was as clear as day on my back. A ticking clock on my life, a storm waiting to rail against me.

As much as I hated to do it, I forced myself to remember what happened the last time I allowed myself to get close to a companion. I had no choice but to kill him before he killed me.

# CHAPTER
# NINE

S enara

"All of you new guards, get in line!" The Royal Guard commander barked his orders, and we scrambled to obey, forming a straight line with bodies stiff and ready for battle, weapons polished and ready at our sides.

The training area and barracks where we'd been instructed to meet were off to one side of the castle. There was a large sparring ring with training weapons on racks at the back, which we were currently standing in front of, straw dummies off to one side for sword and spear practice, targets off to the other side for archery practice. The stables were just around the corner, and of course, the barracks themselves laid in front of us. It was so well set up that I couldn't wait to try it all out. I felt like a child looking at a sweet roll.

Coming off the side of the barracks was one of the castle's towers. I had no idea what was inside it, but it loomed over the training area, casting a large shadow that kept the area cool as the sun crept higher in the sky.

There were ten of us in all, myself and nine men, and even though we were on the same side, fighting for Eaorin and to keep the kingdom safe, they all gave me skeptical looks. I wasn't sure what the hell they were looking at. We were each chosen because we were the best warriors the kingdom had to offer, so they had to know I could take out the enemy just as fast as any of them could. Maybe faster.

"Your new job entails several responsibilities, all of which are required to meet one goal, protecting the King and to a lesser extent the castle." The commander paused and adjusted his hat which only cast a bigger shadow over his face. Not that I needed to see him. Technically, I was supposed to stand rigid and face forward anyway. I didn't need to make eye contact with my commanding officer to take orders.

"You'll be required to patrol at various periods and in multiple locations on the premises. Additionally, you will take stationary shifts, and some of you will even be chosen to guard the King himself if you're found to be worthy of such an honor."

I wanted that. So badly.

It wasn't that I gave a shit about the King really, but I wanted that honor. I wanted to be one of the best warriors in the land, to be recognized as such by being entrusted with King Roth's life was just about the only way I could prove it.

I wondered what we needed to do in order to earn such a high clearance position as protecting the king himself. I couldn't qualify to do what I didn't know. And there was no telling if King Roth would trust that I was qualified. Certainly, the men I worked with wouldn't.

It was clear from their glances that they all thought of me as fragile and feeble because I was a woman. I supposed only time would tell, but based on the looks the other new guards were giving me, this would be an uphill battle. Fortunately, I was up for the fight.

The commander paced in front of us. "You will not meet King Roth or be in the same chamber as him until you have proven yourselves worthy. If you are not able to perform your duties, then you will be sent back to the front, and as such, the King wouldn't need to waste his time meeting you. You would also need to look a lot more presentable than you do now if you were to meet the king."

The commander sneered at us. It wasn't our fault that we'd just been dragged from the front lines and shoved on a ship. "Next, I will give you a short tour, and then you will meet the Blade of the King, the head of the King's Guard. As you are probably already aware, he is the highest authority outside of the King himself. You will treat him with respect and obey his orders without question."

That was the job I wanted. The *Blade of the King*. Certainly, there was something about the title that commanded respect, whether or not its holder did. I had to imagine that to get to such a position others would have to have at least a modicum of respect for him.

The commander turned on his heels and motioned for us to follow him. We stayed in line, with me following the other men, bringing up the rear.

He led us through the lower level of the castle. I wasn't sure how I managed to keep my jaw closed when it felt like it should be hanging open the whole time, but I did.

The main hall was enormous, wide enough for five of us to stand, arms spread side to side before we reached the pillars that lined the room on either side, and there would still be enough space to do the same thing again on the other side of the pillars. The ceiling was high enough we could all stand on one another's shoulders and still not reach the top, like the king who had built this place had been trying to touch the sky itself. As though that wasn't enough, there were multiple hallways that undoubtedly led to numerous off-chuting rooms.

I knew the castle was big, but I had no idea just how big. It was honestly hard to wrap my head around.

There were candles lit every few feet in wall sconces that gave the castle an eerie feeling but provided enough light for me to take in the interior, which was a sight to behold. The sconces themselves were gold, and gold-damask tufted benches lined the walls. Great swathes of red and gold fabric hung from the ceiling every so often, resting against the wall, with the king's banner in front of them.

The grandeur and elegance were second to none. Between the large pieces of fabric, the walls were decorated with intricate tapestries, gold-trimmed paintings, and sculptures depicting kings and queens of bygone eras. In the center of the main room sat a large fireplace that lit up the entire hall with its roaring flames.

We followed the commander through some gardens and into another massive hall before looping back into one of the towers that were situated on either side of the main building. After conquering a tall flight of stairs, we were led into a massive office.

"Sir, I have the new guards for you," the commander said, sounding less bullish than he had outside.

The rustle of papers was the only thing that told me that we weren't alone in the office since the Blade of the King didn't respond verbally to the commander, but I couldn't see anything past the men standing in front of me.

In fact the only thing I could see was one small window that was situated on the far wall, letting in precious little light for such a large room. A fireplace popped and crackled on the side wall, and candles had been placed on stands, sconces, and tables throughout the room, providing a warm glow and lighting the corners that the fireplace couldn't.

"Line up," the commander grunted.

The other guards moved out of the way, pushing themselves into two lines of five, as we had before. Even though the office was big, there wasn't enough room for us all to stand shoulder to shoulder. I claimed my place at the end and could finally see what was going on in the room. I spotted a large man towering over his desk at the back of the room. Dark locks of hair fell down, obscuring his face for a moment, before he lifted his head.

Thorn.

*That* was why his name had sounded so familiar. He was the Blade of the King. I was such an idiot. Beyond an idiot. What the hell had I been thinking?

Of all the people in the bar, this was the guy I'd chosen to... be with. I blinked rapidly and reminded myself that I had to keep my composure.

I stood taller and stared stone faced at the man I'd been with the night prior. I hadn't meant to, but my eyes seemed to have a mind of their own as I glanced at his hands and remembered the way he'd touched me, kneaded my skin, caressed all the best places. Warmth rushed through me, and I shuddered. Then wanted to die because of it.

Thorn glanced down the line of guards, his eyes skimming over me as if he hadn't been inside me mere hours ago. "As the commander has already pointed out, I am Branock Thorn, the Blade of the King." He breathed in, glanced at me again, then away. It was as if he was trying not to know me, or at least trying not to act like he knew me. "I'd like you to introduce yourselves and tell me where you're from."

Thorn walked to the end of the line and listened as each man explained where he hailed from and his full name. There was Arthur Pitvey, Freoc Nancekivell, Tomas Pengelly, Evan Kerleau, and Erwan Le Boudec in the front row. When the second row started introducing themselves, I stopped paying attention, too focused on the fact that he was making his way down the line to me, he stared coldly at me. His gaze was so frigid, I could've grown icicles in my hair.

"And you?" he asked.

"Senara Willow. I'm from Veilhelm, sir, born and raised."

Thorn's single amber eye pierced me with its intensity. "Willow? Isn't that an orphan name?"

"Yes, sir. Orphan's gain their last names from the tree they are found closest to." The same as I was Senara Willow, Wyn's last name was Oak because she'd been caught reading under a massive oak tree. It took everything I had to keep my stare trained over Thorn's shoulder and not making eye contact with him, even though I could feel his gaze on me like ants running over my skin.

"I can do more research into her history if you would like, sir," the commander offered.

Finally Thorn looked away from me as he waved the other man off, and I could breathe again. "That won't be necessary. She will prove herself or she won't. That is the way of the King's Guard, is it not?"

The commander made a noise of agreement but didn't seem to like that I wasn't as highly bred as some of the other soldiers.

He moved back toward his desk and leaned against the edge of it, kicking one of his long legs out in front of him as though he hadn't a care in the world. The giveaway was in his fingers as he gripped the edge of the desk, squeezing hard enough that I was surprised the wood didn't start splintering.

"The reason you've been summoned to protect the King is due to an infiltration of the castle walls." I almost wanted to point out that it was likely a failure on his part that allowed such a breach, but I remained silent because I had some preservation instincts. "The King chose to recall his best warriors in an effort to keep unwanted criminals out of the castle walls."

Thorn stood once more, crossing his arms over his chest as though he was challenging us. "The attackers were of unknown origin, no matter what you have heard otherwise.

Though we had hoped to spot some type of mark or symbol on their armor, they wore no political symbols or any type of identifying items. Even more confusing, they weren't carrying anything other than weapons."

How strange. Any foreign entity we'd come in contact with in battle had always worn their land's emblem proudly and had a member of their army carrying a flag that identified them in the field of battle. What type of clan would choose to stay unidentified?

Thorn continued, breaking through my thoughts. "The attack came too close. In fact, the attackers came closer than anyone outside of the King's Guard knows." That was a pretty big admission for a guy who was responsible for keeping the attackers as far away from the King as possible. "So let me make myself perfectly clear. You are not allowed to speak of this matter with anyone outside of the barracks. And, yes, that is a direct order."

We all nodded our heads in unison, agreeing to Thorn's instructions.

"Although we recognize that this attack was unexpected, those who were responsible for the lax security that resulted in the infiltration have been dealt with in a swift manner, as will be the case for anyone who fails to protect the king. I'm well aware of the rumors that have been floating around of fae and other such creatures returning to our lands, and there is no evidence to support any of that. The Veil is intact, and the number of magic users continues to dwindle under our fair king's rule. If you are caught spreading any of these rumors, you will be punished if not dismissed. Is that clear?"

When we started to nod he added, "Say it."

"Yes, sir," we called, almost as one.

Thorn cleared his throat and stood straight, relaxing his arms at his side. "You will only have a partial training-day today, which will include a round of sparring in the training area for a mild assessment. Then we will give you some time to get settled in. But before you go, I'd like to offer a warning. Although this job might seem dull and easy at times, it's not. So you should take advantage of this rare, free evening. You are dismissed." He didn't look at me, but more through me, as he spoke.

The men shuffled out of the office, and I followed closely behind them, almost to the door. I couldn't wait to put some distance between myself and Thorn. As I walked, I could feel his gaze on my back, that tingling sensation erupting all over me once more.

"Willow."

Thorn's call surprised me and I jumped, turned to see what he needed, and noticed that he'd settled into his desk chair.

"Please stay behind."

# CHAPTER
## TEN

S enara

My breath caught in my throat as I met his gaze. I was unsure of everything at that moment, but more than anything was what to say to assure him I could handle this—that I could handle being the King's Guard and the woman who'd slept with his Blade. It was that lack of certainty that kept my lips still.

Not that I could have said much, not while my mind was busy reminding me of the way he'd caressed my body and pleasured me to the point that my bones were liquid and my breaths little more than whimpers and moans.

Visions swirled through my head. And because it was probably more important than I could actually comprehend, I worked hard to push the thoughts aside, to think of anything else as I walked closer to Thorn's desk, my feet thankfully not tripping over themselves.

More than anything, I was curious to know how he would react to this increasingly uncomfortable situation we found ourselves in. Maybe I could take a prompt from him on how to work through it without making it worse. I just needed a hint as to which direction to go.

He stared at me from across the room, that single amber orb burning through me. I was still further away from him than I would like, but I didn't trust myself to get closer and not do something foolish. A shudder of fear and uncertainty ran through me. I'd slept with him before I knew who he was and before he knew who I was. Certainly we couldn't be held accountable for what we didn't know. Right?

Thorn seemed to sense my hesitation, for me to say that I could handle myself in the face of our... interlude. I could handle it. I didn't have another choice. But I didn't want to lie about it, didn't want to admit the effect he had on me.

He spoke first, his voice a deep reverberation that filled the room with an uncomfortable tension. "Will last night be the cause of problems for you?"

I closed my eyes and forced the mental visions of him hovering above my body, moving in all the right ways and hitting each delicate spot with perfect precision, to a far corner of my mind. Far enough they weren't front and center anymore but still within reach if the opportunity to be alone with my thoughts occurred.

He moved around the desk, coming closer, and I felt my heart rate increase as his familiar scent of cedar and spice surrounded me, reminding me of summers roaming around the woods looking for things I could sell. He was as intoxicating as the ale at the inn, as the feel of his body pressed against mine.

His voice was stern yet gentle as he repeated the question, "Do you understand what I'm asking? Is our association going to cause a problem for you?"

I could feel his gaze studying me intently, searching my face as I made him wait for an answer. I wanted to tell him that everything would be alright, that I wouldn't picture him naked every time he walked past, but the words caught in my throat. For a second. Then I shook it off. I wanted this job. The shaking hands, sweaty palms, and racing heart all inspired by the thoughts which might have been stronger than my will to dispense with them, meant nothing.

"No, of course not." I shook my head and clenched my hands until my nails dug into the skin of my palms, helping to clear my head.

He stepped so close that I could feel the heat of his presence looming over me. The smell of his scent mixed with the subtle hint of the ocean sent shivers down my spine.

"I want you to understand the seriousness of this," Thorn continued, his voice low and deep, husky and a memory in itself.

I craned my neck to stare up at him because he'd moved even closer. My body yearned for his touch, yearned to experience the whole night over and over again. We couldn't. I knew that now. My daydream of afternoon or evening dalliances from my walk this morning were well and truly dashed against the rocks.

"What happened between us must remain a secret. If others find out about it, the consequences will be far worse than you can imagine." His voice softened slightly. "If it's a problem, I'll send you back to the front and you won't be recalled again."

His words hit like a hammer against a blade. He'd worded it as a threat almost, and I didn't appreciate that he thought I would be the one who couldn't control herself. I was here precisely because I could. He was the one who'd allowed an attack at his post. But being sent back would almost certainly be a death sentence.

"It won't be," I whispered. A wave of memories flooded my mind as all romantic notions fled in the face of the recollections of war. Myself and the other soldiers in my regiment had fought so long and hard. Most of us had been on the front for years, moving from one location to another as the generals and commanders dictated. I had seen so many die around me, and I had saved others as well, which made me wonder how many of my comrades had fallen now because I wasn't there.

I could almost hear the screams of agony ringing in my mind, from friend and foe alike, and feel the torturous pain of a slow death, knowing that I couldn't help them in any way. At the same time I also had no idea if *I* would live from one second to the next. The idea that we were expendable was one I had made peace with, but after seeing Grimsby and Wyn again, that peace had fled. There was no way in hell I wanted to be sent back to the front.

"If you had been honest with me from the beginning, all of this could have been avoided." Thorn crossed his arms. His voice silenced the screams, the clash of steel on steel, and the roars of men as they gave the fight everything they had, including their lives. For a moment, I just breathed, relishing the silence as the memories faded.

I hadn't told anyone else in the bar that I was a soldier in the army either. And he hadn't been forthcoming either. But now he was my superior, the man who controlled my fate. I couldn't afford to make this an issue. I took a deep breath. "What do you need from me?" My voice sounded strangled to my own ears, but he didn't even blink.

"If you can prove your loyalty and respect for me, I will do my best to forgive what has been done." I bristled because forgive was the wrong choice of word, but I held my tongue. Sending me back to the front was clearly at the forefront of his mind, and I didn't want to give him an excuse to do just that. "But make no mistake. If you don't obey my orders, there will be consequences." Thorn cracked his knuckles and stared, waiting for my reaction.

Heat crept up my neck as I nodded slowly in agreement,

unable to form any words. Part of me wanted to rage at him, to tell him that the war had probably claimed more good lives because myself and the other warriors that worked to keep everyone safe were no longer at the front. I wanted to scream at him that this was all his fault, that it was his shoddy security that was responsible for us being recalled, and to throw his own line back at him. After all, if he had told me who he was, I wouldn't have invited him back to my room.

There were a few moments of silence as I looked into his eyes, getting myself under control while simultaneously wishing I could figure out what he was thinking.

His expression remained neutral as he spoke, his voice was void of emotion. Aside from the one very brief moment we shared when the tension in the room was so thick it was like another person in the room with us, there seemed to be no trace of the passion that overtook us the night before. Nothing of the man who had smiled and arm wrestled with me, nor of the man who had pleasured me so thoroughly.

Part of me wanted to ask him if things would ever be like they were at the tavern, if they could be like that, but good common sense overrode emotion and held me back from speaking my thoughts aloud. I knew they couldn't, but standing there, so close I could watch his pupils dilate and constrict, I was more than a little tempted by him.

It was almost as if Thorn had read my mind. Stepping closer, he lowered his voice to that sexy purr of his that seemed to dance over my skin as he spoke. "You must understand that this is not a game we are playing here. There are serious consequences for our actions which cannot be taken lightly. The King does not tolerate such infractions, no matter how high up the officers may be." He paused and fixed me with a stern but sympathetic look.

My heart raced as his words hung in the air between us, an almost tangible reminder of what we had done and why we should never—could never—do it again. I dug my fingernails into my palms once more, hard enough that I felt the skin give way, pain trickling through me like a heavy fog.

I swallowed hard and nodded silently in agreement, though my stomach turned over uneasily at the thought of taking orders from him after this encounter. And then it turned again at the same thought, only the second time was with anticipation rather than apprehension.

At the sound of heavy footsteps from the nearby hallway, Thorn glanced over my shoulder. His face darkened before turning back to look at me.

He spoke quickly and with a sense of urgency in his tone. "We shouldn't be seen alone in this room together. It is not a good idea."

Thorn stepped back and gestured for me to leave, his face expressionless.

Numbly, I made my way out of the room without saying another word. Thoughts raced through my mind as I tried to make sense of the hurried meeting.

This would be a whole lot more difficult than I anticipated, not just because of the orders I would have to follow and the looks he had given me, but also because of whatever unexplainable connection we seemed to share. Not to mention the memories I had of his body and the way he knew to use it to make mine sing.

I had to be the only warrior in the land who could screw up an assignment before it even started. How in the name of the old gods was I going to make this work?

# CHAPTER
# ELEVEN

Thorn

A heavy sigh escaped my lips as I watched Senara walk out of the room. She had a sway to her hips that wasn't natural for a warrior but I supposed suited a woman fine. I didn't want to watch her, but I couldn't look away either.

Nor could I forget the feeling of that ass in my hands or the softness of her skin under my fingertips.

I felt an old, familiar pull toward her, something I hadn't experienced in a long time but I'd discovered at the inn. It was something I missed when I woke up without her. I couldn't deny that I was disappointed when I didn't get to go for a second round, and I was surprised that she was the one who snuck out. Usually that was my role.

Unfortunately, now more than ever, it was abundantly clear that this draw I felt toward her could never be acted upon. Desires aside. Feelings aside. It couldn't happen, and I needed to get my head around that. There were reasons she was off limits.

The least of which was the king not wanting her there in the first place. Old bastard still thought women couldn't fight.

Another being that she was now part of the King's Guard, which meant I was her superior. I was the person who would decide what happened to the rest of her life, or at least as much of it as was in the King's Guard. I would be who graded her on the job she did, who could promote or dismiss her.

All of that meant she was off limits to me. No matter how much I wanted the situation to be otherwise, it was impossible for us.

I gritted my teeth and raked my hands through my hair in frustration. I would've sworn if there was a point to it, but there wasn't.

After an entire emotionless life, I had finally felt something for someone, a connection, and now it was all slipping away before I even had the chance to properly grasp onto it. And there was nothing I could do to save it. The rules were the rules, regardless of how much I disagreed with them. There was nothing I could do about it now except to accept it and move on.

I took a couple of steps away from where she'd been standing, needing to put space between myself and the air that still smelled of her, and paced, careful not to make too much noise. The last thing I wanted was for the men to gossip about Senara being in my office alone and me being upset when she left.

Each step was heavy with the emotions running through me, steps of disappointment, guilt, and longing. And each step tantalized me with the scent of her that still lingered in the room, jasmine and something that made me think of the clear, open night sky of my home—something that made me long to leave this place and take her with me.

Part of me wished I had been honest with her before we'd

spent the night together, but I knew doing so would've only made things worse. Because if we had known, I wouldn't have felt her skin against mine, wouldn't know the taste of her lips, the touch of her hand, the heat of her body, or the sound of her pleasure. Of course, I also wouldn't know the loss of those things which I felt keenly.

I was torn between wanting to stay in the moment and run away as far as possible. I couldn't do both, but a part of me didn't want to give up what I'd had with her. There was something about her that set me on fire and made me feel like I was standing in the sun for the first time in years.

When she entered the room earlier, a jolt of energy had surged through me.

Even though I'd told myself to stay away, my desire for her was strong, a pull, and an insistent tug at my heart. I hadn't even managed to stay on my side of the desk once we were alone, needing to be close to her, which was the opposite of what I'd told myself I would do.

My hands ached from the way I balled them into fists at my sides, desperate to keep myself from reaching out and touching her once again. She was almost more than I could resist.

Memories of our night together played in my mind over and over, making it hard to concentrate on anything else in the present moment. I could still hear her cries, her moans as I devoured her and lapped up her sweet nectar, the way she had taken a fistful of the blanket as she'd cried out with her climax. I couldn't stop remembering, wanting more of her.

Her lithe, sinewy figure, the curve of her hips, and her plump breasts all beckoned me to her. Her body didn't come close to touching her fiery personality or the inner strength that radiated out of her. There was also something to the mysterious past she clearly had. Before I'd approached her about arm wrestling, I'd heard her friend talking about knocking the men out and robbing them blind, and I didn't blame them for considering it. Then finding out she was an orphan today... It all came together in a puzzle I wanted to solve.

Unfortunately, I was painfully aware that if I wanted to protect both of us from further pain, I needed to find a way to avoid her each and every day. I didn't have a choice. Avoiding Senara was the only option if I wanted to save my job and hers, to have any chance at fulfilling my purpose, the entire reason I was in this stars-forsaken castle.

With heavy feet and an even heavier heart, I took one last lingering glance in Senara's direction before turning away resolutely. This would be best for both of us in the long run—even if it hurt more than it should. I didn't understand the hurt since we'd only just met, had only spent one night together, and I only had a single memory of what we shared.

I moved around the side of my desk and pulled the chair out before determining that I needed a break.

Before I could sit down, a knock on the door rattled the room, and I sighed. Being the Blade of the King was a never-ending job. The job didn't care if I needed a minute.

My jaw tightened as I glared at Ronan, my right hand man. His blond hair was pulled back into a top knot and he was clean shaven, so I knew that he'd been guarding the King today. That meant since he was here, he needed something or at the very least had a message for me.

He stood expectantly in the doorway before finally stepping into my office without waiting to be invited in. It was something of a sore spot with me. No matter how many times I told him to wait for an invitation, Ronan never seemed to listen. It wasn't a big deal, but if he couldn't obey a simple order, the chances he would obey the big ones weren't in his favor. It also made him look entirely too comfortable with me in front of the other men.

"I don't remember telling you to come in. I believe we've talked about this before," I growled. "You're getting far too familiar for your own good." I might've been angry about something else and was taking it out on him, but it didn't matter. Nothing bothered Ronan.

He shrugged it off. "Sorry, boss." There was a snarky tone to the easy dismissal that made me want to show him who was in command, but I stayed where I was and simply scowled at him, waiting for him to back down. The tension between us grew until our gazes were locked and neither looked away.

Finally, after what felt like an eternity of staring each other down, Ronan shifted his weight and tilted his head, eyes wide with what could only have been curiosity.

"So," he began slowly, "is this foul mood of yours something to do with the beautiful woman who just walked out of your office?"

As I listened to Ronan call Senara beautiful, my anger mingled with jealousy and boiled higher in my gut. I didn't need him to point out for me that she was beautiful. I saw it the moment we met. But hearing someone else say it pushed a strange, unfamiliar feeling deep within me, like a thorn burying itself in my foot.

It wasn't something I'd ever suffered before, this odd form of jealousy. It was so pure and so simple, so easy to identify, and inconceivably strong considering we'd only spent one night together. Somehow that made the feeling all the more powerful, possibly because of how our relationship began and knowing where it could have led if things had been different between us. That door was firmly closed though because of who we were.

I knew that whatever I was feeling now didn't matter at all. I merely wanted Senara to be safe and to keep myself from getting hurt in the process. It would be easier said than done because being around her without giving in was going to be a challenge greater than any other.

I didn't answer right away and, instead, took a deep breath and released it slowly before turning away sharply. He didn't need to see the myriad of emotions that were probably visible on my face. And I didn't want to have to explain anything to him.

Even though there was no denying the truth, sharing it would only make it worse. And so I simply kept silent, fiddling absentmindedly with the various pages and a paperweight on the set of drawers that sat behind my desk in order to avoid the inevitable questions from Ronan.

"What do you want, Ronan?" I snapped in annoyance as I turned back to him.

"The King would like to speak with you," Ronan replied calmly. "He needs a report on the new guards you summoned and their progress."

I snorted. Of course he wanted a progress update. They'd only just arrived, so of course he would think a progress report was appropriate. It would probably be best that I didn't tell him I bedded the first warrior I met. I turned sharply from the door, storming off without another word.

"Hey!" Ronan called after me with a mischievous tone in his voice. "Is the girl fair game then?"

I didn't acknowledge the question for a couple of reasons. First, I had somewhere to be, and second, I didn't want to kill him. Instead, I only quickened my pace out of the office. My fists involuntarily clenched at the thought of someone else thinking they could lay claim to Senara, but there was nothing I could do about it now.

The only thing I knew was that I had to get control of these feelings. She was a beautiful woman living with a barracks of men. It was inevitable that after shutting down any possibility of something between us, she would eventually find a companion among them. Though I bet they couldn't make her scream like I could.

Violence brewed within me at the thought of someone else touching her, tasting her, feeling her come around their cock. And if that someone was Ronan, I wasn't sure how this would end, but it would probably be bloody.

# CHAPTER
# TWELVE

S enara

I stepped into the tiny room, taking in its entirety with a smirk. It was small with only a bed, the narrowest of windows, and a table pushed against the wall. All of the other female guards shared rooms, but I had been given my own little closet while the guys were stuck sleeping in bunks in a large common room.

A guard named Allynna had shown me to my room, explaining that there weren't any others available and no one wanted a third roommate when the rooms were barely big enough for two people. I understood that, but I couldn't deny that I was both relieved to be alone but a little disappointed as well.

There hadn't been any women in my regiment, so I'd been looking forward to potentially bonding with other females who had similar experiences. Not that I could ever truly let my guard down with the mark on my back, but it would have been nice to have made some friends.

With Allynna gone, I took a seat on my cot and kicked off

my shoes, leaning back against the wall before closing my eyes.

I could hear muffled conversations and laughter coming from the other guards' rooms down the hall, yet here in this tiny space, it was almost silent. Despite its size, there was something comforting about having a place to myself, a respite from all the chaos that came with training and sparring most of the day.

It was also a place where I didn't have to be on guard all the time. I could actually let myself relax, something I hadn't been able to do in years while fighting at the front. In that way, the privacy was worth more than potential friendships.

With a content sigh, I curled up on the cot and recalled the training session. It went well, even though the trainer pressed me harder, faster than he had any of the others, as if he was going out of his way to show me that I still had a thing or two to learn about sparring. And that there was nothing special about me having been chosen or the fact that I was a woman.

Nevertheless, I left the ring feeling confident and proud of my abilities. And I couldn't help but wonder if I'd surprised him.

When we walked into the training area, the other guards didn't spar with me, talk to me, or have anything to do with me in general, but by the time the training session was over, there was some staring, some watching, and some nods of respect. It would take time, but this was a step forward.

After a few moments of rest, I sat up, remembering that we had the night to ourselves. We could roam the grounds or the castle in the areas restricted to our rank. And I knew exactly where I wanted to go.

One would have thought, with the training, exhausting as it was, I would want to sleep or, but I was filled with a sense of excitement as I headed off toward the Royal Library. This was exactly the break I needed, and it would be a welcome distraction from my thoughts of Thorn.

After taking several wrong turns down long hallways that sent me in circles, I finally managed to make my way there and went in search of Wyn. Sure enough, she was there, standing with a library assistant, both looking lively and chatty.

I couldn't help but notice that her cheeks were flushed with color which, given how quickly we'd grown up and how experienced we were with handling people, was quite an achievement on its own. Something inside of me stirred. I was happy for my friend, who seemed to be living her own version of a real-life fairytale, but at the same time, the tiniest sliver of jealousy stirred deep within my heart as I watched her enjoy this special moment with her very own someone new.

When I stepped forward, my boots thunked against the stone floor and caught Wyn's attention. Her eyes went wide and excitement shone in them as soon as she saw me, her smile huge and genuine.

She gestured to the tall figure next to her. "Senara, meet Tower. Roderik's his real name, but everyone calls him Tower because of his height and the fact that most people assume he's dumb as a rock."

I glanced at him curiously. He wasn't just tall and broad, he had boyish features and blonde hair. I completely understood the nickname.

Wyn cleared her throat before adding, "Don't let the rock-dumb assumption fool you. Tower here is smart as a whip."

He blushed and shifted his weight from one foot to the other as if I was the intimidating one in this introduction. "Wyn's too kind," he mumbled quietly. I didn't miss the evaluating glance that swept over me, and I couldn't help but wonder what he was thinking. Was he surprised by a female guard? Or was it that I was friends with Wyn?

My friend beamed at him before looking back to me with a

raised eyebrow. "Do you want to see the library? Come on. I'll show you around." She tucked some errant red hair behind her ear and walked out from around her desk. As soon as she was close enough, she hooked her arm through mine and gave it a light squeeze.

I laughed because we were each so excited, it would've been hard to tell who was more so. "Yes, I would love to see where you work." I turned in as much of a circle as I could given the way she was holding on to me, marveling at the shelves and shelves of books that seemed to climb multiple stories and stretched out in several directions. There were stairs leading to the next floor and ladders attached to every set of shelves. I could spend a lifetime here and not see all the books, scrolls, and the shelves on which they sat.

Tower gazed at me with intense curiosity in his eye, clearly eager to know more. "So what brings you to this library?" he asked.

I shrugged and glanced at Wyn, who was standing next to me, ready to show me all the secret nooks and her favorite places. I knew if we didn't leave soon, we wouldn't get to see more than a few shelves. "I'm just here for a little adventure. I hear that it's easy to find between the pages of a good book," I replied with a smile, repeating what Wyn had said to me on more than one occasion as we were growing up.

Tower nodded and seemed about to say something else when Wyn suddenly tugged my arm and pulled me away. "Come on," she said with a giggle. "We don't want to take up too much of Tower's time."

But Tower wasn't ready to let us go just yet. He stepped in front of us and stopped me in my tracks, which made the hairs on the back of my neck rise. I pushed the feeling aside, reminding myself that I wasn't at the front any more and he wasn't an attacker, just a librarian, as unlikely as that may seem by looking at him.

"Hey! No need to rush off like that," he protested, a hint of amusement in his voice. He then fixed his gaze on me again as if trying to read my mind before continuing. "Wouldn't it be better if you hung around for a bit? There's still so much I'd like to learn about you. After all, you are quite intriguing." He smiled like he'd just extended an invitation to the King himself.

I smiled awkwardly at him and tried not to show how uncomfortable I was feeling. Still, I could appreciate the effort, so I replied politely, "That would be really nice, but unfortunately we don't have any time right now. Maybe some other time?"

"It's settled then," Tower grinned before taking my hand in his and shaking it firmly. "Dinner tonight?" He cocked his head and waited, his tongue sliding along his lower lip.

He then shot an amused glance at Wyn, and I felt like I was about to be the butt of some joke.

"Sure." I glanced at Wyn, surprised by her ready acceptance. "That sounds lovely. Right, Senara?" Wyn raised her eyebrows, nodded and widened her eyes further in what I knew was her agree-with-me look.

"Of course." I nodded. "Dinner would be nice."

As we walked away, I felt his gaze following us until we were completely out of sight. I glanced over my shoulder at the last second to see him taking Wyn's place behind the desk, which apparently had to be staffed at all times.

Wyn pulled me through a corridor and giggled. "You sure have a way with the men this week, don't you?" I'd thought she was interested in him, but maybe not. And I didn't have an answer for her, so I ignored her question and instead turned my attention to the rows and rows of ancient literature.

We eventually ventured off into the archives. It felt like another world entirely with thousands of pristine books lining shelves. I expected that the air would be musty from age and neglect, since I doubted very many people traveled into the archives, but it just smelled like books. The rich scent of leather and ink wafted into my nose as we progressed further and further into the library, which seemed to go back further and be even bigger than I initially thought.

Wyn walked slowly at my side, her eyes bright with an excitement that I wasn't used to witnessing. Eventually, she stopped and turned to me, her voice barely above a whisper.

"I found something here," she said quietly, but the excitement was still there. "It's something special."

My heart began to race as I realized the type of books we were suddenly surrounded by. Magic pulsed against my skin, making me feel like I was drowning in it. Wyn had been searching for magic books and had apparently found them, hidden away in the back room of the archives.

I had to know if she still practiced magic. When we'd gone to the market I'd assumed it had been for something that she just couldn't get at the castle, but now I wondered if it was something more. Something worse.

Magic was dangerous, as was the practice of it, and suddenly my friend's safety was more important than a tour of an old library. Anxiety washed over me making my chest tighten and my stomach twist.

Taking a deep breath, I asked her hesitantly, "How much do you still...play in the dirt?"

The code phrase hung between us for a moment before Wyn gave me a side glance. She knew I'd be upset that she still practiced magic, after all we'd talked about her giving it up once she got the job in the library. I knew she didn't want to lie to me, which I appreciated, but I doubted she wanted to tell me the extent of it either.

"I build a mud pie or two... occasionally. Just for practice," she said softly.

Fear churned in my stomach, and my blood ran cold. Practicing magic wasn't just dangerous, it was forbidden. It didn't matter who she was or where she worked. If she was caught, she would be punished. I shook my head at her. This was the last thing Wyn should be involved with.

She was playing with fire. There were rules, *laws,* and I couldn't help but worry about what might happen if she were ever caught messing with something so dangerous. Toying with magic, inside the castle, no less, was punishable by death.

If I were to lose her then, I'd lose the only family I had. "You know better," I hissed before marching out of the section.

"There you two are!" Tower's voice rang out from the other end of the row. A grin spread over his face as I turned to him, struggling to lock down my own emotions.

"You found us!" Wyn chirped from just behind me as she bounded out of the section. "We got turned around by the battle scrolls." She linked her arm through mine once more, and I took a slow deep breath. He couldn't have heard us from where he was, so there was no reason to worry. And yet I couldn't stop the needling suspicion that he'd been around for longer than either of us wanted to believe. Had he been following us?

# THIRTEEN

Senara

"I could eat a horse." Wyn rubbed her stomach as we walked to the dining hall. Since the castle employees had their meals provided to them, we would dine with the rest of the castle staff.

I'd practiced hard all day and hadn't had anything other than the roll first thing this morning, so I was quite hungry as well. I hadn't been here yet, and I wanted to see it all, taking in as many details as I could.

The long hall was filled with people, more than I'd expected. The walls were stone, and the floor was black and white marble that gleamed as if it was cleaned thoroughly after every step taken. I didn't see anyone specifically responsible for such a task, but I didn't doubt there was someone waiting for us to be seated to wipe away evidence of our steps.

The emblem of the king hung on banners on each wall in a paltry mockery of the banners I'd seen elsewhere in the castle during my tour, especially where the elite socialized. There were two large fireplaces, one on each side of the hall, which I was sure people would cluster around in winter, emitting light and heat that helped the room feel more open than it would otherwise. The crack and pop of the wood was barely audible over the din of everyone talking.

Tables lined the entire room, some more bench like, while others were round. Some sat on a platform, but most were just on the floor. Tower was seated at a table near the entrance, and he stood to wave us over.

My hope that he'd got distracted or found some other form of entertainment was crushed. The brief respite from him had been thanks to a bathroom break where I'd used the time to get myself together.

Finding out Wyn was still practicing her magic was not where I'd expected the day to lead me.

The atmosphere was lively as people laughed and ate together. As I looked around the room, I realized I didn't know many of the men seated at the tables of warriors, and I didn't know the ladies in waiting, the cleaners, or the king's entertainers. I found myself feeling like an intruder. It was almost awkward to be amongst so many different kinds of people.

As we passed a round table, I heard one of the guards say something that caught my attention. "She should transfer to the library. It seems more comfortable for her there." He hadn't bothered to whisper even though the subject of his conversation was walking right past.

My blood started a slow boil knowing he was talking about me.

His companion laughed and added his own thoughts. "I bet she won't make it two months here!"

I tensed up, my fury burning red-hot. These strangers didn't have any right to make assumptions about my capabilities.

The anger built inside of me as I processed what the guards said. It was one thing to ridicule me behind my back, but to openly talk about me was something else entirely. If I let it slide, it would only get worse and they would think I was weak and submissive, not wanting to cause a fuss, which was definitely not the case.

I spun around and glared at them, my voice rich with indignation. "What do you think you're doing?" I demanded angrily. "Do you want to say it directly to my face, or are your balls so shrunken up that all you can do is whisper insults under your breath?"

Tower scrambled to step between us and attempted to intervene, but I didn't need help. And I damned sure wasn't going to let him help shield them. They needed to answer for their comments.

The guard side-eyed his companions and let out a hearty laugh. "I'm sorry, little girl. Did I say something that offended you? I was merely speculating." And now he was laughing at me while his friends joined in.

"Oh, you enjoy speculating out loud, do you?" I stepped forward, fists balled and muscles coiled. I could take this guy. Size wasn't everything. I had speed. I had agility. I had rage. I could make him sorry. "Why don't you come a little closer, so I can shut your mouth for you?"

The over-sized mutant of a guard stood and towered above me. "Oh, yeah? May the Veil take you."

The dining hall quieted as everyone turned their attention to our argument. This was probably as much excitement as any of them had ever seen in the dining hall.

"It saddens me to see such a large man overcompensating for his little dick." I glanced at his britches and then rolled my eyes. "Such a pity."

The guard stopped laughing. Must've been true, or he wouldn't have been so sensitive about it. That was my mindset anyway. His face reddened.

His companions roared with laughter as they watched our

interaction, which only caused his cheeks and forehead to turn a deeper crimson, the shade bordering on purple.

"If we're listing things that we pity, it breaks my heart to watch a sweet, young thing using her body to climb the ranks of the Royal Guard." He cocked an eyebrow and gave me an up and down that made me want to cringe, but I wouldn't give him or anyone else the satisfaction. "First you turn down the lower ranking officers, and then you spend time alone with the Blade? Your cunt might be warm and wet, but it will only get you so far, whore."

"Spend a lot of time thinking about my cunt, do you?" I asked as I grabbed myself between the legs. This was exactly the kind of shit I'd had to put up with when I first arrived at the front, and until I put my fist in the face of everyone who dared speak about me that way, it continued. Soldiers respected strength, and I needed to show that I wasn't afraid, nor was I some weak timid thing just because I had a vagina and tits.

"Probably stinks of fish and old cum," the big man grunted as he pinched his nose with his fingers.

Before I had a chance to respond with my fist, Wyn stepped in between us and spread her arms wide in an effort to separate us. Her voice was calm and soothing as she said, "Let's just simmer down now and not cause a scene. We don't want people thinking we're troublemakers, do we?" She shot him a pointed look and then motioned toward the door where undoubtedly she meant the King would be lurking or having someone lurk for him. He was, after all, that kind of king.

I couldn't afford to step back. I had to wait for him to make a move. The last thing I needed was someone to interpret me coming to my senses as weakness, and they would. If I so much as slid a foot away, then I'd become the one who backed down, so I kept staring at him with my teeth bared, ready to fight if he determined that was how this was going to go.

But somehow her words worked. The guards glanced toward the door, looked down in shame before moving away. I took a deep breath to steady myself before reluctantly turning from them and continuing on our path to the table Tower had saved for us.

The moment we sat down, I couldn't help but wonder if Wyn had used some kind of magical influence on those guards. They certainly hadn't seemed the kind to back down due to an abundance of caution. Or an abundance of anything else. To my way of thinking, the only thing they had in abundance was musculature they misused and didn't deserve.

Perhaps she'd done something subtle enough that no one would notice it, yet strong enough for her words to have such a powerful effect on them.

Of course, there was no way for me to know for sure. So I leaned over and asked quietly, "Did you... use any kind of dirt back there?" I knew she'd understand the meaning of my question, even if it sounded crazy to anyone trying to listen in. I wouldn't even utter the word magic in the castle if I didn't absolutely have to. It was just too damn risky.

Wyn smiled at me, wrinkled her nose, and half-winked before turning her attention to Tower, leaving me with more questions than answers. I would have more luck if I asked her again later when we were alone.

Like a blanket thrown over my skin, or a jolt of energy that passed over the room and landed on me, I suddenly sensed a presence in the room and glanced around nervously. My gaze settled on a figure seated in the corner, and my heart skipped a beat. It was Thorn.

I quickly averted my gaze, and like I'd never wanted anything else before in my life, I hoped he hadn't seen me looking.

But of course, I wasn't quick enough because Wyn had already noticed him and gasped in shock. I shook my head sternly at her, indicating that she shouldn't make a scene. I didn't need any more attention.

"Why don't we get some food?" Wyn asked, sounding like she didn't have a care in the world as she pointed out the food line for me.

I pushed to my feet. "Keep the table for us?" I asked Tower since I'd noticed there was nowhere else to sit. Apparently they needed more seating in the staff dining area or people needed to learn to eat in shifts.

"As my lady desires," he replied, dipping his head before glancing at me with a smile.

It didn't do anything to warm me to him, though. In fact, it only served to irritate me further. I just nodded at him and led Wyn in the direction of the food. There were sweetmeats and a stew, roasted vegetables, some bread, fruit, some sort of porridge that seemed to be swirled with honey, and, of course, sweet rolls.

The rich spiced scent of the stew and the warm sugar from the sweet rolls made my stomach rumble. The smell of the food alone was making my mouth water.

I grabbed two bowls of hearty stew and handed one to Wyn before moving on to the bread and sweet rolls. If I didn't have to pay for them, I was definitely going to enjoy them every once in a while. Once I had all my food, I moved away from Thorn's direction and succeeded in avoiding eye contact with him again.

Because I didn't want to seem as shaken up as I truly was, I took my time with my stew and only occasionally glanced back in Thorn's direction. The wooly feeling of a gaze that hadn't wavered rasped against my skin. He was watching me. Though maybe it was just my imagination and my own paranoia. And I was ashamed of it, but I hoped more than anything that Thorn actually had kept his gaze on me.

Tower leaned over and touched my arm lightly. "You sure

were riled up back there, huh?" He nodded to where the altercation with the other guards had taken place, although I half-expected that he was referring to Thorn. It took me a second to realize we were on different subjects. And when I did, I nodded at him.

Although, the way he looked at me left me feeling a little uneasy. Whenever he thought I wasn't looking his gaze would travel over my body hungrily and he would lean toward me a little more as though he couldn't stay away. The poor guy obviously was interested in me.

"Yeah, sorry you had to witness that." I shoved a spoonful of stew in my mouth, hoping Tower would shift his attention to something other than me. It made me uneasy, at best.

"I kind of wish Wyn hadn't jumped in between you and that idiot." Tower gestured to the table across the room. "Seeing you fight would've been the highlight of my day." He didn't seem inclined to let me quietly enjoy my food. "You should've"—he jabbed the air. "I would've loved to see something like that."

This guy didn't know when to stop. Couldn't he see that all I wanted to do was eat my stew in peace?

I glanced at Wyn, noting her stormy glare. Oh no. She did like this guy, and he was ignoring her to talk to me. This asshole. And there was no easy way to sidestep his attention.

Why hadn't I noticed it? All the signs were there that Wyn had a crush on Tower, and if he noticed the signs he didn't seem to care about them. I'd let one comment sway my initial opinion when I should have just gone with my gut.

I gritted my teeth in frustration. Tower wasn't even worth the time of day, let alone the attention of someone like Wyn. But it was more than that. His flirting made me uncomfortable, particularly now that I could see how Wyn felt, but I wasn't sure how to put an end to it without making our dinner even more awkward.

Taking a deep breath, I added this latest incident to the growing list of things that I needed to discuss privately with Wyn. I made a mental note to find a moment when we could talk without anyone else around. I needed answers to questions that no one else could overhear, and more than anything else, I needed Wyn to be honest with those answers and not give me mixed signals.

I shoved another spoonful of stew into my mouth, the food which had started out rich and delicious had turned to ash in my mouth as Tower kept talking. Telling me how much it looked like I could fight, and how a female warrior was so rare, and I should be so proud. All his words did was make me feel sick.

The only thing I could think of was to come up with some way of extracting myself from the dinner and leaving Wyn alone with Tower in the process, though I hoped she saw what an idiot he was and was no longer interested in him. I doubted it, though. I'd seen the adoration in her eyes when I first went into the library, and it would take a message from the old gods themselves to get her to see the reality of the situation at this point.

Between feeling like he'd been following us around the library and the way he was excited at the prospect of violence, he gave me a bad feeling—one that I wasn't sure I'd be able to shake any time soon.

CHAPTER
# FOURTEEN

T horn

My legs tensed with the need to move as I watched them from across the room. The librarian boy, Tower if I remembered correctly, didn't need to touch Senara, but his hand grazed her arm in a way that made my gut burn with anger. My jaw was sore from clenching my teeth so tightly.

Tower laughed, and I glared through narrowed eyes. This bastard was too loud, chortling too long at something she said, and he didn't deserve the polite smile she turned on him. The whole scene only served to fill me with rage.

When he mimicked fighting, punching at the air, my lip curled in response. The boy couldn't even throw a punch.

I looked down and realized that my fists were balled so tightly that my knuckles were turning white as I tried to digest what was happening in front of me. He was too close, watching her, trying to find reasons to touch her.

I could see it in his face.

He wanted her.

With a gargantuan amount of effort, I forced myself to pick

up my fork and eat something. My knuckles were still white around the tiny piece of metal, and I was honestly surprised I hadn't crushed it to dust.

I wanted to rush at him, knock him off the chair that he'd pulled too close to her, and scream, shout, and pound my chest. If it was up to me, I would mark my territory, find a way to force Tower, that bumbling mountain of an oaf, out of the room and away from Senara. But none of that was an option.

The rage in my heart far exceeded the confines of my body, and for a second, I stood, ready to move in, to take out Tower and show him why I was the Blade of the King—why I was the one in charge. But I looked around, and I saw other people in the room. This was not the place, nor the time, for me to act on my impulses.

Still, part of me wished that something could be done about Tower's behavior. Judging from the way she kept trying to move away from him, and hardly looked at him, she clearly didn't want his hands on her or anything else he might've been trying to offer. Had he no respect for boundaries? He was treating Senara like she was some toy, something he could just play with when it pleased him.

I forced myself to look away because I couldn't watch this anymore. It was too much. Taking a deep breath, I tried to calm the rage bubbling in my chest. I knew violence wasn't the answer, but all I could think of was how good it would feel to grab a fistful of Tower's tunic, swing him around by it, and toss him out of the dining hall so that he skidded on his face to the end of the hallway. It was a two-fold kind of fantasy. It would successfully get him away from Senara, and Tower would know he'd done wrong. Two-fold was my favorite.

Ronan paused from stuffing his face with food and looked at me with a quizzical expression. "What's going on?"

"Nothing, I'm just getting a sweet roll," I ground out before stalking away from the table. Turning my gaze from Senara was one of the hardest things I'd done, but I couldn't watch her and make it to the food line at the same time.

The polite thing to do would be to wait, but I didn't even really want the damn roll, so I cut to the end, snatched a roll off the tray and kept moving back to my seat. I just needed a reason to move, something to do that would let my body think it was getting its way and I was going to go and claim Senara the way I wanted to. Only that wasn't what was going to happen.

It could never happen.

"Want to try that again? You don't even like those things," Ronan said as I sat down.

He was right. The rolls were too sweet for me most of the time. I sighed, pausing for a moment to gather my thoughts before explaining what I'd been glaring at. "I was watching one of the new recruits stand up for herself," I said.

I had watched her speaking to the other guards that were there having dinner. Gawen, the guard who was more mountain than man, had apparently upset her. Seeing her fury rise like that, the way she stood in front of him, challenging him even though she barely came up to his armpit, reminded me of why I'd been so attracted to her in the first place.

When she grabbed herself, I'd almost spit my drink across the table. The way her face flushed with rage at his response almost drug me out of my seat.

Somehow, none of that was as bad as watching her with Tower.

Ronan smiled as if he had a bird's eye view to the inside workings of my mind. "Ahh, could it possibly have been the same beautiful girl as before?"

Allynna, one of the few female guards, sat on the other side of Ronan. She was listening, there was no other reason for her to have perked up at the mention of another beautiful woman. "The new guard? I thought she was rather plain and unimpressive in the training ring today, if you ask me." No one had, but neither did anyone mention it.

The thought crossed my mind that Allynna would think differently of Senara if she challenged her to an arm wrestling match. I knew better than to say it out loud because it would only bring more questions and suspicions.

"She looks like she'd like some more company, or maybe just some better company." Ronan stood from the table and took one last sip from his mug.

I watched in disbelief as he approached the table and sat down next to Senara. Tower's face darkened to a deep rage-filled red. He obviously wasn't expecting another male to impede on his flirt-fest with Senara.

Sitting next to her, Ronan's hair looked blonder than normal, and his eyes sparkled as he picked some imaginary lint from her tunic. He knew exactly what he was doing to me. He grinned at her, and she smiled back at him, clearly more at ease with a fellow warrior than the lusty librarian.

She wasn't the only one who looked relieved for Ronan's presence, though. Her friend, the one from The Red Kraken was clearly a librarian also, and even though I hadn't been able to see her face for most of the dinner, I'd noticed her shoulders inching higher and higher the more Tower flirted with Senara. When Ronan pulled up a chair, she relaxed slightly.

Wishing I could overhear what was being said, I leaned forward as though the few inches it brought me closer would serve me in that regard. However, the din of chatter and the occasional roar of laughter in the dining hall left me in the dark.

My palms grew sweaty as I tried to figure out what was going on. Why was I letting Ronan sit over there with Senara? The answer was simple. I didn't have another choice. I couldn't do anything about it even though it was tearing me up inside. I also knew that if I were to intervene, it would only prove Ronan right.

That man was intolerable when he was proven to be correct about something, especially something I'd been trying to hide from him. No, I was going to have to deal with it and let him have his fun. At least I knew he wouldn't lead Senara on or do anything against her wishes.

When he pushed to his feet and held his hand out to Senara, my mouth almost fell open. It was only the fact that Allynna was right there that kept me acting like none of this affected me.

I felt powerless as Senara took Ronan's hand, standing before following him from the room.

I watched powerlessly as they walked away, and it mixed my emotions. First, and I truly didn't understand why, but I was unreasonably unhappy with Ronan. He didn't belong with Senara. And second because it took most of an eternity before they finally turned the corner. A sense of jealousy overtook me, and I wished I could be the one walking by her side.

But instead, I was stuck watching from afar as Allynna moved closer, laying her hand on my arm in an effort to get my attention. She'd seen an opportunity and seized it by sliding into Ronan's empty chair. She obviously wanted something from me, but if I was going to make the decision to go down the road of unethical behavior, it wasn't going to be with Allynna.

Not because Allynna wasn't gorgeous. Any man with two eyes would attest to her sheer beauty. Her long, blonde hair and full, pouty lips typically allowed her to convince men to give her whatever, or whomever, she wanted. Unfortunately, for her anyway, she had her eyes set on me, and as was typically so, she refused to back down.

"So, tell me." Allynna traced her lower lip with her finger, probably because she knew men dreamed about those lips and what they wanted her to do with them. This was a woman who knew the value of her beauty. "What is it that you find so attractive about that girl?"

Oh no. No, no, no. There wasn't a good way to answer such a question. Also, there was nothing I could say to Allynna that wouldn't be met with further advances. If I said Senara was simply beautiful, she would ask what was the good of beauty if I couldn't have it. And we all knew I couldn't. But I couldn't have Allyna for the same reason. I debated not saying anything at all and ignoring the question.

I also knew if I stayed at the table alone with Allyna, she'd only try harder to win me over. So I took a deep breath and pushed back my chair, looking down at her. I hated that her eyes were full of hope as she sat up taller, arching her back. She knew the value of and how to use her breasts, too. But it was the hope that I had to dash. And to do it, I was going to have to be blunt.

"There are many things I find attractive," I said, forcing my voice to a frosty coldness. "But the most notable quality is that she isn't you."

Her face fell as the words hit her. And with that line drawn between us, I turned and stormed out of the dining hall.

Everything in me wanted to stop by the table Tower still sat at with Wyn and teach him not to touch what was mine, and yet I couldn't. Wouldn't. Senara wasn't mine. She never would be.

Even as I told myself that, I found that I was following the same path that she had taken with Ronan. I knew because her scent lingered in the air, driving me to madness. The seductive jasmine called to me like a siren of old or like the song of the Veil itself. Impossible to resist.

I hadn't even realized that I'd almost been running after them until I bumped into one of the guards on their way to dinner. After a brief apology, I took the next turn I could, pushing myself to get away from her scent and the way I knew they were probably going.

After the encounter with her this morning, I'd told the commander to put her on nights. That would at least keep her away from me for the most part. All I had to do was outlast this craving and figure out a way to resist the pull I had to her, and then this would all be fine. I just needed to avoid her until then, which seemed impossible when she was all I could think about.

After moving through the corridors for a while, I had lost track of where I was and found myself in the gardens that I often wandered through when I couldn't sleep. The nature and clean air here reminded me of my home, one I hadn't been to in more years than I cared to count. But it did remind me of how Senara reminded me of my home as well. What I couldn't figure out was *why*.

# FIFTEEN

S enara

"Let me know if you need anything." Ronan turned and walked away, all business with his head held high, his back straight. He was stern, but he'd taken time out of his free evening to show me around. And I was appreciative. I would've been more appreciative, but after the tour, he informed me that I had the first night shift out of the new group of recruits. Right now, gratitude for a tour that was less tour and more training was a stretch.

At least he'd given me my new armor, so I looked official, even if I had no idea what I was doing other than looking for anything suspicious.

It certainly would've been nice if someone had shared my duty station for the night with me earlier. Because when Thorn gave us the night off, I had assumed that he meant all of us. I also thought he meant the entire night, meaning I would have the entire night free to meet new people, roam the castle, and get a good night's sleep.

Turned out that I was wrong. And now it was going to be a

very long night. At least I had a decent meal beforehand, even if Tower made it almost unbearable.

After I quickly changed into my guard uniform and armor, I made my way to the patrol area Ronan had so kindly given me a tour of only a few minutes earlier. If Ronan hadn't interrupted our meal, I would've been late for my first official castle duty, which wasn't the impression I wanted to make. And it infuriated me that no one else had bothered to tell me.

It was almost as if everyone wanted me to fail as they sat back and mocked me from afar. Not that I'd seen anything or been told by anyone. But then, who would tell me? Who would be the one brave enough to say something? It was just a feeling in my gut.

Maybe I was being paranoid, but it seemed like ever since I got on that stars-damned ship, I had been labeled as an outcast or something, unfit to be part of the general population. Sometimes I wondered if people could somehow sense that I was Moon Marked, or at least that I was hiding something, and that was why they were so eager to keep their distance from me. Usually, I appreciated it, but this time, it was coming with a sense of negativity that I wasn't used to.

Moving slowly and searching every inch of the grounds I could see from one side to the other, I patrolled the area as I'd been trained to do. Ronan emphasized that I was to leave no corner unviewed since the king was on high alert after the last attack. "It's your job to ensure his safety, so that means no distractions and keeping your eyes peeled all night."

I didn't want to let Ronan down, especially since he had gone out of his way to be kind to me. But I especially didn't want to disappoint Thorn. His warning rang in my head, strong and powerfully, making me remember how his strong arms had felt wrapped around my body, while also reminding me that he wouldn't hesitate to send me away again.

I shook my head, silently scolding myself. Now was not

the time to daydream about the sex god who also happened to be my superior. Although, were they really daydreams if they happened in the night and were more memories than fantasy?

As I continued on my assigned path, I made mental notes of everything I saw, and each time another member of the staff passed me, I resolved to try and learn the names of as many people who worked at the castle as I could. Having the ability to greet people by name was a good first step in becoming part of the group who devoted their lives to the service of the King. At least, that was my thought at the time. In my mind, it made sense.

After the insults that were made about me in the dining hall, I knew I was going to have to spend some time proving I was worthy of the position I'd been given. Proving myself was probably as vital as being able to also show everyone that I could be a team player.

I rounded a corner and immediately stopped in my tracks. Thorn and Ronan were heading off on a trail toward the city together. Luckily, they hadn't seen me, but for as long as I could see them, there wasn't a reason I couldn't watch or notice the way Thorn smiled at something Ronan said.

A spike of jealousy pierced my heart at the sight of someone other than me making him smile like that, even if it was only Ronan.

It was such a ridiculous thought. I hadn't even known the guy for a week. Barely an entire day. I had exceeded ridiculousness.

Twenty-four hours.

That was how long it had been since I'd met Thorn back at The Red Kraken.

Just because the man gave me two of the best orgasms of my life did not mean that I was suddenly attached to him or had any right to him. Besides, he was my supervisor and had made it clear that what happened would never happen again, so I was going to have to put up with him smiling at other people, probably even flirting with other people. The thought made my stomach twist.

He wasn't mine. Never would be.

I sighed again and stole one more glance as the men walked off together. For a moment, actually longer, if I was honest, I stood there wishing I could join them for whatever fun they were about to have in the city. Instead, I continued my route, patrolling back and forth, checking the shadows and staring into the blackness for shifting figures and shapes. I saw nothing.

As I made my way back to the same corner an hour later, my heart raced as my gaze landed on a spot in the darkness that seemed out of place. There was someone there, hunched by a pillar.

I didn't know much about castle life, but I knew enough to realize that this person wasn't supposed to be there. I shifted my stance, my senses on alert as I stepped forward, careful to tread lightly to not make a sound as I attempted to get a better look.

Whoever they were, they were dressed in all black, which only made me even more suspicious of their motives. In my experiences, bandits and thieves preferred dark colors. It made their jobs easier and those of the guards who chased them much more difficult. Despite the darkness of the night, I was determined to use this knowledge to my advantage and cautiously follow after them. It was my goal to pursue without them noticing me, but time would tell if I was successful.

Anyone lurking around at such a late hour had to have some hidden agenda, and I was ready for anything. I stepped carefully, avoiding loose stones and twigs and trailed behind them while staying close in the shadows. My body tensed with anticipation of what I might uncover.

I was hellbent on catching this shady figure. Maybe it was

because I wanted to prove myself to Thorn and the rest of the seasoned guards. And to myself, too. Regardless, I needed to follow through with my agreement to protect the King. Bandits of any kind were a threat to the King and his rule.

And if I could capture this intruder alive, maybe the King's spymasters could even get some answers about who was trying to attack the King and why. Just the thought made me want to dart forward and tackle the figure, but there was too much ground between us. I knew as soon as I moved with any kind of speed, they would notice.

I stalked the figure through the black night, my heart pounding, watching them as I inched ever closer. My heart raced, but I kept my eyes trained on the dark character in the distance. I silently crept through the shadows, edging closer and closer until I was almost within range of being able to take them down without risking them getting away.

My breathing grew shallow as I steeled myself for what I was about to do. But just as I was ready to make my move, a cloud moved and a beam of moonlight cast down and illuminated my brightly shining armor.

I froze, but it was too late, the sudden brightness of my armor had alerted the person to my presence, and they took off running. That was the problem with this armor.

I cursed myself for not having the foresight to be less noticeable and ditch the armor when I had the chance. Of course they would see me. I was in armor that had been polished to a high glossy sheen, gleaming like a beacon in the pale light of night.

Determined to catch up, I ran like hell after them, which was hard to do given that this armor weighed more than my battle armor. With each step I took, hatred for the intruder grew inside me. Beyond that, there was an unbearable feeling of shame that weighed heavily on my shoulders for not being more prepared and nimble-footed.

I chased for as long as it was worthwhile, but the intruder eventually jumped onto a wall, and I knew I wouldn't be able to follow, or at least by the time I could, they would be long gone. Before they disappeared over the wall, the intruder turned and glanced at me over their shoulder, the hood they had been wearing falling back to reveal a pointed ear decorated with more gold rings than I could count before they disappeared.

My breath froze in my chest.

Pointed ears.

That could only mean that the intruder was fae.

We'd been told that the idea of intruders being fae was merely a rumor, not an actual possibility, but that was what I'd seen. Though according to what I knew about fae, the intruder would be a giant among their kind. They were supposed to be small but vicious.

As the shock faded, I was left alone with nothing but frustration and self-pity. I was overcome with a sense of foolishness as I ran back toward my post, my mind racing with the fear that maybe the intruder had been a decoy. Something used to lure me away. It wasn't like I was guarding a particularly vital piece of the castle, so if I was the guard they picked to distract, they'd chosen the wrong one.

But it wasn't just anger that tore through me. There was also an overwhelming shame that threatened to wash away all of my ambition. How could I have been so stupid? Why hadn't I taken better precautions? I had approached the suspect as I would have someone in battle and because of that, they'd gotten away. Maybe I wasn't cut out to be a member of the Royal Guard.

As these thoughts crossed my mind, so did a feeling of hatred toward the bandit, no, fae who had outwitted me so easily. It was a personal affront, as if this thief had deliberately chosen to make sport of me, or chose my path because I was a new guard, a lesser protector amongst all the other, more seasoned, guards.

I stood there, empty-handed and miserable, and the dark figure escaped unscathed into the darkness. I had no one to blame but myself.

Now I was left to figure out how to break the news to my superiors. To Thorn. Not just that the intruder got away, but that whoever they were, the one thing I knew for sure was that they were fae. I was certain of it. The only question that needled at me was whether or not anyone would believe me.

# CHAPTER
# SIXTEEN

Senara

"How many corridors does this damn place have?" I asked no one in particular at a volume no one in the world could've heard, but I was frustrated. The hallways were long and twisted in one direction or another as they wound into one another. It was all very confusing. Especially as this was a trip I didn't really want to make, to an office I didn't really want to go into, to make a confession I would have preferred to never speak aloud. So yeah. The number of corridors and the distance between each one was an annoyance that might have seemed petty, but in my opinion wasn't.

My attitude could've been better, but I'd been walking in circles for what felt like ages before I finally made my way to the commander's office.

Knocking gently, I strained to hear him respond. I almost wished he wouldn't.

"Come in." His tone was deep and gravelly, and I wasn't looking forward to listening to him yell. That type of voice always made my throat ache in sympathy. As I reached to shut the door behind me, he shook his head. "Leave it open."

There were ten or so guards waiting outside his office, and I didn't want them to hear this. I didn't want to be the new recruit who got yelled at after her first shift. But that was probably what was going to happen.

The commander sat behind his desk, looking as if the last thing he wanted to deal with was one of the new recruits, and since the last thing I wanted was to be there, we were both in the shape to not want any part of this. Unfortunately, the choice wasn't ours.

"I'm very sorry to disturb you, sir." I cleared my throat and clasped my hands behind my back. I didn't look at him but rather a point on the wall behind him as I'd been trained. It didn't matter because he didn't even look up. Yet. "I wanted to make you aware that while patrolling my area last night, I saw a dark figure dressed in all black." I wanted to tell him that I'd come to his office right away since I'd been unsure what to do, but no one else had been around, as though legitimate attacks could only happen during the day or something.

It was a start to the story, and though I didn't need to pause before I went further with the previous night's happenings, I took a short, shallow breath so I could watch for a reaction from the commander out of the corner of my eye. He finally looked up at me, waiting for me to continue, but when I still paused, he leaned back in his chair and folded his hands over his stomach. As I struggled to find the words, he raised his bushy salt-and-pepper eyebrows expectantly.

I didn't care if he was the guy who was going to decide where I worked every night from here to the end of time, I wasn't going to let him intimidate me. After taking a calming breath, I continued undaunted by the narrow stare. "I attempted to pursue the intruder, but they saw me and ran off. They knew the terrain, sir, and I'm sorry to say that I wasn't able to catch up to them. As they fled over the wall, their hood dropped back and I saw their ear. They were fae sir, I'm sure of it."

"Oh, I see." The commander crossed his arms. His lips turned up into a slight smirk. "I'll look into it."

He'd look into it? That was his response?

I announced that I'd see a fae, our sworn enemies since the Hundred Year War, enemies we thought were banished by the Veil, and that was all I got?

My face flushed with the anger that bubbled up inside me as the commander sat in front of me, looking as if I'd just told a joke. It was one thing to expect a level of excellence that far exceeded my level of training—since I'd been here one day and sent out on my own, but it was another thing to act as if my report of a marauder was meant for his amusement.

I wanted to scream in his face, but I wasn't a child who needed to throw a tantrum. Aside from that, it wouldn't do any good to yell at my superior for not taking something seriously, especially a legitimate threat to the Crown. If he wanted to risk the King's life and Thorn's wrath, that was on him. All I managed to bite out without losing my temper was a quick, "Thank you, sir."

The other guards that had been standing just outside the commander's office laughed quietly behind me, which only made the matter of my humiliation worse. As they snickered with one another, I realized that they were clearly enjoying the show and likely believed me even less than the commander did.

I could understand why they weren't welcoming and hadn't gone out of their way to accept someone new right away–after all, who knew how long new recruits to the King's Guard normally lasted–but certainly they didn't need to act with such blatant hostility. It simply didn't make sense for all of them to hate me from the start. I thought that maybe yesterday's training sessions would have softened them a bit but apparently not.

"You're all dismissed. Head down to training, and then you'll have time to sleep the rest of the day." The commander turned his attention back to the map that was sprawled across his desk and the stack of papers that sat next to it. He either didn't want to entertain the idea of a suspicious intruder gallivanting through the castle grounds, or he was no longer interested in speaking to me.

As I walked toward the door, I noticed the guards eyeing me and whispering to one another. Anger boiled just under the surface of my skin. Even though I had no interest in hearing what the other guards had to say about my encounter, I couldn't help it. One of the men leaned in and commented to the others. "She's so desperate to make a name for herself that she made up a mysterious figure, frolicking through the night air. Fae no less. And then she *admitted* she let him go. Can you imagine? Fae showing up and then just letting him go?"

The other guards burst into laughter, no longer trying to hide their amusement. "What else could she do? Claim the mystery man was invisible, too?" Their laughter was raucous and loud.

This time, I chose to ignore them. I wasn't about to make a scene in front of the commander, especially when we were about to go train for battle by fighting one another. There was another way to work out my anger, and they were going to be on the wrong side of it.

How many of them were used to fighting on little to no sleep? On the front lines of war, where I'd served my king and my country, attacks were known to come at any time, and never had my commanders been afraid to call on me and ask me to fight for as many hours as it took until we were able to beat the opposition back.

I stood alone among the other Royal Guards, but my face was a mask of determination. It would be the day that the Veil took me when I allowed these horrible people to get me down.

As we marched back out to the training area, I was taken aback when my mind wandered and I found myself thinking of how long it had been since I first joined the royal army. Wasn't it just a few years ago that I'd been pleading with the recruitment captain to let me in? Then I'd been whisked away to lands I never expected to see in my lifetime before I arrived here, having come full circle. It felt like I had been back a lot longer than a day or so, that much I was sure of.

Between my awkward meeting with Thorn, a confrontation with one of the guards, and now seeing a suspicious person and not being taken seriously when I reported it, I was so tired it felt as if I hadn't slept in several days. When I took into consideration how miserable I'd been from the unrelenting sea sickness and everything that had happened on the voyage over from Balaise, it was no surprise that I was starting to feel run down. It had been well over a week at this point since I'd had more than a few hours of sleep at a time.

Sweeping a piece of loose hair from my eye, I looked around at the guards walking with me to the training yard.

There were dozens of them walking in formation next to me, each of them scowling at me whenever our gazes happened to meet. I wondered again what I could have done to make them hate me so much already. I hadn't even been given the chance to prove myself as the championed warrior I knew I was.

Was it the other new guards? Had they been spreading rumors about me? We hadn't exactly started off on the right foot, and ever since, they'd been cold and cruel to me at every opportunity. If their distaste for me was the plague, they'd infected all of the other guards with the same illness. And for the life of me, I couldn't figure out what the cure was or if I even wanted to spend time and energy on getting these men to like me.

My hopes of having some form of friendship with the few female guards were pretty much dead in the water since they were acting as though *I* was the one with the plague and avoiding me as such. It was exhausting, and in some ways, I'd rather be back at the front fighting. At least then it was black and white. Enemy, friend. Kill, don't kill. Live, die. I wouldn't have to deal with any of this petty bullshit.

As we stepped out onto the practice field, the trainers barked orders at us. No matter who was yelling, or whose spittle was landing on our faces, we were expected to stay in line and do as we were told or suffer the consequences regardless of rank or experience.

"Do you think just because you were up all night you can give me half of your effort?" One of the trainers stepped toward a guard standing next to me. "Unacceptable! March! Pick those knees up!"

The guard picked up the pace, running as fast as he could toward his next target and slamming his body into the stuffed dummy.

The grueling hours passed quickly as we practiced formations and combat techniques with the dummy targets stuffed with hay and sand. It was mind-numbing and made my muscles ache, but I kept up with the guards that had been there a while better than some.

Despite being incredibly exhausted, I couldn't help but think back on what happened last night. The mysterious figure in all black had seemed oddly familiar, but then again, maybe I'd imagined it. The familiarity anyway. I certainly hadn't imagined the man running through the castle. Even if no one wanted to acknowledge it as a real event. And even if no one believed me. My only hope was for them to try again so I could catch them and prove to everyone else that I wasn't lying.

# CHAPTER
# SEVENTEEN

S enara

When the hours-long training finally ended, I was instructed to use the bathing area set aside for female guards. It was a small bathhouse with only three bathing pools, a few benches, and an area for dressing, but I didn't need a castle. I just needed some water and a little bit of soap.

The sunken terracotta tiled pools were already filled with water, but I knew from experience that they usually needed a bit of a top up to get the heat back to where I liked it. Back when our only choice was the river or the public bathhouses, Wyn and I used to save up so every once in a while we could take a bath together in warm water instead of the frigid water of the Zorah River. She used to joke that I'd end up boiling myself accidentally one day, and honestly, she might be right. She would always wait until the water had cooled off to get in.

The very idea of hot water rinsing away the sweat and grime from a grueling night shift and even harder training session sounded like pure perfection. I carefully placed my uniform on one of the benches, only bringing my towel with me to the bath itself since I didn't want anything else to get wet, and turned the water on, giving it time to warm up to a skin-scalding temperature as it refreshed what was already in the pool.

Steam billowed off the top of the water, and I sank down into it letting it work its magic on my sore muscles. The lavender scent of the shampoo filled my nose and made me feel fancier than I had in a long time as I washed my hair. With that done, I topped up the water a little more and grabbed the soap. The yellow bar smelled of honey and berries, and I couldn't wait to get rid of the week of grime from the ship, the night of passion with Thorn, and the sweat from training and running after that damn fae.

By the time I was ready to get out, the water had started to cool and my fingers were pruney. I could have fallen asleep in the water, I was so relaxed. Maybe that was why I didn't hear them come in.

"Oh, look at little miss fancy hair, splashing about. Are you pretending to be a mermaid? Probably believe in those if you believe in fae." I knew the voice. It was one of the guards I'd trained with today. He'd entered the bathing area and stood with his arms crossed, leaning against the sink. He looked relaxed, but the tick in his jaw and the throb of his temple told me otherwise. "Did your mama help braid your hair for you this morning?"

I didn't know what my braid had to do with anything, let alone the fact that I was taking a bath and cleaning myself. Whatever it was that had upset him didn't matter to me, but my stomach was churning. It didn't take a genius to know that he wasn't here to make friends. He was either going to try the same thing as the soldiers on the ship or he was going to attack me.

Three other guards joined him, one at each of his sides and one behind him, each of them staring at me as if I were a piece of meat. The one on the right I recognized as one of the other new members of the King's Guard. One of the men who had been on the ship with me. The fact that he was there made my blood run cold.

Quickly I pushed up out of the water and grabbed my towel to cover myself. "I don't want any trouble." I held up my hands as much as I could while keeping my towel around me and backed toward the wall. Looking around the small, closed quarters, I realized I was trapped. The odds were not in my favor.

The one thing I knew was that I couldn't let them see the mark on my back. If they saw that, they may as well kill me right then and there because it would mean my death either way. As far as I knew, I was still able to hide it with a towel, but that was the tricky thing about these stars-damned marks. They got bigger with each full moon, which is why they were always discovered eventually, no matter how much people tried to hide it.

The four of them edged closer, careful not to step into the baths accidentally. "Please, let's just talk about this," I tried.

"She wants to talk!" The lead guard, Chambers was his last name if I remembered right, said. "Want to tell us all about your meeting with the Fair Folk? Or maybe offer to suck our cocks thinking we'll help her, tell the commander we saw the wee man too?"

"Didn't even bat an eye about showing us everything, did you see that?" One of the other guards mumbled as he leered at me.

Reflexively, I tightened the towel around myself.

"Aye, I did see that. Feroc warned us that she was a whore, and it seems like he was right." The leader gave the new guard a nod, and my stomach soured even further. So this was related to what had happened on the ship.

Without warning, the first guard lunged toward me, and the other three followed suit. The first blow landed against my temple and shot pain through my head before I was tackled to the ground. My head hit the hard floor and caused stars to appear in the place where my attackers' faces should have been.

Everything blurred as they piled on top of my body. All I could focus on was the pain as blow after blow landed in all the wrong places. I tried to get up, but they were too strong, so I instead focused on keeping my towel wrapped around my body.

There wasn't enough room for them all to be around me at once, not without risking falling into the bathing pool I'd just been using, so they took turns. When that wasn't enough, Chambers grabbed me by the hair and dragged me to a more open spot. I had to fight not to scream in pain, but I didn't want to give them anything more to use against me.

With more room, they were all able to get in on the action at the same time. One or two held me down while the others hit and kicked me before they traded positions.

The cowards wasted no time in beating me to a pulp. Honestly, I was just thankful that all they seemed to be interested in was physical violence, not the sexual kind.

Desperately, I tried to defend myself, curling into a ball to try and protect my organs, but they were too fast, too strong, and they kept me pinned so the blows could land in the worst places. I was truly trapped.

Each punch landed with a sickening thud. And every minute passed slower than the one before. I was sure before they finished—and I didn't think they would any time soon—I'd pass out from the pain. But when it seemed like it would never end, it all stopped.

I knew I'd cried out, that at some point I'd screamed for help and none had come since that had earned me a boot to the face. But once I stopped fighting back, stopped trying to resist, they seemed to get bored faster.

They stood, leaving me crumpled on the ground, breathless and whimpering against the cold floor.

The guards stood back, and I could feel them looking at me, surveying the aftermath of their assault. I was little more than a rag doll that I'd seen carried by other children when I was little. My limbs were at odd angles as I lay discarded on the floor with no hope of escape.

Despite every part of my body crying out in agony from the beating, I had to stay put. There was no way I could move even if I wanted to, and I didn't want to. I needed them to think I couldn't move as much as I actually was unable to. As it was, my limbs shook and refused to do as I commanded them.

For several moments, none of us moved or said anything, until finally one of them stepped forward. He didn't reach for me, although I curled into myself, trying to protect the parts of me that I could since there was no way I could take any more.

"Get up!" His voice echoed off the bare walls around us and penetrated my battered skull. I was half-blind, probably because my eye was beginning to swell shut. I couldn't fully breathe, but I heard him.

"Get up, or we'll come down to you," Chambers commanded, his voice going quiet with the threat at the end. His breath stank of ale, and I was both surprised and not. Clearly the men here didn't have enough to do, so as soon as they were done, they went drinking and wenching. I was just surprised at how quickly he, and probably the others, had managed to get so inebriated they thought this was a good idea.

His threat hung in the air, and I didn't want to find out if he would follow through or not. I didn't have a choice. I had to move. Struggling against the pain, I slowly regained my footing and tried to lift my head enough to look him straight in the eye despite all the pain and the terror inside me. He stared right back at me without emotion on his face or a litany of threats coming from his lips. Just stared.

It was almost as if he was sizing me up, trying to decide if I could withstand any more punishment.

With one parting blow that snapped my head to the side hard enough to knock me backward, I sprawled on the floor once more, my head dipping down into the bathing pool so I came up coughing. I pushed away from the edge of the water with as much force as I could muster, but stayed down as my head spun and rang.

Chambers moved closer to me once more, and I braced for another hit, but he just stared down at me. "Let's go," he snarled before spitting in my face, turning on his heel, and storming out. The other three followed suit, each stopping by to spit on me before leaving.

I could still feel the heat from their angry glares as they all stalked away in silence. As soon as they were gone, I fell onto my back, trying to focus through a haze of tears and pain as I muttered a drowsy curse under my breath. I didn't know how I was going to manage to get up again since the intense pain was everywhere, but I had to. I didn't want to die naked in a bathhouse.

I lay there on the ground for a few moments, trying to catch my breath and willing my trembling limbs to stop shaking. I gingerly touched my face, trying not to wince as I examined the extent of the damage. I didn't think anything was broken, but it was hard to tell given the amount of pain I was in. What I did know was that my lip was split and one of my eyes was already swollen shut. And it hurt. The pain made me wish I could pass out until my body stopped hurting.

My eyes darted around the room, looking for something to help hide my injuries from Wyn. She would lose it if she saw me right now.

After a few moments of searching, I finally spotted a

raggedy old scarf hanging on the wall. Grabbing it gently, I slowly wrapped it around my head and stood up cautiously. I snatched my uniform from the bench and pulled it back on, whimpering with each movement.

I couldn't bear putting the metal pieces on, but it was either that or walk them back to my room so I could stash them there. Neither option was one I relished, but my room wasn't too far away, so I thought I could make it. At least that was until I started walking.

There was a third option that I ended up choosing because it was all I could manage, which was to bring it all with me. Taking a deep breath, I tried to project more confidence and a whole mess more stability than I felt as I stumbled out into the corridor.

Wyn had no idea what was coming her way.

Every step was a struggle, and I had to remind myself that I'd been injured worse than this before. This time though, I hadn't expected to be injured taking a bath, so I wasn't prepared for it. Somehow, that made it all the more difficult to deal with.

I tried to focus on putting one foot in front of the other, but it was hard when I could barely see through the swelling of my eye and the pain that made my head pound. There were a few strange looks thrown my way from people who passed me, but no one stopped to help or ask if I was okay.

A couple wrong turns later, I finally made it to Wyn's door, or at least what I hoped was her door based on her description of how to find her room. The relief I felt was almost enough for me to pass out. As it was, I stumbled with my hand in the air, ready to knock with my heart pounding against my ribs, which ached with every beat.

I moved my hand, mimicked the knocking motion to test for pain, then barely found enough actual strength to knock softly. Seconds passed without an answer or any sound from inside whatsoever. Just as I was about to turn away, the door suddenly swung open.

Wyn stood in the doorway, and her eyelids opened ever wider at the sight of me. She gasped and ushered me inside, quickly closing the door behind me. "What in the name of the stars happened to you?" she demanded.

My vision dimmed, and I managed to gasp, "I made some new friends. Can you help?"

She knew what I was asking, and she knew that I wouldn't ask if I thought I could handle it by myself at all, but I couldn't. This was just too much, but so was asking her to use magic within the castle. Still, if I went to a healer like this, or worse if Thorn or the commander saw me like this, I'd be classed as unable to fight and dismissed.

Wyn was my only hope of making it out of this situation without permanent damage and with my job intact. I just hoped she was willing to help me.

S enara

"Ouch." Every gasp for air made me gasp again. It was a never ending circle, and I closed my eyes and allowed Wyn to examine my beaten body as I perched on the edge of her bed.

Her room was bigger than mine, which wasn't a surprise, but a relief nonetheless. The stone walls had no windows, but she had a nice bed from the feel of it, a desk, a chair, a dresser, and a bookcase that was packed with all different kinds of things. There was no free space on the walls. Shelves that were stuffed with books took up the majority of the space, while the actual bookcase and large dresser took up the rest of it.

The only place that didn't have shelves was the area above her bed, and I had to assume that's because she didn't want to hit her head, otherwise there would be no stopping her from filling that space with books as well. Wyn felt safe around books, which was why I'd worked so hard to get her an interview for the librarian apprenticeship. I knew if she interviewed, the head librarian would see her passion and she'd get the position without any issue, and I was right.

Wyn delicately lifted my top, and I watched her face flicker through a range of emotions, everything from rage to pity. It wasn't like she had to look hard to see the evidence of what happened. There were bumps and bruises, red marks, winces of pain, and remembrance of the terror that I had only just endured.

She leaned onto the bed so she could see my back as she ran her hands over my skin with a featherlight touch. A frustrated sigh escaped her before she spoke. "They broke a couple of your ribs."

Yeah. I didn't need the recount of my injuries. I could feel every single one. "I thought I heard something crack at one point." I attempted a laugh, paid for it with another deep wince and a sharp gasp, and then held my side, which helped very little.

The pain radiated up into my chest and around to my back. It was a sliver less intense and possibly more manageable. But only a sliver.

"Why are you laughing, Senara?" Wyn grimaced, but for being the only person who really knew me, she still didn't quite understand me. "Those monsters could have killed you." Her tone said she had no patience for those monsters. I pitied them if she happened to run into them before I did.

Fortunately, she had no idea who they were since I hadn't said any names. The last thing I wanted was for her to confront them and get a beating of her own, or worse, use magic and get caught because she wanted to get retribution on my behalf.

"Well, they didn't." I took a sip of water from the cup Wyn had placed on the small table by my side. It was cold and somehow managed to burn on its way down. "So I guess I'm just happy to be alive." Wasn't that the truth? Or maybe it wasn't. I couldn't tell right now. My head hurt too much to be able to decide, or to know the difference.

I could have been hanging on by a thread, knocking on death's door, and I would have still tried to make a joke or laugh in order for Wyn to not feel scared. I never wanted to be the cause of pain for her when she'd already experienced so much in her life.

It took me a minute, a few more swabs of my blood on the cloth as Wyn dabbed at the worst of the cuts on my face, to decide it was a lie. I sure as hell wasn't content being alive. It wasn't enough for me to barely survive or merely exist in the castle.

I had been chosen to be a Royal Guard, yet I was being treated like a worthless street rat. Worse, really. Street rats were generally ignored, not beaten half to death.

There had to be a reason, and I wouldn't rest until I figured out why. I didn't want to believe it had anything to do with what happened on the ship, but I wouldn't put it past the guards that I'd traveled with to spread rumors about me either. Rumors that made everyone else hate me.

Wyn gently lifted my arm. It dangled at an odd angle from my shoulder. "Looks like this is broken, as well. And don't get me started on the black eyes and the multiple bruises all over your body." She spoke the words like they tasted bad in her mouth, and she grimaced. "Those bastards." And for her, that was strong language. The strongest I'd ever heard from her, anyway.

I had been warned about the dangers of being a Royal Guard, but I hadn't expected it to be this hard. And I certainly hadn't expected the dangers to come directly from the other guards instead of the King's enemies. That had been a most unpleasant surprise.

After only one day on duty, I had already been beaten and left for dead. By the king's own men. His personal guard, much the same as I was. If that didn't say something, nothing would.

As Wyn examined my bruised body, I realized that if I wanted to survive in this castle and prove myself worthy of being a guard, then I was going to have to fight twice as hard as everyone else.

Wyn left to get a fresh bowl of water to clean me up a little more. Curiosity got the better of me, and I tried to stand, but with my broken ribs and arm, it proved difficult. Just as I was able to get to my feet, Wyn came back in. The scowl that took over her face made me sink back to the bed before I'd even taken a single step.

Honestly, I wasn't sure how the assholes had managed to not significantly hurt my legs, but I was thankful for it. As far as I could tell, nothing there was broken or sprained, which meant that the main part of the pain came from the movement of my arms and torso. My head spun, but I just tried to ignore that.

Wyn marched back over and set to cleaning me up once more, the fresh water turning pink much too quickly. The clean rag barely lasted more than a minute. Apparently, I was in even worse shape than I thought.

Over the years, I'd developed a couple of interests that helped me as a member of the royal army. I knew about tinctures and herbs and salves that helped healing. Nothing that could be construed as magic, but things that would help ease pain.

Wincing with every movement, I looked around the room for something that would help me heal faster. There were only about three herbs and a handful of ointments that I knew of which could ease the swelling and potentially stop the bleeding.

On the front lines, we hadn't had much since all our supplies were limited due to budget cuts from the King's court. All we were provided with was basic salves and bandages, neither of which did much against broken bones and internal bleeding, but they had helped a little. Wyn had a few bottles of things stashed here and there, but I had no idea what most of it was.

I knew if I wanted any chance of recovering quickly enough that Thorn or the commander didn't find out what happened, drastic measures needed to be taken. I hated to ask, but I didn't have a choice. Not this time.

"Can you use your magic to heal the worst of it? I'm not worried about the bruising and other superficial wounds." As a warrior, it was custom to wear your battle scars proudly, but broken bones wouldn't serve me well as one of the King's Guard. And maybe they'd serve as a reminder to me that I absolutely couldn't let my guard down. Not for now, at least. Likely not ever.

Wyn let out a breath as though she'd been waiting for me to ask that very question and was relieved that she didn't have to bring it up. "Yes, I can try." She set the bowl and rag to the side. "Please lie down flat."

I did as I was told, slowly allowing my body to sprawl out on Wyn's cot. My head spun at the change, and a wave of nausea filled me until all I could focus on was breathing through it. Just as I opened my eyes once more, she raised her arms over my body and began chanting in a language I didn't understand. It didn't matter what she said so long as it worked. Within moments, a warm sensation blanketed my broken body.

As Wyn concentrated on healing my injuries, the glamour she had been using to hide her Magic Touch began to slip.

I stared in disbelief as blackness spread along her fingers and lips. It was more than a little shocking to see the effects of her magic practice. It looked as if she'd dipped her fingers in an ink jar and then gave it a big kiss.

"Is the illusion of normal-colored skin hard for you to

construct?" I asked, not able to pull my eyes away from the charcoal skin.

"No, it's not." Wyn opened one eye then looked at me before closing it again as she refocused on healing me.

I could tell that she was lying. Wyn and I had been around each other long enough to catch each other in half-truths and blatant lies. I didn't know why we bothered pretending to keep things from each other at that point.

"Will healing me weaken your glamour?" I squinted, paying close attention to her body language. I knew I was asking too late, and that it would be next to impossible for me to stop her now, but I still needed to know. That way if this happened again, and I prayed to the stars that it didn't, I would know not to come to her.

"Oh, no. I don't think so." Her eyelids fluttered when she spoke. A tell-tell sign that she was lying to me. But I had to be healed. It was selfish, but I needed her.

I closed my eyes and focused on the healing process. The warmth that had at first spread through my whole body had now shifted to the main areas that needed healing the most.

And before long, I could bend my arm without pain. It felt completely fine, as if someone had sucked the pain up through my arm and out the tip of my shoulder.

"Stop," I instructed Wyn. "That's good enough." I could move it, and I didn't want to drain her magic any more than healing me this much already had. My ribs felt better, too. I didn't want to scream every time I took a deep breath anymore, so I knew the worst of my injuries were taken care of.

"What do you mean?" Wyn's eyes flew open and she cocked an eyebrow, her version of a confused look. "You're not completely healed yet."

"Right, I know." I sat up on the side of the cot, letting my much less achy legs dangle. "This is good enough, I promise."

Wyn lowered her hands and took a seat by my side. "If the pain is too much, please let me know."

I nodded, and now we'd both told a lie or two. "Can you tell me about the instance in the dining hall last night?" I pushed to my feet testing out the places that felt stiff or still a little sore.

"What do you mean?" Wyn asked without making eye contact with me, suddenly engrossed in cleaning up the rags and bowl she'd been using.

"You know exactly what I'm talking about, Wyn." I gave her a bump with my shoulder, pulling a small grin from her. "Did you use magic to calm the argument between me and those other guards?"

She shrugged, but it was obvious what the truth was. I couldn't let her take these kinds of chances. If she was discovered, the situation would be dire.

"Listen to me." I gripped her by the shoulders and turned her to face me. "You are being way too reckless. I'm so happy that you've found a position, in the castle no less, that you enjoy. But you're using magic. In the castle. Literal rooms away from the King himself, who abhors magic and all those who possess it." I shouldn't have had to tell her this stuff. We hadn't survived this long and become who we were by playing loose with the risks.

I was relieved that my own magic had never presented itself. All I had to live with was the mark. If I had random bursts of magic as well, I would have been safer on the front lines, fighting until an enemy took me down.

She frowned at me, not acknowledging what I'd said.

I didn't want to fight with her, especially after she'd just healed me, so I let it go for now, but I hoped she listened to me. "I need to get some rest," I said as I reached out and pulled her into a hug.

When I released her and started to move away, she

suddenly grabbed my arm and pulled me back toward her cot. "I don't trust that you're safe in your own room. You'll be sleeping here until I have to go to work." Her look was as fierce as her tone.

I didn't want to impose on Wyn. I'd already taken up too much of her time. Besides, I was anxious to see what my own cot and room felt like. But I didn't have much of a choice because with a gentle shove, she pushed me down onto the bed. My eyes closed before I could verbalize my protest.

She had to have used magic to stop me, but as the darkness pulled me under, I couldn't find it in myself to care. My body needed the rest and wasn't being shy about letting me know. I just hoped that it didn't take too much out of her to do that after healing me.

# CHAPTER
# NINETEEN

S enara

The night shift was nothing more than a tedious waiting game. A series of laps spent marching up and down a trail, checking the shadows and watching the open spaces. It was completely uneventful. Though, if something had happened, I probably wouldn't have reported it unless I had hard evidence in my hands.

At the end of our shift, we were once again dismissed to the training yard. As we walked through the corridors and passed the barracks, the guards that were around but didn't have shifts turned and looked, whispers quickly spreading through those who were more discreet and jeers coming from those who weren't. They stared, which wasn't surprising since I looked as if I was beaten to hell and back. And their assumptions were correct. I probably shouldn't have been alive after the beating I received, and I definitely shouldn't be up and walking, let alone going to training.

A part of me worried that it might arouse suspicion from some of them, but the more I thought about it, the less convinced I became of that possibility. A lot of the guards just weren't aware enough to think about something like that.

It irritated me that I still had to work with the asses who used me as their fighting dummy, but I was more worried about Wyn's use of magic on the castle grounds. I couldn't have been more grateful that she was able to help me the day before. If it weren't for her magic, I'd still be in bed attempting to recover.

There was no telling what Thorn would have done if he discovered I was out of commission. Chances were he would have sent me back to the front lines on a gurney. I'd already pushed him to the point of anger by not telling him the truth about who I was, so I doubted he would believe me if I told him that several guards had beat me up, completely unprompted. It happened to me, and I still couldn't quite believe it.

Plus, I had history to back up my thought process. Guards stood by guards—commanders protected their troops, even if what they were doing was wrong. They didn't want to be guilty by association, so they refused to believe the truth when one of the soldiers or, in this case, guards, was accused of something.

The scent of dirt and hay greeted me as we stepped out of the castle proper and into the morning sun. Someone must have just fed the horses for the hay smell to be so strong. I raised my hand to shield my eyes as they adjusted to the sudden brightness while we walked across to the training area. I wished I could go and see the gentle giants in the stalls around the corner instead of having to stand in the muck with these pigs that called themselves guards.

Our trainer stepped into the center of the dirt circle. His goatee looked a bit raggedy, as though he hadn't had time to get ready in the morning. Maybe he'd had a late night judging from the bloodshot eyes that squinted at us. "Today, you'll be sparring against each other in hand-to-hand combat to practice the skills learned yesterday. No weapons or shields will be allowed."

He eyed each of us, and I didn't cringe, though I wondered how my body would hold up considering what I'd already been through. "Each of you can choose an opponent. When one person wins, they can move on to choose another opponent." There were quiet murmurs of excitement as if this was a good thing. And on another day, I might have thought it to be so, but today, I wasn't impressed. "At the end of the session, we should have one guard who reigns victorious over the others."

I knew this was my chance to prove myself, even if it was only to our trainer. With only a slight second of hesitation, I challenged myself to beat every single one of the guards who had attacked me. I would put them on their asses in front of all their friends.

The first fight, I was chosen by a large guard, both in height and width, who—and I could tell by the smug smirk on his face—thought he could easily defeat me. His hair was closely cropped to his scalp, trying to hide the fact that he was balding, and his brown eyes were dull except for the spark of violence lurking within. I couldn't remember his name, but he was one of Chambers' lackeys. Of course, when he'd laid hands on me the day before, he'd had back up. Today, we were one on one. And I had the ache for revenge on my side.

My mind flashed back to him slamming my head against the cold, hard ground. This time, though, I wasn't penned in and trying to hold my towel in place. Without his buddies to help him, his punches were slow and predictable. I used my agility to dodge them with ease.

Part way through the fight, I realized that he had a blind spot on his right side. Not completely, but more like his mind wasn't fast enough to realize when someone was in his peripheral vision. It was a weakness I could exploit. I took a couple of good shots of my own but eventually put him on his back on the ground, looking up at me with my foot on his throat.

All it would take was a little more pressure and I could crush his windpipe, giving him a slow, painful death that he probably deserved. We weren't on the battlefield, though, so I settled for just resting my boot on his neck.

The trainer came over and declared me the victor. The thrill of it gave me a burst of strength and adrenaline.

"How?" the guard asked as he scrambled to his feet and moved to the loser's side of the arena. He grumbled under his breath as his friends taunted him from the sidelines. The sound was like a salve to my soul.

The second opponent was shorter and leaner than the first, but with better reflexes. His gray eyes snapped with hardness like winter ice. I knew I had to be quicker if I wanted to have any chance against him, so I focused on using my speed before leaning in to hit him where it hurt. It took a few rounds of sparring, but eventually, I forced him into a submission hold that had him begging for reprieve unless he wanted to break his arm to get out of it, much like he had done to mine the day before. The jeers of his friends sounded as though they couldn't believe what they were seeing.

The third man stepped forward with a smug grin, probably thinking that I was tiring and wouldn't be able to take him down as well as his two comrades. He probably looked at me and thought that with the damage his friends had done the day before, a full shift of guard work, and the two fights already under my belt, I would be ripe for taking down.

He couldn't have been more wrong. There was nothing remarkable about him as I deftly parried his blows, letting his own momentum work against him as I landed punch after punch until he too was laid out on the dirt in embarrassment.

Even though he hadn't been in the bathing room when they were beating me, he clearly knew what had happened, so I couldn't help but wonder if he'd acted as a lookout or something.

I made my way through the ranks of men until there was one last fighter left. Chambers. The leader of the shady pack who'd beaten me. His brown eyes were shrewd and reminded me of a fox's. Conniving, that was what the townsfolk had always said about foxes as I was growing up, and if this man was anything to go by, they were right. It wouldn't surprise me if he had a dagger on his person somewhere, one that might accidentally find its way into my gut.

This was the man who had instructed the other guards when they could stop pounding their fists into my limp body. He had been their ringleader the day prior, and even the ones I'd already sent to the loser's side seemed certain it would end the same way once again as they grinned and elbowed one another in the ribs. Their cheers bolstered their leader, though I had the cool clarity of battle settling on me like morning dew on grass.

No one was cheering for me, but I didn't need them to. I knew my worth and skill, and I wouldn't be cowed by lesser men.

"So." Chambers stepped forward, his warped grin stretching across his face. "We meet again."

I nodded my head, not willing to give him the satisfaction of a verbal response. He hadn't earned a response more than a fist between the eyes. And I was going to make sure he got it.

"I'm sorry to do this." He cracked his knuckles, flexed his fingers, and then smiled. "But orders are orders."

Just as he ran toward me, I unleashed all the strength and determination, the fury and pride I kept hidden from them all until now. With each move faster than lightning, I stunned the crowd that had gathered to watch the fight. There were gasps and murmurs, chortles and oohs.

I claimed victory over my final opponent, and probably faster than anyone expected, leaving only awe in my wake as everyone gasped when I went in for the kill. It was only the clock chiming the hour that pulled me back from putting Chambers into the ground permanently. There were no clocks on the battlefield, at least not that I'd encountered, so the sound helped ground me and bring me back to the present.

My final blow left the big man lying on the ground, shocked. He'd toppled over backward, rolled into a ball. and went for another spin before he ended up on his back, staring up at me as if he'd never seen a woman warrior. I hadn't shown him much yesterday since I'd been too concerned with holding onto my towel, so perhaps he hadn't until now.

"You all must've gone easier on her last night than you claimed," a friend of the guard called from the loser's side of the training area. "There's no way you beat her into a sniveling mess if she's able to fight like this." He looked me up and down, and while I could assure him they'd most definitely beaten me to within a couple inches of life, we all had our secrets. I wasn't about to reveal mine.

This other guard wasn't the only one who seemed to know what happened. Even some of the other female guards who were around didn't look surprised, which made me wonder if they had been through something similar when they first arrived. Did people not believe them? Dismiss anything they said? Is that why they kept silent now?

I waited for the trainer to show up and declare victory, but he was chatting with the commander off to the side, completely uninterested in who won his little contest. The prick of rage still made my skin itch as I listened to the comments before finally deciding to speak up for myself.

"Have any of you been to the front lines recently?" Oh, I had a point to make all right.

Glancing around the circle, only a few hands were raised, and they all belonged to the new recruits. I knew that it had probably been several years since the other Royal Guards had stepped foot onto a battleground. And so the better, the more seasoned fighters with the most combat skills were the new recruits.

I gestured to the bruises all over my body. "Most people who are fighting at the front look like this or have fought like this. Some fight with broken arms, missing limbs, you name it." The things I'd seen in my time at the front had defied logic and reason and on some occasions, even magic. There was an endless supply of stories I could've shared.

"They're fighting in the worst conditions possible. And, yet, none of them stop until they are dead or until they have driven the enemy back." Otherwise the fighting continued, and while we'd all had a common goal, we also had no ally to save us. That was up to the individual. And some days, when the battle raged through long nights, when the man next to me had fallen and died, I continued to fight on because to fight was to survive,

I stood over the guard who coordinated the attack against me. "*I* fought in the worst conditions possible. Maybe you all should remember that while you're on patrol today."

With that, I turned to leave and walked toward the bathing pools. This time, though, I brought my weapon with me.

# CHAPTER
# TWENTY

Senara

I walked back to my room, chest filled with a swell of pride for beating the four guards in my sparring assignment. They'd gotten the better of me in the women's bathhouse because they'd attacked as a group and I hadn't been able to fight back without potentially revealing my mark. But I'd certainly shown them that I wasn't one to be messed with, and I'd delivered their beatings in front of their friends, no less.

That could backfire and make them even more likely to attack me again, but I refused to let that concern tarnish my current victory. I would celebrate this win the best way I could, with a bath and a good sleep.

It had been a long day, and I was happy to be on my way to my room to get some rest. Fighting and taking a beating was a lot harder than fighting and winning, but neither was easy, and I was tired.

As soon as I stepped through my door, my mouth fell open in surprise to see Wyn there waiting for me, wearing gloves. It wasn't particularly cold outside, so there was only one explanation.

I knew immediately why she was wearing them, of course. Wyn's magic was special, although she suffered the same addiction as everyone who'd been touched by magic. I had no doubt that when she used her magic to heal me, it weakened her own magical strength and allowed her true form to show through. Helping repair my broken bones and hiding the injured state I'd been left in had caused her glamour to slip in a way that she couldn't fix for some reason, so she'd had to cover her hands before someone noticed they were black. The stain embedded in her skin was a grim reminder of the cost of using magic. Sometimes, it was too steep of a price to pay.

Without saying anything, I shut the door and turned around to face her, dropping the armor on the floor behind the door and crossing to her.

"How are you feeling?" Wyn fiddled with the fingers of her gloves. She hated wearing them, but they were a necessity. Although she seldom brought attention to them by touching them.

Completely ignoring her nicety, I knelt down in front of her, close enough that I could touch her, but I waited. "What's wrong?

"I haven't been able to wash the mud off my hands after playing in the dirt last night." Wyn stared at the floor. I could see her lips, and for some reason the glamour there had held, but it made me wonder why.

It didn't matter though, not really. In that moment, I couldn't help but to be proud of Wyn for talking in code. We were, after all, in an unfamiliar place, and it was too risky to discuss magic at all, let alone that she had done magic or that she was marked by it. Magic was dangerous. Period. We had to be extra careful.

I reached out my own hand and covered hers with it,

giving a comforting squeeze through the gloves. I smiled at her, letting her know it was going to be alright even though I wasn't sure of it. I wasn't sure of anything. "What do you need to get cleaned up?"

"There are specific ingredients I need. Usually I'd go to the market, but they won't be up and running again yet. The only other place I've found them is in the Moonlit Garden," Wyn explained in hushed tones, her voice more frantic than usual. She pushed to her feet, almost knocking me over in the process and began pacing as I took her spot on the bed. It was very unlike her, but I understood. This was the kind of thing that could get her killed. She'd done it for me, and I owed her help, but I didn't know how. "Usually, I sneak to the market at night, or go to the garden when there's a guard on shift that I can butter up, but that's typically when I have time to plan it all out."

"What difference does it make?" I sat on my cot and removed my boots. It had been a long night, and I was aching. Partly from the previous beating and partly from the night of marching and the day of training. Wiggling my toes, I realized how wonderful it felt to not wear the clunky and tight shoes.

"Since this happened unexpectedly, I need to get the ingredients now. There's no time for elaborate planning." Wyn continued to pace the small room, her red hair frizzing around her temples as though the stress was causing it to behave poorly.

"It will be okay, Wyn." I stood and walked to her side, stopping her movement and pulling her into a hug, her cinnamon and vanilla scent filling my nose and reminding me of how much I had missed her while I'd been away. When I pulled away, I said, "Listen to me, I'll be your escort tonight, and we can get the ingredients so that you can do whatever you need to—" I paused and looked around as if the entire castle was in my room listening before continuing, "To get the mud off your hands."

"Thank you." Wyn let out a loud and visible sigh of relief. Her shoulders rose and fell as tears gathered in her umber eyes. She didn't let them fall.

I knew that feeling all too well. How many times had Wyn come to my rescue when I believed I was all alone? She'd proven to me over and over again that she was on my side, and I tried to make sure she knew I would always be here when she needed me. And now, it was my pleasure to do the same for her.

Wyn cleared her throat. "But I still don't know if we'll be able to get in. You're a new guard, and there's no guarantee that the guard on duty will allow you to pass."

"Who said anything about asking permission?" I winked at Wyn as I redid my side braid. "You know my motto. Easier to ask forgiveness as opposed to asking for permission." Also, on occasion, it was necessary.

Wyn giggled. "If you say so." I certainly said so and would always say so when it came to keeping her safe.

But as that was a quest for a later time, I yawned and pushed my arms over my head, clasping my hands. My arms and back were extra sore after today's training. "I'm exhausted, so I really need to take a nap." I pulled my under armor off so I was just in my thin chemise and slipped down under my covers. "Are you okay hanging out here for a few hours?"

"Sure." Wyn sat on the end of the bed, resting against the wall. "Yours is getting bigger. I noticed it last night." Her voice was barely above a whisper, but it was a dagger to my heart.

"I know." It was all I could say because I *did* know. I wasn't sure exactly how big it was, but I'd known since I was a child that it grew slightly with every full moon.

She sighed, clearly not liking my answer. "At some point,

you're not going to be able to be a guard anymore. Not if you want to keep it hidden."

Her words made me nervous about exactly how big it had grown, but I didn't want to worry about that today, so I forced it from my mind. "One problem at a time, okay?"

Wyn didn't say anything for a long time, but then she began to sing softly under her breath. Her gentle tone quickly lulled me to sleep, and before I knew it, Wyn was shaking me awake.

I looked at the window in my room. It was dark, the sun having already set. "Wow. It's so late."

Wyn nodded. "We better get going if we're going to have time to retrieve the ingredients so I can create the glamour tonight." Wyn had dark circles under her eyes, and I couldn't decide if it was from lack of sleep or just part of the Magic Touch seeping through her skin.

I stretched and yawned. "Yes, of course."

After pulling my guard uniform back on, I turned to Wyn. "You have to stay close."

She nodded, and we quietly left my room.

As we made our way toward my designated patrol area, one of the guards stepped into our path.

"You're supposed to be at work." He looked Wyn up and down. "Not hanging out with friends."

Squinting at the guard, I realized that he was one of the men who'd attacked me. The last time I saw him, I had my boot on his throat. He caught me staring at him and smirked, seeming to assume that even though I had showed him up earlier, I was scared of him now.

Wyn glanced around nervously. I could sense the anxiety permeating from her body. Neither of us wanted to be seen together tonight, and now we were having to answer to a burly guard in the middle of a main corridor.

"Where do you think I'm going? My patrol is this way." I

stepped to the side, prepared to ignore and walk around the guard. "Just leave us alone."

"Aww, look at the precious, little girl, pretending to be a guard." He pretended to cry with a mocking tone. "I'm surprised your friend here lets you out after bedtime."

My fists clenched tightly at my side as I took a deep breath. I knew I should ignore him, but I couldn't pull myself away. "Maybe if you'd stop being an asshole, you'd actually fulfill your duties and protect the kingdom, and I wouldn't have been called back from the front where I was actually appreciated. Unfortunately for both of us, I'm here, and you're just going to have to deal with it."

Maybe that would shut him up.

I was wrong. He stepped forward, sizing me up and glaring down at me from his seven inch height vantage point. "I'd hate to kick your ass in front of your pretty, little friend. Or maybe your friend would like some attention. Maybe she needs a drink to relax a little after being dragged around by a cunt like you."

Wyn scowled and stepped to the side, obviously uncomfortable with the guard's attention.

"Leave her alone." I took another step forward, leaving only an inch between us. "Don't you have somewhere to be?"

Just then, another guard on the opposite end of the corridor called the guard's name. Jarek. His name was as annoying as the guard himself, but at least I knew it now.

"Be right there," he called. He snarled and spat on my boots before turning to walk away. "This isn't over, bitch," he hissed.

I lunged forward to teach him a lesson, but Wyn grabbed my shoulders and pulled me back.

"Don't do it," she warned.

Wyn was right. We didn't need any more attention on us as we made our way to the Moonlit Garden.

"I'm surprised how much the other guards dislike you." Wyn patted my shoulder as we continued our trek down the long corridor.

I shrugged, pretending like it didn't bother me. "I think someone's been telling tales because I turned down his advances."

"Really? That's why?"

A weary sigh escaped me. "Honestly, I have no idea. None of them are exactly forthcoming with details, you know?"

"Bastards, the lot of them," she whispered as she slipped her arm through mine.

I couldn't help but grin at her words. She wasn't wrong.

"What about the female guards? I'm sure I've seen some."

I nodded. "Yeah, they seem hesitant to interact with me, and I can't help but wonder if they're reserving judgment, seeing if I can handle it."

"Rude. Women should support other women. It's hard enough to get any respect as it is." She huffed angrily on my behalf before she dropped her voice to a whisper. "It's just up here on the left."

Anxiety flooded me. This had to work. I needed her to be okay, which meant that we needed to get into the garden and get whatever it was that would make the glamour work again, and I'd do whatever was necessary to make that happen.

# CHAPTER
# TWENTY-ONE

Senara

Wyn and I made it to the garden with surprisingly little trouble outside of our encounter with Jarek. There weren't many people walking through the corridors of the castle at that hour, so we didn't receive any odd looks or questions from those in important roles, the ones who worked diligently to keep the King abreast of all kingdom happenings and would know that we were somewhere we didn't belong.

Just as we turned to walk toward the garden, Wyn held up a hand and stopped me. "There's the guard." She whispered and pointed toward one of the men who jumped me in the bathhouse.

It was the fox-like man with his hard gray eyes. Why couldn't I seem to get a break from these stars-damned idiots? I had to bite my tongue to keep from saying something I shouldn't to Wyn. If she knew he was one of the men who had beaten me, I wasn't sure how she would react. The woman had a vengeful streak that no one ever expected.

"He's not one to allow leniency." Wyn sounded defeated

already, but I wasn't about to let one man stop us. We needed in there, and whether he was going to go easy or not, Wyn needed supplies. I already knew he was a terrible human being, so I wasn't opposed to doing what was necessary if it came down to that to keep my sister safe.

Only if it became necessary, though. With a heavy sigh, I observed the guard. He patrolled the garden by walking slowly, making large loops around the perimeter of the wall.

"He's completely predictable." I motioned for Wyn to follow me. "We'll wait a minute, but then..." I pulled her down so if he looked our way, he wouldn't see her. When he was around the side, I took her by the arm and pulled her behind me.

Wyn nodded her head and looped her arm through mine. The gesture was as familiar as brushing my hair out of my eyes.

Her dependency on me in this situation reminded me of her frail body when we found each other years ago. We had both been starving, had both been discarded by parents that neither of us could quite remember. She stuck to my side as if my two inches height difference would save her from all the world's enemies. And maybe that was what made me so tough, knowing she needed me to be. It was the only thing I could think of that explained why I was the tough one and she was the flower.

It helped that I had a natural aptitude for movement and fighting, whereas she was the one who was always more interested in books and learning. She felt safest with a book in her hands and her head between the pages, but I felt safest with steel in my hand and my eyes open watching for the next attack. There was always another attack for one reason or another..

Wyn's parents had abandoned her when she first

displayed signs of magic, just like mine had when they realized my mark would only grow as I got older. When we found each other and began to trust one another, it was like a weight was lifted from my shoulders. I had someone to share the world with that I could be completely honest with.

"Now's our chance to sneak into the garden. We'll have about three minutes before he loops back around. Think you can grab your flowers and herbs in that amount of time?"

Wyn nodded sharply.

Three minutes wasn't much, but it was the best we could do unless we wanted to make more than one attempt, but that was risky, and meant waiting longer, which delayed me from getting to my own post. Not ideal for a new guard.

I turned my attention back to our mission as we crossed over the garden walls. We were surrounded by blooming roses, herbs of all sorts, leaves, and vegetable plants. Wyn's eyes lit up as she raced to the place she knew the plants she needed grew.

The Moonlit Garden was designed to be enjoyed at night, with all different kinds of night-blooming flowers scattered throughout, but no one was around. I doubted anyone ever really got to experience its beauty.

I moved to stand in the shadows and keep watch as Wyn gathered her supplies. My heart pounded in my chest at the thought of us being discovered, especially with her in her current state. I didn't want to think about what would have to happen then. There was plenty of blood on my hands already, but that didn't mean I wanted to add to it.

"I can have this ready in less than two minutes." Her voice was a hiss next to me as she plucked leaves and flowers alike. This was a woman who knew things, how to save people, how to work a potion or a poultice. This was a woman who could be of value to the King if only he let her. But he wouldn't.

And as she'd promised, in less than two minutes, she had what she needed.

She'd known exactly where she was going, probably because she'd done this more than a few times before. She was in and out before I had a chance to look around properly. But the scent stayed with me. The smell of life was in that garden.

With a handful of flowers, Wyn smiled as I led her back out of the garden and down to the area where I'd been patrolling the past few nights.

I looked over my shoulder just in time to see the changing of the guards at the garden entrance. We'd missed them with only a few seconds to spare. I shuddered at the thought of the repercussions if the guards discovered me helping a citizen in and out of the royal gardens. Even if she did work at the castle, there were rules, and the garden was off limits to everyone but the king, his advisors, and those he deemed worthy. I was fairly certain that Thorn would send me back to the front for such a blatant act of insubordination.

Breathing a sigh of relief, I turned to Wyn. "Wait out of the way over here while I get rid of the guard on duty."

She nodded and sat against the wall in a shadow where the moonlight didn't reach. She was busy taking inventory of her harvest.

Once I'd sent the guard off to bed and taken over the post, I walked back to Wyn. "Follow me."

It was only when I was safely in my own patrolling area with the previous guard long gone that I felt like I could take a deep breath, like we had actually gotten away with it. The intensity of it all was hard to come down from, though, and it wasn't over yet. She still needed to do whatever it was she did to make the glamour work.

"Where are we going?" she asked but came along with me, knowing I would never take a chance with her safety. I would leave this section of the castle wall unguarded, the entrance unprotected, but I wouldn't let anyone hurt my friend.

"There's an alcove where you can mix your potion without being seen." I stopped at a corner and looked both ways. We were in the clear. "I'll stand guard in case someone walks our way. Although, there's never any foot traffic this time of night." It was a small assurance but an important one. And it was true. If anyone saw her mixing a potion, they would cry magic user and Wyn would be discovered. She was still wearing the evidence of her magic on her fingers and her face.

She followed quietly behind me until we reached the recess in the far wall of the castle's foundation. She wasted no time in setting up in the corner. She had a pestle, a bowl, and a small vial of water in her pocket.

Deftly, she dropped the petals from one flower, leaves from another, and seeds from a third into the mortar bowl, grinding them with the pestle before she added some ingredients that she pulled from a pouch, although where she'd been keeping it remained a mystery to me. I had my secrets, and she had hers, which apparently involved a very complex set of pockets in her cloak.

Just when I felt confident that whatever she was doing was safe and the mixture or potion was mixed thoroughly, a puff of smoke leaped into the air. I shot her a look and a hushed whisper. "Wyn!"

Coughing, Wyn shook her head. "The leaves from the plant I picked were too old. But the potion should get me through to the next time I can speak with a guard and be allowed into the garden for more than a few minutes. I didn't have time to examine the plants thoroughly."

Without warning, she tipped the bowl back and took a long swig of the potion, and immediately burped.

The abrupt sound splitting through the silence of the night startled me, and I jumped.

I couldn't help but laugh. "Well, it looks like you won't have to worry about forgetting the ingredients since you just drank them all. That should hold you over for at least a year, right?"

She rolled her eyes and sat calmly, waiting for the potion to take effect.

Watching closely, I wasn't sure what to expect. I didn't know if the magical transformation I expected would be quick and blunt or slow and steady. I didn't even know if I would be able to see the transformation.

A few moments later, she stood to her feet and slowly pulled one of her leather gloves off. She held up her fingers, gave them a wiggle, and turned her hand over and back again then grinned from ear to ear. "Look. It worked."

Sure enough, the blackness had disappeared to the point that it just looked like she'd been holding coal or ink. To anyone who didn't know she'd just ingested a magic potion to fade the color, her fingers looked stained, not Magic Touched.

Before either of us could celebrate the effective potion, a rock scraped along the pavement nearby. Maybe it had been kicked, or pushed, or just touched so that it rolled, but it certainly wasn't a purposeful throw.

We both jumped and turned toward the noise just in time to see a dark figure running away in the opposite direction. I thought about giving chase, but there was no explanation I could give that would pass for why we were where we were and what we were doing.

My heart skipped a beat as I remembered from my patrolling the past few nights that there was an alcove in that area, too. It was possible that someone had been quietly watching us. Whoever it was could have seen Wyn perform her magic, and death wasn't something I was going to let that happen to Wyn.

We'd made a stupid mistake that could have cost us our lives. It was nothing more.

Thinking quickly, I turned to Wyn. "Take your potion and hide in the bushes until I return."

I didn't wait for her to respond and, instead took off running after the person who saw us.

# CHAPTER
## TWENTY-TWO

S enara
It felt like it had been a while since I had a day off, and while one couldn't come quickly enough, only a week had passed since I started as a Royal Guard. It didn't stop the relief that surged through me when my commander told me I had the day and night to myself, and I spent the majority of it sleeping in my room. Now that I'd rested, my thoughts were clearer, and I was ready to spend a full day protecting the castle.

My commander assigned me to patrol around the royal gardens, the irony of which wasn't lost on me. And it would've been easy to let Wyn in today, to let her have time with the plants, and then she could've gone to her room and made her potion without anyone seeing.

It was a matter of one day. A few hours even.

Even though I only had a limited amount of time to adjust to the day shift, I'd forced myself to return to the spot where I last saw the man fleeing from Wyn and me.

He was tall, built big, and moved with all the grace of a fish out of water, but there were many big, clumsy men in the castle. Unfortunately, I hadn't been able to make out any more distinct features. His darkly colored cloak with its hood pulled up firmly hid his identity from my sight as I'd chased him around the castle until he just seemed to vanish into thin air. There were no tracks, not a disruption in the soil and the castle floors didn't give away any secrets of those who passed over them either.

His quick disappearance was so startling that I wondered if he had magical abilities, too. Wouldn't that be hilarious? A Magic Touched spotting another Magic Touched. But then, why run?

I'd been looking for any type of clue that might lead me to where he went. He had seen Wyn using her magic and that could get her killed. I had to ensure that the cloaked individual wouldn't blab to anyone about what he may, or may not have, seen. But first, I had to actually find him, or at least figure out who he was. The task was proving next to impossible.

I spent all of my patrol shift getting more and more agitated since I couldn't figure out how to find the person who saw Wyn. And what made the whole situation even worse was the fact that I was supposed to be protecting her while she mixed her potion. Shame ached in my bones. Poor Wyn trusted me, and I let her down.

To top it all off, if the mysterious person chose to tell others about Wyn, we would both be punished, even though I hadn't actually performed any magic. In fact, the one who reported it may even be punished just for being in the presence of magic.

None of it mattered in the eyes of the King. Anyone involved with magic, anyone who knew it was used and didn't inform, anyone who benefited from it, or allowed it, whether it be directly or indirectly, would be brought before the royal court and sentenced to harsh punishment. It was almost always death.

Wyn and I could very well be as good as dead and just not know it yet.

My stomach gurgled, aching a bit, and I realized I hadn't eaten all day. My mind was so focused on the possibility of us being turned in that I hadn't even taken care of my basic needs.

When a guard showed up to relieve me of my duties, he didn't say anything, just jerked his head in the general direction of the rest of the castle. I had no idea if I was supposed to check in with the commander or if I was just free to do as I pleased, but I wasn't going to take chances.

As I hurried through the halls toward the tower of the King's Guard, I had to fight the urge to look for any secret passageways or alcoves I may have missed the first few times I'd scoured the area. The last thing I needed was to make the commander angry by showing up late to my debriefing.

It turned out I was worried for nothing though because the commander was already gone and his office door closed and locked. I hoped that meant that I was free to do as I pleased for the evening because I was starving and didn't hesitate to turn around and head to the dining hall.

Loud voices echoed down the corridor as light spilled out from the open doors. The scent of various dishes filled my nose, and my stomach twisted with hunger. It was the general mealtime. I knew that meant that not only would castle staff be there but so would the guards that had just got off day shift, unless they'd gone straight to the taverns, which some of them did.

It also meant that I would have to endure the dirty looks and cold shoulders of my fellow guards. But I needed to eat, so I would brave it.

Pushing past my insecurities, I strode in and headed straight for the food line, grabbing a plate of meat and potatoes along with a sweet roll before I walked to a corner table to sit and eat, alone. I didn't look at them, but plenty of them looked at me, their gazes crawling over my skin like ants. Plenty of them chortled at whatever joke they made at my expense that they weren't brave enough to say so I could hear. It didn't matter. I was only here for the food.

I hunched over my meal, eating quickly and keeping my eyes down. There was no need to draw attention to myself. I couldn't risk another quarrel that could very well lead to my return to the front lines, one death sentence exchanged for another. And if that happened, then I wouldn't be around to protect Wyn either.

A realization hit me. If I were gone, I wouldn't even know if she'd been turned in and executed since no one knew we were friends outside of Tower and Thorn. Neither of them seemed likely to write to me to tell me of the death of the woman who may as well have been my sister. She could be gone, and I would never even know it.

My stomach went from empty to agitated in only a matter of minutes. I'd eaten so quickly that I probably hadn't chewed the meat long enough or given my body a chance to object to the large quantity I'd just shoved into it. I ate like it could have been my last meal, but I hadn't savored any of it, just scarfed it down.

With a heaviness in my chest and a lump in my belly from all the food, I decided to walk around the castle, allowing my stomach to settle. Stars knew that there were plenty of hallways to walk down to work off the stomach cramps.

I made my way through the winding corridors of the castle, stopping from time to time to admire a painting or sculpture. There was a statue of the king, adorned with jewels and his robes, a crown so big it made his head look too small. Just one of those jewels could keep most of the kingdom fed for a year or more. The thought had me shaking my head, trying not to borrow more trouble than I already had, before I continued walking.

My time here had been so rushed that I hadn't allowed myself a moment to really absorb the magnificence of the castle. It was stunning. Yet the intricate, gold-trimmed draperies and marble statues of heroes from a bygone era were just a reminder that I didn't really belong here.

I was fooling myself to believe that an orphan who had lived on the streets for so many years, with no real family to speak of, could be found a worthy enough warrior to guard the castle walls. I wondered if one of the reasons Thorn had allowed me to stay was because he realized I had nothing to lose. Because he realized that being a guard was all I had and I would fight for it accordingly. Not that any of that mattered. I would do whatever it took to not get sent back to the front lines.

Right now, I needed to focus on finding the man in the cloak before he could tell anyone what he saw, so I pushed all my speculation away. With Wyn's future at stake, I couldn't let myself get distracted by my own self-pity and anxiety. Plus, I still had to make sure I paid attention to everything going on. I'd let a bandit go once—well, twice if I counted the one who'd seen me and Wyn. I wasn't about to do it again.

I instinctively rubbed my back, suddenly acutely aware of its markings. When I was alone and I touched the skin there through my chemise, I could feel the rough dips and valleys that the mark consisted of. The skin there was harder, more unyielding than the rest. Now, even though I was touching it through my armor, it was almost like I could still feel it.

I shook the thoughts from my head and attributed the unusual amount of time I'd spent dwelling on my mark to my lack of sleep. My eyes burned from the abrupt change in my sleeping schedule. It was going to take time for my body to adjust to my new sleeping hours, but I could tell I needed rest.

I was too wound up, though. Anxiety crept in, and I thought I might crawl out of my own skin. When I returned to my room, instead of feeling peace and relishing the solitude, it felt like the walls were closing in around me. I knew I couldn't stay in there, so I turned around and walked back out.

Fresh air was the only thing that helped when I was like this, and before I knew it, I found myself walking around the edge of the training yard. I moved to a rock on the side of the outer markings where Thorn sometimes stood to watch us train, and I took a seat, watching as others practiced their sparring.

They were working with swords and shields today, which I had to admit I was a little jealous of. According to our training officer, he wanted to make sure we were proficient in hand-to-hand before we moved on to weapons. At least in any significant manner.

But time passed, training slowed, and men tired. Slowly but surely, they all left. More than likely, they had somewhere to be, shadows to patrol, hallways to watch. In my mind, it was a different story though, my paranoia was telling me that they couldn't even stand the thought of me watching them. I was convinced that they didn't want to be around me, and I knew deep down that my assessment wasn't far from the truth.

I didn't blame them. Especially with my current mood. The stranger in the cape had escaped me, and that meant Wyn was still in danger. I had to find out who it was, and fast. But how?

My face scrunched up as my mind raced with ideas, each one more outrageous than the last. I even considered asking Wyn if she knew any magic that would help. Using magic again, especially something as powerful as a spell like that would have to be, was just asking to be caught, so I quickly trashed the idea. I hadn't even realized that the sun was setting until it was already dark and twinkling stars had appeared above.

There was a sky full of bright points of light tonight, and as I looked up for a moment, I watched as one fell out of the sky. The moon glowed in all her glory, and I felt a sense of certainty and peace as I watched it rise over the horizon, casting the city below the castle in its pale light.

Gazing above, the sense of calm I'd been searching for all day washed over me. Maybe I could finally get some sleep. Though, there was a part of me that didn't want to go inside or move away from where I was for fear that the calm I'd found would vanish.

I always wondered if I felt such a connection to the moon because of the mark on my skin. The Moon Mark was named as such, to my knowledge, because it looked like the texture of the moon itself. What if it was more, though?

Before I could indulge in thoughts I usually kept locked away, a strange sensation crawled over my skin. I looked around, confirming that everyone was gone. Yet I could still feel someone watching me.

# CHAPTER
# TWENTY-THREE

Senara

I turned around, practically spinning in a circle where I was standing as I looked for whomever was watching me. I was shocked to see Thorn standing in the darkened doorway of the guard's watch tower. I paused as I looked deep into the shadows—all my training was coming in handy after all—to see if anyone else was with him, but he appeared to be alone. Since we weren't supposed to know each other, I looked away as I would with any other guard.

He didn't stop watching me, though, and the prickling sensation that he always gave me erupted all over my skin. It didn't help that he had been staring at me like I was water in the middle of a desert.

I didn't know how to respond to that, whether I should have waved or stared back. And because I didn't know how to respond, I simply pretended like I hadn't spotted him.

He'd practically ignored me the entire time I had been a guard at the castle, which was fine by me. I didn't need any more drama, and I certainly didn't want to listen to him telling me how *I* had created an uncomfortable situation for both of us.

Instead of being the adult and acting like we were just colleagues, which was all we should have been, I bent over and pretended to tie the laces on my boot, hoping he'd just go away.

He didn't. The dirt and gravel of the training ground crunched under his boots as he walked, and suddenly my heart was in my throat. When his boots stopped in front of me, filling my field of vision, I had no choice but to look up at him.

"Oh, Thorn. You startled me." I lied. "I didn't see you there."

"Sorry." He crossed his arms as I pushed off the rock I'd perched on to fake tie my laces. "I need a good workout and wondered if you'd like to join me."

What? My mind stuttered as I remember the last work out we'd had together. He wanted to—

"I prefer fighting over other activities, and I thought you might be a worthy opponent." Ah, not what I was thinking then. He cleared his throat and shifted his weight nervously. "Your form is good, and it seems you might last longer than thirty seconds against me."

He'd been having a rough time finding sparring partners, especially ones who could last long enough to give him a bit of competition. Whenever I saw him in the ring, I tried not to watch, not wanting him to think that I was obsessed with him or something. I'd turn away, find something else to busy myself with, but as soon as I let my thoughts wander I'd find myself staring at him again with a sharp sense of longing in my chest.

Now was not the time to think about how much I wanted him though. Especially not if he wanted to spar. Even though I didn't see anyone around, I couldn't bring myself to believe that he'd chosen to spar with me over someone like Ronan. I scoffed and looked over my shoulder to see if other guards were listening to the conversation. If he was mocking me for their benefit, I would be angry on a whole other plane of being and would likely end up doing something beyond reckless.

He looked around as though he was trying to figure out what was going on with me before he looked me up and down. "I saw you training the other day. You beat some of the best fighters here. Your speed and agility will prove challenging, and I don't expect that you'll hold back."

My jaw almost fell open with the realization that Thorn was actually being sincere. He'd gone from fucking me, to threatening me, to ignoring me, and now complimenting me? I was starting to get whiplash from his mood swings.

If he wanted a fight, I had plenty of rage I'd been storing up to unleash on him, especially since I knew he could take it. "I won't."

Belatedly, I remembered how difficult it had been to arm wrestle Thorn. He may as well have been a stone wall. He might have been cocky, but he wasn't exaggerating his abilities either. The man was abnormally strong. I probably couldn't beat him hand-to-hand, but I had some anger to work out. I nodded.

"And I wouldn't mind releasing some pent-up energy before bed," I added as I removed my weapons and put them in a pile out of the way of the fighting ring.

Once I returned to the center of the arena, some of the clouds had shifted, passing away from the moon. The night was even clearer than before, and I couldn't help but glance up at the moon once more.

When I looked over at Thorn, I was struck by just how handsome he was. It was as if I was seeing him for the first time. Looking at him now, I didn't see the dark, brooding man I'd become used to seeing around the tower. I didn't see the fact that he'd ignored me ever since that first meeting in his office, not even the fact that he wanted to use me as a punching bag now. Nor did I think that his eyepatch diminished his handsomeness. This guy was the definition of attractive.

But right now, he was eyeing me as he gritted his teeth, his jaw muscles moving. The mood seemed to have shifted from tentative trust to anger, but the way his features hardened only made him that much more striking.

Maybe it was just his sparring face as he amped himself up for a match. Or perhaps I had already annoyed him somehow? Maybe he'd expected me to use weapons in the fight? I couldn't decide which one, but it didn't matter.

He slowly inched closer to me, never breaking the death stare I was locked into. I couldn't tell if the sparring had started or if this was all a part of his warm-up, so I kept still. I wouldn't give in just because he was staring me down.

I kept my knees slightly bent with my hands in loose fists at my sides, just waiting to be called to action.

To my surprise, he reached a finger toward my face and gently ran it over my cheek. I winced at the twinge of pain, realizing that he had noticed one of the many nasty bruises on my body. For a moment, I wondered what the big deal was, until I realized that Thorn hadn't seen me since I was attacked by the guards in the bathhouse. We hadn't so much as run into one another in a hallway, and I'd had no reason to seek him out. In fact, I may have been actively avoiding him, just to keep myself from temptation and thoughts that I didn't really want to have.

Instinctively, I turned away, but Thorn caught my chin and gently, but firmly, raised my face so he could look closer at my injuries. He tilted my head left then right. And he stared hard, anger burning in his eye. I knew it must have been a trick of the light, but I could swear it seemed to glow to a deeper amber, one that made me think of fire instead of stone.

He blinked, and the spell was broken. "Who did this to you?" His voice was soft and lethal.

"It doesn't matter." I twisted my chin out of his hold, and he dropped his hand as I stared at the ground. "It's been taken care of."

"Oh, really?" He smirked and shook his head, smiling. I could tell he wanted to disagree with me, but he didn't. Instead, he seemed to consider me for a moment before asking, "Why don't we place a bet?"

I looked up, intrigued by his suggestion.

"If you beat me, you can ask for anything you want and, if it's in my power, I'll give it to you." Well, wasn't that interesting? He raised his eyebrows and searched my face for a reaction I certainly wasn't going to give him. "But if I win, you have to answer my questions."

I cocked an eyebrow before I grinned at him. "You'll regret the bet being weighted so unfairly."

"Ahh, I see." He rubbed his chin as if in deep thought, the sound of his stubble scratching against his skin ringing in my ears. "Okay, fair enough. We'll revise the terms. If you win, you can ask for anything you want to the tune of one hundred gold pieces. And if I win, then I get to ask you three questions and you have no choice but to answer honestly."

Cracking my knuckles, I considered the terms of the bet. He was powerful enough to get whatever answers he wanted, whether I was the one who spoke them or not. But this was a rare opportunity to line my pockets with a hefty amount of gold coins. Coins that could mean life or death if Wyn and I needed to make a run for it.

I shrugged. "Okay. You're on." My heart thumped hard, racing in anticipation as he stepped forward to meet me.

The match had begun.

As soon as he grabbed my shoulders, I realized it wouldn't take a seer or one of the knowledgeable elders to explain why he was so confident in betting that amount of gold. His skill was unlike that of anyone I'd fought against, recreationally or on the battlefields. Beating him would take every ounce of skill I had, plus some luck. He would have to trip, fall, and maybe hit his head on a stone, and I'd have to be right next to him to take advantage of it.

We circled each other, jabbing and ducking. He swept his leg and I jumped; I punched, and he sidestepped. We were testing our skills against each other as well as our limits.

His moves were smooth and precise, but I managed to anticipate most of them, parrying away his moves time and time again. I could see the admiration behind his eyes as we exchanged blows and blocks.

I had speed and flexibility, and he had strength and reach. Despite our differences in height and weight, we were evenly matched. At least it seemed that way at the beginning.

When I went on the offensive for a moment, trying to catch him by surprise with a flurry of strokes meant to overwhelm him, it didn't work. Thorn just smiled as he pushed back against me, matching my speed and strength without breaking a sweat. At that moment, I realized just how much more powerful he was than me—but instead of feeling intimidated, it only served to strengthen my resolve. I wanted to win those coins. I wanted to show him I was a worthy opponent. I wanted everyone to know I held my own with the Blade of the King, even if no one else was there to witness it.

Most of the men I'd sparred with since I arrived at the castle couldn't last against me, but Thorn held his ground. I attempted my signature moves, twisting and turning at fast speeds and unexpected times. He never missed a beat, always in my face before finally pinning my arms to my side.

I kicked out, using my weight to throw him off balance, intending to take him down, but it just ended with both of us falling to the ground.

Where he pinned me.

The sensation of him holding me down, his body pressing into mine, pinning my arms over my head, sent shivers running up and down my spine. In a moment that should've been filled with disappointment from losing the bet, all I could think about was my desire for him. My body hummed, longing and want burning in my belly. He was strong and virile, and there was something about him holding me down that made me wish he would lean in while he did it.

My cheeks flushed as I realized I was flustered for all the wrong reasons. He won, though it definitely took him longer than thirty seconds.

We froze in that position, and while I couldn't tell what he was thinking, I was remembering our night together. As I struggled to catch my breath, I saw desire flash in Thorn's eyes. Desire that I wanted to reach out and grab, and it took everything in me not to roll my hips against him, not to react to the need racing through my own body.

"I win," he growled from above me, and I nodded, not trusting my voice. Stars help me, I was glad he won just to feel him pressed against me like that. And if that wasn't pathetic, I didn't know what was.Yet, I didn't care. Whether it was because Thorn was treating me like a valued warrior or just because of who he was, all I wanted was to go another round with him.

In the ring.

Or in bed.

I didn't mind which if I was being honest.

To my disappointment he pushed to his feet, leaving me

alone on the ground as he ran a hand through the hair that had come loose while we were sparring. I lay there a moment more before I pushed to my feet as well, my blood still pumping hard through my body for a variety of reasons, all of which had to do with the man in front of me. A man who was now looking at me the same way I looked at a sweet roll. A man who I didn't seem to be able to resist.

# CHAPTER
# TWENTY-FOUR

Senara

Since he won, Thorn suggested we go back to his office to talk. I nodded in agreement, uttering a mumbled, "Sure," before I followed behind him. His office was up a couple of floors in the tower by the training area, and I realized as I walked in that he could look out of his window and watch us work in the yard below.

The first time I'd been in the office, I'd been too turned around from the tour to recognize that he was so close. There was still plenty to the tower outside of the guards and our use of it, but I had a feeling that Thorn had this office specifically so he could watch over us.

Once in the office, he gestured toward a bench I didn't remember seeing the last time I'd been in the room, though I had been slightly distracted by the sight of the man I'd just slept with being my new boss. It was hardly more than a few pieces of wood that had been put together, but at least it had some pillows on the seat and back, as if he was trying to make it look comfortable.

His voice rolled over my skin like rain in a storm as he said, "Have a seat."

I did as I was told, still too surprised by this turn of events to do much else. Mentally, I was preparing myself since I knew this was the part where he got to ask his three questions. I had a feeling I didn't want to stand as I answered.

The soft snick of the door closing made my skin pebble, even as I sat next to the fire that blazed in the hearth. The hint of smoke in the air wasn't enough to drown out the scent of Thorn, and it seemed like the smell of him was everywhere. Each time I adjusted the way I sat, another wave of it hit me.

Thorn moved about the office, and I tried not to pay too much attention. "How about a drink?" He uncorked a bottle without waiting for my response, then poured the ale into two cups. He handed me one with the amber-colored ale, and I nodded in thanks.

"Thank you," I said as I took a sip. It wasn't the watered down stuff I was used to drinking, this was rich in flavor. The warmth of the liquid spread through my body and seemed to ease my apprehension a bit. I didn't know what the questions would be, but my word was my word, and I'd given it. The idea of owing him answers to unknown questions made me nervous, though.

Thorn took a seat in the armchair directly across from me and took a sip of his drink. "Are you ready to answer my questions?"

There was no choice in the matter. I had made the deal with him, overly confident in my abilities and too eager to line my pockets, even if it was for a good cause. Maybe if I had remembered how it felt to arm wrestle Thorn before I agreed, things might have been different. As it was, there was nothing I could do other than nod in resignation.

Thorn looked at me, his gaze intense and stern as if he

expected that I would try not to answer. "My first question is about your past. Why did you join the army? There aren't many orphans that want to help the king."

His question shocked me because I assumed he would continue his questioning about the bruises on my face, the very ones he'd been careful of when we were fighting. He'd never once gone for my face. I watched him closely as he took a few sips and eyed me over his ale.

There was no denying it. I wanted him. I wanted him so badly that my whole body ached for his touch. But I couldn't. It would be wrong, especially considering that he was my commander's commander. But what I knew in my mind didn't stop me from wanting him.

I took a deep breath and sighed. "I joined the army to keep my sister safe."

It was true enough. I thought of Wyn as a sister. She was honestly closer to me than a sister could be, I thought.

I watched as Thorn placed his cup on a nearby table. Curiosity burned in his gaze, but he didn't ask me about an orphan having a sister. Nor did he break eye contact as I sat, waiting anxiously for his comments or follow-up questions concerning the army. But still, none came.

Instead, he seemed to accept my answer. As we sat in silence, I watched as the curiosity in his eye became tinged with suspicion, as if he thought I might be lying. I was grateful that he didn't push the subject.

"Alright. Time for my second question." He raked his hand through his long, black hair, pushing back the strands that had fallen from the top of his head when we fought. It gave him an even sexier look than he already had. My mouth went dry and that same sense of longing I'd felt before we sparred returned ten-fold. My chest, stars, my whole body ached for him.

"Who hurt you?" he asked. "I want to know exactly what happened."

He may as well have thrown a bucket of cold water over me. Though it was probably for the best. As I gathered my thoughts I almost called him on combining two questions into one but thought better of it. My heart raced, and my palms grew damp. Overall, it was not an attractive feeling. I knew that if I told him the truth, he might be angry with me and assume that I was stirring up trouble. But what choice did I have? He had already seen my bruises, so there was no point in lying or trying to deflect his question.

After clearing my throat, I forced the words out of my mouth. "My first shift as a guard was a night shift, and after training the next day, I was jumped by some guards in the bathhouse. I was in the bath, they showed up and cornered me. I had stupidly left my weapons on the bench, and I was completely defenseless against them."

He abruptly stood, the chair he'd been sitting in screeching against the stone floor in protest of his forceful movement. His hands clenched at his sides before he paced a few steps and smacked a hand against a wall before turning to stare at me for a second. "I want names. Now." His voice told me there was no room for argument.

"Yes, but there's no need for action." I raised my hands defensively–I was in the room with my commander's commander, and I was telling him to mind his business. I was essentially telling him that what had happened between me and the other guards didn't concern him. I'd handled the situation the best I knew how. "I already humiliated them in the training arena. So there's no need for anything else."

"Names, Senara. Now." Rage flashed through Thorn's eyes, and I knew I had no choice but to answer him.

"I don't know their full names, but I know that Chambers

was the ringleader. Other than him it was Jarek, Kenwyn, Ret, Brioc, and Freoc Nancekivell." I wasn't a snitch, never had been, but these men didn't deserve defending or protecting. As I listed them, Thorn scribbled their names down on a loose sheet of paper.

I could tell he wanted to ask me more about it, but he didn't.

"Again, I've already taken care of it." I pushed off the bench and moved toward him, shooting him my best glare. It was the one I usually reserved for enemies rather than a man I'd slept with, but I couldn't think of him that way anymore. Nothing about that would end well for me, no matter how much I wanted him. "Just leave them alone, okay?"

"I'll take your words under advisement." Thorn paced the room until he'd either walked off his anger or had given up trying. After a moment, he returned to his seat, watching me as I followed suit and sat back down on the bench. "Keep in mind that part of my job is to make sure that all of my guards are safe. If some of them are putting others in danger, I have to take that seriously."

"Fair," I muttered, though I was loath to admit it. These men were dangerous, why they had specifically targeted me was still somewhat of a mystery, but I had no doubt that it at least partially had to do with what happened on the ship.

"My third question might come as a surprise to you." He crossed his arms over his broad chest which only served to make it look broader and stronger, more defined in his tunic. If I thought he was my enemy, he would be terrifying, especially after seeing him fight. I waited for the question while he stared and nodded then smiled as if he already knew the answer. "Did you enjoy yourself the other night at the tavern with me?"

Of course I did. But it wasn't a question I could answer

vocally. I couldn't say it to him. I didn't want to look like or sound like some alehouse strumpet.

Instead, I nodded, and even after, didn't trust my own voice.

"Was it just okay for you?" he asked, his eyebrows furrowing as though he thought my nod and lack of verbal response was a mark against him and his performance.

We were both fully aware that he had surpassed his agreed-upon three questions, but I couldn't just leave him hanging. He didn't look like the kind of man who needed his ego stroked, or the kind who needed to be assured he'd hit the mark, so to speak. But he'd asked a question, and I wanted to answer.

He leaned forward in his chair, and with how close our seats were, if I moved forward as well, I could've touched him. He was staring at me, almost defiantly, as though he was challenging me to be honest and tell him it was bad or so-so. The weight of his stare was intoxicating. My mouth was dry as I wondered what he would do if I lied and said his performance wasn't satisfactory.

"It was incredible." I paused, considering whether or not to expand on my compliment. "It was the best I've ever had, in fact." As the words tumbled out of me, I couldn't believe that I'd said them. I wasn't the kind of girl who discussed this sort of thing with anyone. Stars, I'd barely even told Wyn when I'd lost my virginity, and she was my sister.

My cheeks warmed as I waited for Thorn's response.

"I agree." He smiled so genuinely that it reached his eye, making the edges crinkle as his shoulders relaxed. I couldn't help but return it. "It was the best I've had, too."

There were things between us left unspoken, and they would have to stay that way. It was not proper for a soldier to flirt with her commanding officer. But there we were, in a silent agreement of understanding.

Still, I didn't quite understand why he cared about my opinion of our night together, or why he bothered to share his impression of it. It couldn't happen again.

It shouldn't happen again.

But just the thought of the sex we'd had turned me on to the point that it was painful. I ached in a way that was unlike anything I'd ever experienced before.

The longing pulsated with each beat of my heart, moving through my throat and across the tips of my breasts before settling deep within my core.

I shifted slightly in my seat, trying to diminish the sensation, but it was no use. No amount of ignoring or denying it would quell the passion I felt when I looked into Thorn's eye.

I must've made some type of noise, or at the very least looked incredibly uncomfortable, because suddenly Thorn appeared at my side. "Are you okay?"

"Yes, I'm fine." My voice shook against my will. Heat and awareness crept up my body to my cheeks, and I swayed toward him at the same time he leaned his warm body toward mine. He reached for my face and pulled me close, kissing me gently on the mouth.

My whole body turned to jelly as I returned the kiss, my tongue searching his mouth as if my life depended on it.

Moments passed, and we eventually pulled away from one another, breathless and gasping for air.

We stared into each other's eyes, I didn't want the moment to end, didn't want to lose this connection I had with him. And although I knew it went against the rules and regulations of the Royal Guard, I leaned in and kissed him again.

Thorn made no attempt to stop me, claiming me just as thoroughly as he had in The Red Kraken.

The next time we broke apart, though, I panicked. We'd done this before, and he'd threatened to send me back to the front lines. I wouldn't risk that again.

With some force, I pushed him away from me. "I-I can't do this," I muttered before I bolted from the room, my entire body wanting me to turn around and go back, to take advantage of what was clearly on offer. I couldn't, not if I wanted to stay and keep Wyn safe as well.

# CHAPTER
# TWENTY-FIVE

S enara

The previous night had been a mistake. I knew it but trying to resist Thorn was next to impossible. He was too overwhelming for that. Too virile. Too handsome. Too... everything. Especially when he was that close.

It was his fault, after all. He'd closed the door in his private office, and he was the one who'd brought out the ale. He had to know what was going to happen. Had to know that I was more than a little drawn to him, especially if the way I kissed him was anything to go by.

And then I ran away.

If I was a dog, my tail would have been between my legs as I went.

For my entire shift that day, all I was able to do was replay what happened in my mind. At some point, I'd resolved to go talk to him about it, apologize even, if that was what it took. As my shift ended, I walked the long hallway that led to his office and when I was close enough, I could hear his muffled voice through the door of his office. My heart fluttered, and my breaths came in short puffs in anticipation of seeing him again.

But despite my longing, I knew it was impossible. I had to find a way to tamp my need for him down. There had to be a way to forget everything that had happened between us, the way he'd made my body come alive with his touch, the soft strength of his hands, the way his lips demanded my own. He was my commanding officer and forbidden fruit. And my train of thought wasn't helping clear my head of the desire that was clouding my thoughts.

I wasn't about to interrupt a meeting to bring up us kissing, so I walked past as though I was on my way somewhere else. If it weren't for the other guards, I might have stayed just to listen to his conversation. The tone of his voice was rich and decadent, like strawberries dipped in fresh cream or a warm drink on a cold night. As ashamed as I was to admit it, hearing his voice was almost satisfying enough.

This was the kind of man with the power to make me pathetic, and I didn't think pathetic was a look I wanted to portray. I had to leave before anyone noticed my lingering, so I quickly made my way down the hallway. My heart was still pounding, and now my palms were sweaty as I tried to process what had happened between us the night before. It was only a few kisses, but they were definitely not chaste, and if I hadn't run away, we both knew exactly where the night was heading.

I was so wrapped up in my thoughts that I nearly collided with someone coming at me from the opposite direction. I looked up just in time, and I stepped aside, prepared to apologize for almost walking into them.

The guy, a castle employee I'd seen once or twice removing candles from the wall sconces and replacing them with new ones, paid no attention to my blunder. He was far too focused to notice me, and instead, I realized that he was staring at one of the maids as she leaned over to dust a lower bookshelf that lined the corridor in this section of the castle.

I moved on with my business because I had problems of my own. I didn't need to worry about the way a man looked at a woman—with such longing and desire that I could read his intentions on his face. I was knee-deep in a pit of my own desire and longing, and I had to figure out what to do about it before it was my ruin.

It was a problem to feel this way about Thorn. He was a colleague, my commanding officer, in fact, and I couldn't act on how I felt. For a second, I wished he was the guy who replaced the candles in the castle, the guy who baked the bread in the kitchen, or even the guy who cleaned up after the horses in the stables. ONe of those guys I could be with without sacrificing my service to the king. But Thorn was... off limits. He couldn't be more forbidden.

I walked down the corridor, left feeling completely confused. The more I thought about it, the angrier I got with myself for letting my emotions, the need that had been surging through my body, get in the way of our professional relationship. And if I was a fool before to think I could resist Thorn, I was no warrior now. I was no better than a court jester, or whatever was worse than a fool.

I shook my head, determined not to let myself fall into a shame spiral. Wyn's voice echoed in my head with various things she'd called me over the years. She would tell me that I was strong and capable enough to push past any attraction I felt toward Thorn, that I needed to focus on the task at hand, which was finding the man in the black cloak. And though I wasn't the only one who'd succumbed to the feelings and desires, I was the one who would end it. The one who would put a stop to it. For good.

The days progressed slowly, and after so many passing

without coming up with an answer, having no idea who I was looking for, I finally gave up on my search for the man who had seen Wyn performing magic on the castle grounds. Surely if he was going to report us, he would have done so by now. I could only hope that the stranger had kept their mouth shut. But just in case, Wyn and I were going to have to come up with a plausible explanation for what had probably looked like magic. Because it was.

I sighed, feeling the weight of my failed mission on my shoulders. As if I wasn't already wearing the weight of the world already, I reminded myself that protecting Wyn was a priority. Maybe I shouldn't let it go. I couldn't let her down. If I ever saw the mysterious stranger again, I wouldn't let him get away. Not a third time. Though that was linking two unrelated events, which was a stretch.

It seemed like ever since I'd arrived at the castle, things had been going wrong left and right. Like I had become the center of some bad-luck vortex.

The worst part was that in addition to dealing with Wyn's mystery stranger, I was also suffering my own agony. Every day that passed, my desire for Thorn only grew stronger. Almost unmanageably so.

Every day I tried to push him out of my mind, but we shared a castle, worked together, and ran into one another randomly. Not thinking about him was impossible. Running into him was a lot more common than it had been that first week, though.

As soon as I heard him coming, I would try to duck out of sight, or if I wasn't able to, then I refused to make eye contact. Except I found that I still couldn't resist him. I was like a Magic Touched when the need to feel the energy became too strong. I was an addict.

When we made eye contact, my body didn't know what to

do with itself. My heart would thunder in my chest, my palms would sweat, and the urge to run to him was almost overwhelming. Ironically, it was that urge which made me turn and run the other way. I refused to want anyone like that, especially someone I couldn't have.

Everywhere I went in the castle, whether it was in the darkest corners or brightest corridors, in the garden, in the shadows when I patrolled, even alone in my room at night, I felt his presence lingering around me like an invisible force. The memory of our last kiss still played on my lips whenever I watched him speak. I felt the softness of his mouth that had gone harder and more demanding the longer our kiss went on, the feel of his hands as he'd threaded one into my hair and pulled me in closer with the other, the taste of his tongue as it plunged in and out of my mouth. It was exquisite and perfect. Maybe *that* was why I couldn't forget it.

I'd been trying to deny my feelings for Thorn ever since the first night we shared together, but these days, it was becoming increasingly difficult. I felt my skin prickle as though his hot gaze was on me, as if he was always watching me, even when I couldn't see him or knew that he was elsewhere.

Every shift I worked, I imagined I could hear, see, or smell Thorn, even when I knew he wasn't around. The cedar and spice scent tantalized me with the memories it induced. It was almost eerie, as though I'd walked around the corner just after he'd left. He was always there, at the edge of my life but just beyond where I could touch or see him.

And it hadn't escaped my notice that the guards I named as my attackers to Thorn had disappeared. I supposed he'd probably had them reassigned, maybe even sent them to the front lines to wait for the fight to come to them since they'd been so anxious to fight me. But at least he hadn't had them killed. Or if he did, no one talked about them being missing or anything. Probably because men like them had no one to miss them, likely had no one to care about them. Certainly, if he hadn't sent them back to the battle, I was more than willing to bet that wherever they were, they were being punished in some form or fashion.

As though my body still remembered what happened my ribs ached, leaving me holding myself in a funny stance as I waited for the twinge to subside. Maybe it wasn't memory though and was more to do with the fact that I'd been falling into bed recently and barely moving all night, or day, or afternoon, or whenever I happened to get some rest.

The rapid shifting between night and day patrolling wasn't helping with my mental strain. It didn't help my mind stay clear enough to sort a problem or even remain focused long enough that I could try. Even my emotions felt like they were becoming more unmanageable.

And constantly feeling like Thorn was just out of my reach or watching me only made matters worse—only made me want him. Being near him allowed me to imagine the two of us walking through the castle together, training and eating meals together. It would never happen, but it helped me pass my days as I imagined what life as Thorn's companion might look like.

With Wyn almost always working a shift or volunteering in the Royal Library and none of the other guards talking to me, daydreaming about Thorn was therapeutic. I kept telling myself that he was looking out for me and had my back, no matter the circumstance. Slowly, I began to feel less isolated.

I was an outcast. There was no sense in skirting around that fact. I'd always kept to myself out of necessity to survive. I hadn't realized how much being on the front line had created a sense of camaraderie with the other soldiers, and I missed it dearly.

In some ways, the solitary nature of my current job reminded me of when I'd been taken in by the Chantry.

I shook my head and shoved those thoughts to the side, not allowing myself to think about what happened back then any more than I already had. There was a reason I kept those memories locked away, shoved down deep inside my mind where they could never see the light of day.

# CHAPTER
# TWENTY-SIX

Thorn

"These are the documents that need to be signed for the provisions to be sent to the front." Ronan placed a stack of papers on my desk. "And this is the map that the king's cartographer recently updated. It will need your initials in the bottom left-hand corner." I looked at the paper and pushed it aside.

I stared at the pages he'd dropped on my desk, but the words blurred, and I found myself unable to focus. "Thank you."

Ronan nodded and left the office, closing the door behind him. Not before he shot me a worried glance, though. I wasn't acting like myself, and that was a problem for a number of reasons.

Finally, with a moment of peace to myself, I sat back and stared out the window. I was not in the mood for more work. I wanted Senara. Couldn't have her, but I still wanted her.

The kiss that we'd shared on the bench in this room haunted every moment I spent in my office. Each time one of the officers or commanders sat there, I wanted to scream at them for sullying it, distorting the memory of her there with her hair flowing over her shoulders and her eyes heavily lidded with desire.

I tried to keep my distance from Senara, and I was failing. Leaning back in the chair, I closed my eyes and remembered the scent of her hair and the feeling of her naked skin against mine when we were at The Red Kraken. She was soft but muscled, her body taut yet pliant. She was every contrast a woman could be. And I wanted her so much I ached.

It was like I was being drawn to her against my will. My duties kept piling up, so it wasn't as if I didn't have enough to preoccupy my time or my mind. I was the Blade of the King. There were always things that needed my attention. Yet all I could think about was Senara. She was the bane of my existence since she was preventing me from getting any stars-damned work done, official and otherwise.

After an afternoon of studying charts and maps, reading letters from the front line commanders, and ones from inside the castle as well, I needed to move around. I stood and stretched, going to the window and looking out. Even if I wasn't fighting right now, at least some of the guards were.

My gaze caught on some long brown hair that was flying through the air as the owner of it attacked their opponent relentlessly, drilling them to the ground. Suddenly, I needed some fresh air. I had to be down there.

As I made my way to the training yard, I stopped short, halfway between the entrance to the gardens and the training yard itself. Because she was there in the middle of the ring, sparring with a man twice her size.

I'd seen her fight and drill on more than one occasion, more than she would probably even imagine or that I cared to admit. Yet I still found myself captivated by her. Her moves were graceful yet precise, steady and clean. Every part of her body moved in time to some invisible song, rhythmic and calculated.

Had I realized it was her sparring down here before I left my office? I wasn't sure, but now that I knew, I couldn't turn away.

My body hummed with need. Every part of me needed her, and before I knew what I was doing, I broke.

I swiftly walked to Senara's side. "Willow," I called out as I entered the ring, causing the two of them to stop sparring immediately. "I need to speak with you about what you saw the first night you were on guard."

My voice was loud enough that anyone nearby would hear me and not be suspicious of my motives.

Senara looked at me with one eyebrow tilted in what I could only guess was confusion.

"I was told about the incident by your commander, and I'm not sure I agree with his assessment," I continued as if I had any intention of speaking to her about whatever she thought she saw. But I had to make it look good because my body had already made a decision, and now my mouth had to go along. "What you saw should not be dismissed."

It didn't matter that her commander had told me about it as a joke or that it was something that really *should* have been taken seriously. None of that was going to play into what happened after she followed me, not if I had anything to say about it.

Without another word, I turned and walked back into the castle, making a direct line for my office. I glanced over my shoulder a few times to make sure Senara was following. She looked concerned, her normally pouty mouth set into a tight line, and pieces of her brown hair fell into her eyes, hiding the pale blue orbs that haunted my dreams from my sight. I couldn't lead her into my office fast enough.

Once we were both inside, I closed the door behind her.

She began to move away, to walk toward my desk, but I grabbed her hand and spun her toward me. Pulling her against my chest, I leaned down and whispered in her ear. "I can't resist you any longer."

I descended on her with a ferocity I hadn't intended as my own desperate need spilled out. As soon as I felt her soft lips against my own, I stepped closer, kissing her deeply. I could feel the heat of her body melting into mine. I stroked a hand down her side and murmured her name. Merely touching her felt right. "I need you. Now."

She nodded, in either agreement nor acknowledgement. I wanted to take it as her agreement, but she had run away when I kissed her last time.

"I need you to tell me what you want," I said, though my voice sounded more like a beast's than a man's.

"I want you, Thorn," she whispered, her lips brushing against my own with every syllable. I wished she'd called me by my real name but not enough to actually say anything about it.

Wrapping my arms around her, I devoured her mouth in a hungry kiss that took as much from her as I could, not giving her a chance to say anything again. I moved my lips down her jawline to her ear and sucked in her earlobe as I did, backing her against the wall. I needed to pin her against something lest she run away again, not that I would stop her if she really wanted to.

"I don't think I'm ever going to get enough of you." I growled the words against the side of her throat.

She shivered in my hold, and I bit back my smirk. The way her body responded was addicting. I wasn't sure I'd ever tire of it.

I licked and nipped down her neck, inhaling and taking in her naturally sweet and slightly floral scent, a teaser of what was in between her legs. Without wasting a moment, I glided my hand down her stomach and then lower, until I slid my hand between the apex of her thighs. Her pulse raced as I kissed her neck and pushed my mouth to hers to catch the moan that fell through her lips as I flexed my fingers against the material of her pants.

She tasted sweet, and heat seared through the material. I relished the dampness soaking the fabric.

I released her mouth and leaned my forehead against hers, letting her soft breaths hit my skin and her light mewls tickle my ears.

"That feels good, doesn't it?"

She panted, "Yes."

Her hands moved up my arms and grabbed onto my shoulders before twisting in my hair as she pulled me down for another kiss. She teetered a bit as she tried to move closer.

"Eager?" I chuckled even though my body felt the same way. I wanted her naked and riding me, taking her release while I watched her writhe and moan on top of me. Then I'd take her from behind, then against every wall of the castle if I could, until she couldn't go into a room without remembering the way I made her scream with pleasure in that same place. I wanted her to be as addicted to me as I was to her.

"Thorn..." Senara's voice rasped out so quickly that she didn't even know what she was asking for I could see that in the way her gaze skimmed all over my face and couldn't settle.

Quickly, I removed my hand, bent down, and picked her up bridal style.

She yelped, cheeks flushing as I nuzzled her neck. I moved to my desk chair and sat down, making myself comfortable with her sitting on my lap. I buried my face further in her neck and let the tiny tendrils of hair sweep against my nose.

I wanted her hair down like the first night. She looked magical with her long, flowing hair, but it would take too much time to undo the intricate braids, and I needed her now.

She squirmed in my lap, forcing my cock to liven up harder and faster. I'd been at half-mast since our time together, and now that I had her in my arms, I was harder than a rock, my cock was demanding to be somewhere soft and warm inside her.

Leaning forward, I captured her lips and pulled her tightly to me, her thigh grazing against my cock. I groaned at the pleasurable pain it induced. Getting out of my pants was the next thing I needed to do.

Senara discovered my hardness for her, and her small hands snaked their way down from my shoulders and chest to cup the bulge there.

I fell back in the chair and let her torture me.

I growled as she sat up and removed her hand but calmed quickly when she knelt before me and went for the ties of my pants.

Her slender fingers quickly removed the material, and I lifted my ass to give her more access.

Sitting back on her heels, she watched me with a slight smile on her face as she wrapped her hand around my cock firmly. She stroked down, cupping my balls in her other hand before her way back up to the tip.

"That. Keep doing that."

I leaned my head against the chair and watched her work me over with care. My toes curled inside my boots, and my breathing grew labored. My palms itched to be wrapped up in her hair, around her breasts, and to finger her pussy. I wanted to touch all of her.

Then without warning, she lowered her mouth and licked the head of my cock, forcing me to twitch, swell, and chase after her.

"Fuck."

She removed a hand and sucked me in deeper, but I felt

like I was about to burst, and I couldn't have that. I needed her wrapped snugly around me.

My palms wrapped around her shoulders firmly, stopping the up and down motion that she'd been working me with. She looked up at me with big eyes, my cock in her mouth, one hand wrapped around the base and the other cupping my balls. It was an erotic sight to behold, and I'd never forget it.

Her brow furrowed, and she lifted her mouth off me, keeping her cheeks hollowed and sucking the whole way.

"Do you not like it?" Her innocent voice made me want to tell her I loved it and to resume, but that would have to wait for another time.

"Too much. Ride me. I need to be inside you." I was giving her orders, and I wasn't sure how either of us felt about it, but I didn't have enough brain power left to say anything else.

Slowly she stood up, smiling at me as she undid her pants. Once they dropped to the ground, she stepped out of them but left her shirt and belt on, too needy to be bothered with getting completely naked, which in my current state I appreciated. She straddled me on the chair. Her wet heat slicked down her thighs, and my cock jumped at the sight. The fact that she wanted me that badly—almost as badly as I wanted her—with me looking the way I did, was a minor miracle.

Holding me in her hand, she lined me to her center and stroked my head up and down her slit to gather as much of her wetness as she could so I could easily slip into her tight pussy.

With each pass, her breath hitched, and my mouth watered at the covered breasts that dangled before my face.

Without hesitation, I unlooped the tie at the top of her covering, and in an instant, they fell before me. Her creamy breasts, with the pert rosy nipples, beckoned for me. I moaned at the beautiful unveiling. Before I could feast, Senara lowered herself down on me about an inch and lifted herself, biting her lip the whole time.

Then she dropped back down and rose after a couple of inches. Then she seated herself almost half the way down. Her lower lips thoroughly swallowed as much of me as they could every time.

A small whine escaped her, and I hoped it wasn't from pain. "Only take as much as you can. Use me for your pleasure, Senara. Ride me until you come on my cock."

She seemed to have forgotten how big I was, and at this angle, I was sure I probably felt even bigger. Slowly, she rotated her hips up and down, getting lower each time until I felt her hips connect with mine. I let out a groan of satisfaction. As she began to ride me, I knew I wasn't going to last long. I grabbed her hips hard enough to leave ten distinct bruises and lifted her up and down.

We both moaned at the movement. After several deep thrusts, my hands slipped further around her back to grab her ass. She let me grasp her for a moment before she removed my hands and placed them on the arms of the chair. What I hadn't expected was the way she grasped the top of the chair on either side of my head, dangling her soft biteable breasts in front of my mouth as she worked herself up and down on my cock fast and hard.

Her slickness poured over me and down around my shaft. Her breaths were coming out in double time, and her chest bounced in front of me so fast that I couldn't latch on for a taste.

I sat back and watched her work me over, and I couldn't believe this amazing creature was there.

"Oh, oh, I'm almost there." Her hips were losing their rhythm, and she could only jerk. Her thighs had to be on fire.

Grabbing her hips again, I planted my feet firmly against the floor, holding her steady above me, and fucked her from beneath.

"Oh. My. God. Yes. Yes. Yes." She started shouting as her

breasts bounced up and down. I heaved like a racehorse, and sweat ran down my back and temples.

Then Senara bit down on her mouth to muffle her screams as her body tightened and convulsed around my own. Her pussy grabbed onto my cock and didn't want to let go.

My balls tightened, and I came hard into Senara, filling her, pumping every last drop of my cum inside her. Once my cock was done spasming inside her, I fell back into the chair with the fantastic woman sprawled over me.

Fuck, each time with her was intense. I knew before I even withdrew from her that I would need to fuck her again, and often. Whatever was between us would not be denied, and I for one was tired of trying to fight it. I just begged the gods that she felt the same way.

# TWENTY-SEVEN

Senara

As I walked to the training yard, I smoothed my hair and glanced at my uniform. Nothing was out of place, and I looked as I typically did with my side braid keeping my hair out of my face while the rest was loose down my back. Yet I felt vulnerable and wondered if anyone would notice the fact that I'd been alone in Thorn's office for an extended amount of time the night before.

It didn't help that even though we had cleaned up afterward, I still felt as though I was soaking through my uniform pants. Whether it was from how hard I came or how much he came, or maybe even a combo, I wasn't sure. Either way, it felt like a sign pointing at me and telling everyone what I'd just done.

When I left his office after our time together, I noticed a few of the guards watching me as though they could tell what had just happened.

I had been quiet, though. Hadn't I? Hadn't he?

Still, I was worried.

I walked into the training yard, and my stomach sank as I

turned in almost a full circle, realizing that I was right to be concerned. They had all stopped what they were doing to stare at me.

"Whore!" One of the guards yelled from across the yard. I couldn't tell which one it was, but I didn't give so much as a glance because I didn't want them to see how the word affected me. I practiced stoicism. And indifference. Pride on a whole other level of such a thing. And deception because there was that, too.

Holding my head high, I made my way to the opposite side of the circle. As I walked past, another guard, and then another and another, insulted me under their breath. The word *whore* was like their chant.

Word had traveled fast, and my actions certainly weren't winning me any friends. Not that I'd had any to begin with.

I turned my back to them and pulled my sword from its sheath. Grabbing the sharpening stone, I focused all of my nervous energy on making my blade razor-sharp.

"Excuse me." Someone—a voice I didn't immediately recognize—spoke directly into my ear and placed a hand on my shoulder.

I whipped around, my sword held high and ready to take out the person who'd decided to attack me.

"Whoa." Allynna, one of the few female guards, held her hands up high. "I'm not here to fight."

"Oh. Sorry, Allynna." I slid my sword back in its scabbard. "I guess I'm a little jumpy."

Allynna eyed me with one perfect eyebrow raised and a small smile curling her lips, as though she wanted to make a comment about the rumors flying around about me. Instead, she cleared her throat. "There's a gathering for the new recruits to check in on how they're doing. Your commander was looking for you since you've been fighting so well recently." She motioned behind her to the circular structure. "It's at the top of the tower. They said it was a training activity. And it's definitely a chance to impress the higher ups by being up there." Not that I was in it to impress Thorn, but if there was a meeting at the top of the tower, then he was about to be impressed.

I couldn't deny the skepticism that crept into me at her words.

She must have sensed it because she leaned closer, her blue eyes staring into me as she whispered, "It's kind of like an initiation thing for the new guards. Mostly talk and very little action, but it might help you bond with some of the other guards."

In some ways, that made me not want to go. To stay down in the training area out of spite. But if I could win some of them over to my side, or at least push them back to being neutral instead of outright hating me, then I should go.

I tilted my head back and covered my eyes from the glare of the sun. The tower was extremely tall and mainly used by guards to keep watch in the far distance. I couldn't think of another use for it anyway. And there was no visible door that I could see. The bulk of the tower was closed off and used for storage after the floor that Thorn's office was on.

"I'm not sure how to get up there," I admitted, still staring at the massive structure.

Allynna shrugged and gave me a small smile. "No problem. I'll take you." She turned and walked across the training circle, not bothering to see if I was following, which of course, I was. As we walked, I blocked out the whistling and name calling from the other guards.

The stairway leading to the tower was so narrow that I had no choice but to walk directly behind Allynna. As far up as I could see, there were more spirals of steps leading into a skyward abyss. Even though I considered myself to be in great shape, by the time we made it to the top, I was out of breath.

But I would've rather died than panted, especially since Allynna seemed completely unfazed by it. Instead, I concentrated on breathing slowly and deeply.

As much as I hated to admit it, Allynna was the most senior female guard here, and if I wanted a chance to make friends with the other female guards, I knew I had to win her over first. They took their cues from her and paid attention to how she treated people. I had also noticed the fierceness with which she fought in the training ring. The last thing I wanted was for her to think I wasn't capable or that I was unfit to be a guard.

"Here we are." Allynna turned and motioned to the ladder that stood in front of us. The hatch at the top was closed, which made me feel nervous all over again. If they were all up there, then me flinging the hatch open would attract a lot of attention. "It sticks a bit, so you'll have to give it a shove."

I climbed up and did as she said, shoving my shoulder against the hatch which gave way and flipped open more easily than I expected given Allynna's words.

"They're probably just on the other side of the crates," she called up.

As I looked around, I didn't see anyone, but there was a big stack of crates right in front of the hatch. Voices were carrying from somewhere, and I was already late so I hopped out and started to head around the crates. I was surprised that they were able to stay standing with the way the wind howled up here.

A cold breeze took me by surprise, chilling me to the bone. Rubbing my arms, I turned to say thank you to Allynna. " Thanks for showing me the way. It's surprisingly cold up..."

Allynna's smug face disappeared back down the ladder as she quickly closed the hatch and latched it from the other side. This was nothing but a trap. There was no one else up here, just me, and I had no clothing to protect me from a biting wind. She'd left me here to freeze.

The self-recriminations were sharp and swift. How could I have been so stupid to believe her? Especially with everyone else mocking me? Of course Allynna would hate me, too. She wouldn't want to be left out, wouldn't want to stick together with the likes of me. I was an outcast.

It was brutal on the tower with no protection from the wind. It howled around me and the crates by the hatch offered no real protection. The sun would set soon, and I knew I wouldn't survive the already cold winds or the drop in temperature.

I frantically searched for something to use to pick the lock, a pin or a shard of metal or wood, but of course, the tower floors were surprisingly—or maybe not depending on how long she'd had this planned—clean. There wasn't even loose dirt between the stones.

With no other choice, I tried to break down one of the crates, praying to the old gods and the new that there was something in there that I could use. None of them were listening, though, because all I found were empty bottles.

I had no idea why they were out on the roof of the tower, but it was annoying to say the least. Some of the other crates were simply empty, which made me think that they had been put up here to help lure me up there. Other crates held moldy rations. Why was this stuff being held on to?

In the last crate, I found a moth-eaten blanket which gave me hope, even if it did reek of piss. I broke some of the empty crates apart and tried to use the nails and thin pieces of wood to pick the latch, but there was no space to get anything between the hatch door and the ledge that it rested on, no way to lift it up so I could even try to get at the latch.

I had to do something. I couldn't just die up here, and I would if I didn't get down before night fell. It was already frigid with the wind, the air still slightly salty from the sea at this height. Without the sunlight warming me, I had no doubt I would freeze to death overnight unless I could build some kind of shelter from the crates and blanket. I wasn't hopeful.

Allynna wouldn't have the satisfaction of being the one who put an end to my time at the castle. I needed to think. There had to be something I could do. Maybe I could drop something to try and get someone's attention? The only things heavy enough not to be carried away by the wind were my boots, the empty bottles, or the crates themselves. I didn't particularly relish throwing any of them over the side of the tower.

Plus, I would have to calculate the exact time, and if the wind blew harder or softer than expected, it wouldn't work. On top of that, if I wasn't careful, something dropped from this height could seriously hurt someone if it landed directly on top of their unsuspecting head. And depending on how long Allynna planned on leaving me up there, I could easily become sun parched and wind burnt. If I didn't freeze to death first.

I had no choice but to believe that she'd left me at the top of the tower to die.

Shaking my head, I pushed my suspicions about Allynna's intentions away. I couldn't dwell right now because I had other things to concentrate on. Like surviving. And whether or not she wanted me gone wouldn't change my current predicament. I had to figure out a way to alert someone that I was locked on top of the tower.

I glanced between my boots and the empty bottles. This was such a bad idea, but I had no other choice. I was worried about people being hurt as I tried to get their attention, and the thing that seemed less likely to hurt them were my boots. Slipping my foot out of one, I leaned over and peered below.

The shift debriefs would be over soon, and then I could catch someone's attention. I hoped.

The commander walked out into the yard, and I immediately threw my boot, but the timing was off, which I could see as soon as the boot left my hand. It landed just behind him. He turned to see what the sound was, picked my boot up, examined it, checked the men around him—probably looking for a one-shoed wonder—then dropped it back to the ground. He didn't look up, having no idea that the boot had been thrown from the tower above him.

As he turned to continue toward his destination, I desperately threw my other boot, which landed just beside the first. This time, he didn't even look.

Someone else came out of the castle a minute later and glanced at the pair of boots lying on the ground. He promptly kicked them to the side since they were in a walkway and then went along his way.

My eyes filled with tears as I started to lose hope that anyone would find me. It occurred to me that I was to die, trapped in the tower like a princess in need of a heroic rescue. Truthfully, I wouldn't have scoffed or turned my nose up at a heroic rescue.

I had no choice but to drop one of the bottles the next time someone walked out. It smashed against the ground and they turned and looked up, but either they didn't see me or they ignored me as I frantically waved my arms over my head. This whole thing was repeated three more times before one of them hit a guard on his shoulder.

He looked up, and this time I knew he saw me because he gave me a one-fingered salute before he went on his way.

My stomach sank.

Were they all in on this? Was this some kind of punishment because they suspected I'd slept with Thorn?

I pushed the thoughts from my head. Now was not the

time, especially when I realized that I was out of bottles and my boots were already gone.

The next thing I tried was the decaying blanket, but that just floated away on the wind as though it had better places to be, even after I'd knotted it to try to make it heavier.

With most of the heavy things gone, it was either start throwing the crates or use more of my clothes and hope it drew someone's attention. I already felt guilty for that bottle hitting the other guard's shoulder, so I couldn't bring myself to use the wood, not yet at least.

First, I removed my doublet, keeping my jacket around me for warmth. As I hung over the edge of the tower between one of the cutouts for the archers, I waited and watched closely. From this distance I couldn't yell. Well, I could, but the chances anyone would hear me were slim. But still, I had to try.

When another figure emerged, I screamed at the top of my lungs. "Hey! Up here!"

I threw my doublet with all my might and could hear the buckles as they rolled down the length of the wall and hit the stone.

The person looked around but didn't seem to see me at first, so I stripped out of my jacket and waved it over my head like a flag.

Whoever it was who'd come out, turned and went back inside the castle just as a gust of wind snatched the jacket from my hands and blew it the opposite way, to the outer part of the castle walls. At least I had worn a thicker chemise today.

I knew there would barely be anyone around for the rest of the evening now. The night shift was starting, and no one was in the training areas, almost like they'd been told to find somewhere else to be, so I didn't have anyone I could call for help.

The only thing I had left to use was the crates I'd broken apart earlier. I made my way over to them only to discover that a lot of the smaller pieces of wood had blown away while I was trying to get the attention of people leaving the building. Still, I didn't have much of a choice, so I stacked all the pieces of wood together that I could and made a v-shaped shelter.

It hardly blocked the wind at all, with the wood being too rotted and old to do much. It was better than nothing, though. At least I thought so until it started raining as well.

Icy drops hit my skin, making me groan with frustration. If the rain turned to snow, I wouldn't be surprised.

I slumped onto the floor, wrapping my arms around my shivering body. All I could do was hope that the person had seen me and was on their way to investigate. If they didn't, if they ignored me, then my fate was clear.

I would die of exposure on the tower. And there was nothing I could do about it.

# TWENTY-EIGHT

Senara

The longer I sat, the more my teeth chattered and my body shook. Every second of it was against my will. The sun had set, and the temperature dropped dramatically. There I sat without a doublet or a jacket, much more vulnerable to the icy wind than I would've been with them. Add to that the cold rain that was falling and the thunder that was rumbling overhead, and I actually wanted to cry.

If I was going to die, why couldn't it be on the battlefield doing something I was good at instead of being left like rubbish on a rooftop? Maybe, if by some miracle I managed to get out of this situation, I'd ask Thorn if I could go back to the front. I knew it meant leaving Wyn, but with everything that was going on, I wasn't sure where else I belonged. At least there, I'd get an honorable death. Probably.

I was down to my thin undershirt, which was the same as wearing practically nothing. Closing my eyes, I tried to calm my breathing. The chattering and shivering made my whole body ache, but it was no use. As a cold gust whipped through the tower, my body shook harder. There was no defense and no way I was going to survive another hour of this, much less an entire night. It was too cold to cry, even if I wanted to, and too cold for the hopelessness to take root.

A rustling noise on the far side of the tower caught my attention. Probably a bird had landed intending to roost for the night with me in my stone prison. To my surprise, Ronan's head appeared through the hatch at the top of the tower. Thanks to the setting sun, I hadn't been able to see whose attention I was trying to get.

His eyes widened as he looked at me, realizing that I was the one who had been locked on top of the tower, desperate enough to be found that I had sent my shoes and my clothes down in a feeble attempt to be noticed.

Thankfully, the shock only lasted a couple of seconds before he flung the hatch open and jumped out, rushing to me. I tried to move toward him, but I was so cold I was barely able to move my legs, let alone get up from where I was sitting.

My hands and feet had gone numb because I had been so focused on getting down from the tower I forgot that they needed blood circulating to them. I should have rubbed them, used the motion to create heat in both my hands and my feet, but I'd only thought of getting help.

Nothing else had mattered to me, and now I was paying the price.

Even though I'd only been completely still for a little while, my joints already felt like they'd locked up, like I'd be permanently frozen in this curled up position. While I knew the feelings would fade and I'd regain movement, it didn't stop me from panicking slightly as I couldn't get my body to obey and do what I wanted and needed it to do.

Ronan was there to help, though. "You're freezing," he said as he carefully wrapped his jacket around me. His voice was gentle and caring, kind and a not unpleasant warmth spread through me, melting away the chill. I wasn't going to die. At least not today. And it was all because of this man.

"Thank you." I mumbled, my teeth chattering and my whole body shaking.

He picked me up with very little effort. If I hadn't been in such bad shape, I might have been impressed, but instead, as his warmth scorched my frozen body, all I could do was rest my head in the space between his neck and shoulder to rest. He smelled like the heart of the forest, but with a fresh note of citrus on top, like he'd just had a glass of lemonade or orange juice. Those kinds of things were usually reserved for noble families, though, so I had to assume that it was part of his natural scent.

Ronan walked back to the hatch and backed us both out, closing the hatch as he carried me down the ladder. He somehow did all of this without dropping me, or even feeling like he might lose his grip. He continued down the winding staircase, the rhythm of his steps and his confident hold making me feel secure and a little sleepy.

Before I knew where we were, he was turning off the stairs. I forced my eyes open, curious to see where he was taking me. I gasped and would have struggled as we rounded a corner and Ronan walked directly toward Thorn's office, but I didn't have the energy to move much.

Besides that, what would I even say? No, please, not the office of the man I've slept with twice now? How would I explain that my boss' boss and I had an awkward but very intimate relationship. Before I could decide on an excuse, form a sentence, or even open my mouth to protest, we were in the office.

Ronan set me gently on a sheep-skin rug that was positioned in front of the fireplace. Picking up a long fire iron, he poked at the logs, moving them around and adding more onto the pile, causing the tall flames to reach higher and burn harder. The red and orange fingers were tall enough that they were licking the top of the fireplace.

We sat in silence as he worked, and my shivering slowly subsided. For a moment it felt good, but then it was so hot that I backed away. Ronan grabbed me and pulled me to his side. "We have to get you warmed up."

I was too weak to protest as he moved to sit behind me. His arms wrapped around me, and all I could do was spare a brief moment of worry that somehow he might become aware of my mark. I doubted it, though. My head fell back onto his shoulder, and I closed my eyes, allowing the heat that was radiating into me from both sides to thaw my frozen body.

"You have a lot of enemies for someone who's only been here a very short time." Ronan smiled and pulled me closer, adjusted his arms around me so that we were sharing the fire and his body heat.

The door to the office opened, and I jumped, completely startled, not just by the noise of the door opening but the sudden shift in Ronan's mood. He tensed behind me as though ready to face down whatever attacker was there.

When I looked over my shoulder, it wasn't an attacker at all, but it was the owner of the office.

"What's going on here?" Thorn demanded, hands on his hips. His glare was deep and his fists were clenched. He was a man who'd walked in and seen two of his soldiers in an embrace and it was, if not against the rules, at least unadvisable. And worst of all, it was in his office. An office where probably only hours ago he was inside me as I rode him to my own pleasure on his desk chair.

If I didn't know better, I would've thought it was jealousy I saw in his eyes. We'd slept together, twice now, and all I knew was that the desire he had for me was just as strong as my own unnatural desire for him. That didn't mean that there was anything serious between us.

His look was possessive, though, heating my blood. Ronan held up his hands as he moved away from me to stand. Once he stood, he helped me to the bench and stepped away completely.

The tension was suffocating, like another presence in the room. I couldn't turn away as I watched Thorn eyeing Ronan, looking him up and down as if the answer to his question was written somewhere on his uniform. For a moment, I thought Thorn might lunge toward Ronan. Certainly he had the strength and the know-how to kill him with one fell blow, and my mind conjured an image of it happening.

I'd thought that Ronan was Thorn's best, and maybe only, friend. Of course, maybe I'd misread their relationship. Right now, they certainly didn't seem very friendly.

Thorn's face had turned a deep shade of red, almost purple.

Before he looked at Ronan again, before the situation blew up as I feared it was about to, Thorn turned to me. "What happened?"

I shifted my body on the couch so I wouldn't have to strain my back. Wiggling my toes, I realized that the normal sensations had returned. The fire had done its job and so had Ronan. I would be grateful another time because clearly this wasn't a good one for that.

"I was locked on top of the tower. Ronan found me and got me down," I said, hoping that would be enough of an explanation for Thorn to understand why we were there together.

"Where are your shoes?" He looked down at my bare feet.

I tucked them under myself, suddenly self-conscious. "I used them to try to get someone"—I shrugged—"anyone's attention."

"Did it work?" He still sounded stern and angry, but the initial rage seemed to have faded.

"No." My voice was small and timid, and I hated it.

His face softened, and he looked from me to Ronan and then back again. Without a word, he nodded toward Ronan. "You may go."

Ronan walked to the door and didn't look back as he walked out. I probably wouldn't have if I was him either, but I would've liked to thank him. I would have to find him and see to it when this was finished.

Thorn turned his attention back to me. "How did you get locked in the tower?"

His tone brokered no room for anything but the truth, though I didn't want to get into it. Just like the night he'd asked me about the beating, I felt I had no choice but to give him the details.

"I was told there was some sort of training exercise taking place on the tower this afternoon." I rubbed my temples with both hands, still feeling foolish in the wake of Allynna's deception. "Like an idiot, I followed the person up there, and they waited until I was on the roof to close and lock the hatch behind me. I tried to yell for the people below, but no one could hear me over the wind. I threw my shoes and clothes down to grab someone's attention. I even threw some bottles from a crate that was up there which smashed on the ground." I realized then that I was still wearing Ronan's jacket because mine had blown away. I wasn't likely to find it again either, which would mean I had to scrounge for a new one.

I paused and glanced at Thorn, who had walked to the couch and joined me, sitting with one knee resting on the cushion and one arm running along the back ledge.

"Luckily, Ronan walked by and saw my doublet falling and me waving my jacket around like a flag. If it weren't for him, I —I think I would've died up there." I forced myself to look at Thorn, even though I wasn't particularly anxious to hear his response.

I'd been locked in the tower by one guard and beaten by

others. It didn't say much about my abilities to protect the Crown if I wasn't intelligent enough to protect myself. No wonder he was suspicious. I didn't want him to assume I was a troublemaker, but he would think whatever he thought and there wasn't anything I could do about it.

Of course, then he asked the question I'd been hoping to avoid. "Who?" The word was snarled out, and though I knew the anger wasn't directed at me, it was still hard not to flinch at the ferocity of it.

"Allynna."

Thorn's face contorted, and rage flamed to life in his eyes. If his anger was directed at me, I was sure I would have burned to a crisp right then and there. Fortunately, it wasn't. Still, I couldn't shake the feeling that I was the one at fault for this whole situation because I'd trusted her.

"They heard us. Just so you know." The words were barely a whisper as they slipped out.

Shock stole across his face for a moment before he shrugged. "Don't pay any attention to them."

My mouth seemed to have a mind of its own as I found myself asking, "So you're not going to send me back to the front?"

He snorted. "Why would you think that?"

"Because that's what you said you'd do after the first night." I shrugged.

He moved forward on the bench before giving up and coming to kneel in front of me. It was odd to see this large, formidable man on his knees for me. "Senara, if I did that, I'd have no choice but to go with you." He reached out and cupped my face. "Didn't you hear me when I said I couldn't resist you any longer? If you went back to the front, I'd just follow you, then drag you back here. Or somewhere else maybe." An odd light came into his eyes at the last part, but I was too focused on my racing heart to pay it that much attention. "Then I'd claim you over and over again until you had no choice but to admit that you belonged to me."

Thorn's words were heavy, and I felt them wrap around me like a winter cloak. They didn't scare me the way they would coming from anyone else. Instead, they just made me feel safe and cared for. I wanted to kiss him, to lay with him in front of the fire and let him warm my body completely, but I wasn't sure that my advances would be welcomed, so I kept them to myself. I was glad for it when he pulled away a moment later.

# TWENTY-NINE

S enara

Even though I'd been locked on top of the tower and it was the middle of the night, so I hadn't had any sleep, Thorn still demanded that I report for my patrolling shift. I supposed he didn't want to show me any preferential treatment, but I could've certainly used a nap since switching from days to nights was harder for me than the other way around.

I was beyond exhausted, but there was no other choice than to fulfill my duties. Protecting the castle was a job to be done at the cost of all comforts and luxuries.

There were days like this when I'd served on the front, days where sleep seemed to become a thing of the past as we fought and prepared for the next assault. At the front, it would always happen that just when we thought we had a moment to rest and catch our breath, another band of opposing soldiers would make their move.

I would make it through this shift, just as I'd always made it through my sleepless nights on the front. I didn't have to be happy about it, though. And stars help anyone who crossed my path and tried to start shit.

As I made my way through my assigned territory, a flash of movement from the corner of my eye stopped me. I glanced up in time to see a hooded figure. Again.

I couldn't be sure that it was the same person who I'd been tracking that first night, the one who probably witnessed Wyn performing magic, or whether this person's appearance was something else entirely. Either way, I wasn't going to let him get away. Not this time. Not again.

I didn't know if he'd seen me, but if he had, he wasn't running now. He was sneaking through the shadows, trying to stay hidden. Running after him hadn't been a good idea last time, so I quickly yanked off my breastplate and pauldrons, leaving only the forearm braces which were scratched up so not exactly luminous, and decided to follow him, softly creeping, staying in the darkness behind him. A slow and steady approach seemed more reasonable than full out running when last time, he'd clearly outwitted and outran me.

As I tracked him—and I assumed it was a him because of his broad shoulders and height—it became obvious that whoever he was, he knew the ins and outs of the castle. He made his way into the castle, then easily shifted from one room to the next, taking back stairwells I didn't even know existed. Before long, I had followed him from one end of the castle to the other, although it had only been a few minutes.

I also found it interesting that this person was well-versed in the routes the guards took. Each time he came to a new corridor or stairwell, he stopped, waiting until the guard patrolled the area and moved on in his circular route. Then, he waited for the exact moment, when the guard was completely focused on another area, before he moved which gave him the maximum chance of sneaking by the guards unnoticed.

Each time he turned to check for something, almost as

though he wanted to be sure I was following, and I saw the wink of earrings in the low light. Earrings that were much too high up to belong to a human, which meant that he had to be fae and I hadn't imagined it last time. It also made it even more imperative that I caught him. And once again left me confused by his stature.

When we made our way to the inner walls of the castle, I suddenly lost sight of the hooded figure. My heart raced as I frantically searched the area I'd just seen him, but I couldn't find him.

The alcove that he'd been standing in didn't go anywhere but was empty by the time I checked it. I hadn't missed him leaving it, but he was gone nonetheless. When I turned and saw the edge of a cloak disappearing around a corner I chased after it, only to find one of the other guards on their patrol route. We weren't supposed to wear cloaks, but it had been getting colder out.

I backed off from the other guard and looked around once more. It was as if he'd disappeared into thin air. Could fae disappear into shadows? Maybe I was going crazy, but I knew I hadn't been following a ghost. There was a person. I only had to figure out where he'd gone. And if he was even a *he* at all. For all I knew, it could've been a she. But I thought... It didn't matter. Whoever they were, they were gone.

I was infuriated. This was the second time—no matter which instance of hooded figure he was—that he'd gotten away while I was chasing after him in my official capacity as a guard. I'd lost him again. It wasn't every day that a person in a black hood and cape mysteriously made their way through the castle. I should've been better trained to follow the hallways and corridors. I should have known them like the back of my hand to be able to anticipate and head off this bandit's moves. Yet I hadn't been able to.

I expected to have something to show for all of my time and effort spent tracking them this time.

With a deep sigh, I made my way back to my assigned patrolling route. As I walked slowly, I made sure to stay alert, watching for any suspicious activity. I didn't let my mind wander to the identity of the hooded figure but rather where he could've gone. At least my armor was where I'd left it and hadn't vanished into the shadows as well.

I probably needed to inform the commander or Thorn in the morning. If there was a bandit in the castle, someone needed to know. Of course, there was always a chance I would be met with skeptical stares and a good beat-down afterward, but someone had to know. Maybe I'd leave the fae bit out. If I did, they might take it more seriously.

At the very least, if I brought it up again, maybe the commander or some of the other guards would consider changing up their route and not being so predictable since this guy knew where the guards were stationed and what paths they patrolled. They couldn't walk in the exact same pattern, night after night, and not expect something, or someone, to figure out their moves.

I thought of the guard that had allowed Wyn and I to so easily creep into the garden that one night. If Wyn and I could do it, could sneak past or sweet-talk her way into the garden as she'd done before, there were others getting by with the same kinds of thing. People were beating the system, coming and going throughout the castle without anyone knowing, or worse, with someone knowing and not caring. Perhaps that's why the King was taken by surprise during the last attack. His Royal Guards had let him down. And continued to do so for no other reason than them either being lazy or selfish.

If I could convince the commander to let the guards switch their patrolling patterns, we'd have a better chance at catching the mysterious, hooded person. And that was assuming there was only one. The Veil only knew what or who we would be able to catch if we made some changes.

By the time I made it to the morning debriefing, everyone else had taken a seat and was awaiting the commander's instructions. If they saw me come in, they ignored it as if I was invisible. Even Allynna. I was so used to being met with snarls, smirks, and unsolicited insults that I was shocked to take a seat in a room without notice.

The commander stood from behind his desk and made his way to the front of the room.

"Alright, everyone. Did we have another uneventful night?" He scanned his office, looking at the various groups of guards who each nodded their heads.

I was nervous to speak up but pushed those feelings aside. My job was to protect the King, not to please the other guards with a report that lied and said I hadn't seen anything untoward. I raised my hand.

"Yes, Willow?" The commander pointed to me.

"During my patrol, I spotted a hooded figure creeping around the perimeter of the castle." I paused and glanced at the other guards as they groaned and snickered in equal amounts. I wouldn't let them get to me and instead raised my voice louder.

"I followed the person as they continued to easily make their way through the castle. They had no issue navigating the corridors, various as they are. As a matter of fact, they seemed very familiar with the hallways and doorways." No one looked at me except the commander, but I had his attention, so I continued. "The most disturbing part is that this bandit knew the exact moment a guard would walk past their location, so they waited until the perfect time to continue on their route, remaining unseen by all of the other guards."

The commander raised his eyebrows. "Since I don't have a prisoner report, I assume you didn't apprehend the bandit?"

My eyes shifted to the floor. "No. Unfortunately, I lost him somehow." And now came the part that required courage. An extra bit, even. I cleared my throat and stared at the commander as if I was a woman of confidence. "Regardless, I suggest that we change our patrolling routes and make sure everyone is aware of the potential of an intruder."

"Such a liar!" One of the guards shouted as a few others murmured. "The only hooded figure you saw was your reflection in the mirror as you left the Blade's office last night."

"Is screwing the Blade of the King not enough attention for you?" The other guards broke into laughter, not concerned that we were all in front of the commander.

"That's enough." The commander raised his hand. "You're all dismissed."

I stood, frozen, unwilling to leave my spot as the guards filed out of the room, some bold enough to hurl insults as they walked past me, though the commander had yet to move from where he'd stood near his desk.

After everyone was gone, I glanced at the commander. "You, too, Willow."

As I turned to leave, I considered whether or not to attend training. There was no way I'd show up just to be berated the entire time, so I chose instead to head back to my room and sleep.

I locked my door behind me and quickly removed my uniform. Falling face-first into my bed, I closed my eyes and allowed my body to relax.

Maybe when I awoke things would be better. Honestly, they couldn't get much worse.

# CHAPTER
# THIRTY

S enara

It turned out that when I woke up, nothing was better, and in a few moments, it was going to get worse.

I was at the edge of sleep when someone knocked on my door, waking me from a dream I would've liked to continue. It was about Thorn. Most of my dreams these days were.

But as the knocking was persistent, I lifted my heavy eyelids and squinted against the light. Outside of the window, the midday rays of daylight still showed through from a velvety blue sky dotted with fluffy white clouds. Thankfully, for whatever reason I'd been roused from my sleep, it was well before my next patrol was due to begin and hopefully, I would have time to return to my room to sleep before it.

"Come in." I cleared my throat and forced my body to sit upright in the bed, expecting Wyn to pop her head through.

Whoever was on the other side attempted to open the door but failed because I'd locked it. Groggily, I pushed out of bed and went to the door, snagging a dagger from my boots on the way, just in case.

To my surprise, when I swung open the door, Ronan stood there. I shuffled back toward the bed intending to lay back down as soon as he'd said whatever it was he came to say. As I sat, I stretched out the aches from not enough sleep and from lying too long in one position.

"Oh." He averted his eyes, his cheeks turning red with color. I was in undergarments and my chemise but no more. I'd been a soldier for so long I sometimes forgot that men didn't always see women dressing. His voice was a bit higher in pitch and tone than normal. "Would you like me to come back once you're dressed? I can wait outside."

"No, you're fine." Luckily, I had bathed earlier, or I would've felt extremely gross from all the sweating at the top of the tower, at the strain of being rescued, and the stress of not knowing before that. "Just tell me why you're here." If I sounded gruff, I certainly didn't mean to. Especially since I owed Ronan my life, but I hadn't slept long enough for it to do more than upset me that I'd been awoken.

"Thorn has called a meeting for all of the guards. He sent me to get you and make sure you arrive okay." Ronan ran his fingers through his straw blond hair, smoothing it away from his forehead. Was he nervous? I hoped not. I didn't want that to be how we were together from now on.

Careful to keep my back to the wall, I grabbed one of the clean chemises from my drawers and swiftly changed out the one I'd been sleeping in for the clean one, then I pulled on the pants that I wore underneath my guard uniform to keep it from chafing my skin. Ronan watched me the entire time, his gaze hot even though his face remained passive. Still, it made me feel oddly sexy, which wasn't a feeling I was used to. My cheeks grew warm as I watched Ronan watching me, and I liked the attention of gaze burning a trail up and down my body.

Taking a deep breath just to calm my nerves, because I was

unsettled by his attention, I focused on getting what I could of my uniform on and followed Ronan out the door. I still needed to find a new doublet and jacket, so all I really had on was my chemise and the big waist belt that usually went over the doublet. The lack of weight on my top was both unsettling and freeing.

Ronan was waiting for me, so I didn't want to mess around with trying to find a new doublet or jacket on the way, even though I didn't know where I was going. Still, he led me toward the training grounds, where a couple of other stragglers were being rounded up for the meeting. We were being herded into the ring like sheep in a pen.

I moved past them into the ring. I didn't want everyone waiting for me to arrive. The last thing I needed was another reason for everyone to blame me for something new—like being stuck all together because I was late.

I tried to blend into the crowd unnoticed, but no one, other than Ronan, would stand next to me. They all shifted to the side, essentially leaving a gap around me. That was fine, too. Some of them didn't take well to bathing and others rarely changed the clothes under their armor. And I just didn't need the others nudging me harder than necessary to prove they could.

Thorn was in the center of the sparring ring holding a wooden practice sword. He stood like a bronze statue, unwavering, unflinching, just watching the crowd. What was he up to?

When he was satisfied that all of the guards were present, he pointed the sword directly at me.

"What's wrong with Willow?" he asked.

I opened my mouth to answer that I was completely fine, with no issues whatsoever, even though it was a bold-faced lie. I'd been beaten, abused, ostracized. The treatment had its effects.

When a murmur rolled through the ring, angry and louder than normal, Thorn smacked the wooden sword against his greaves. "Silence!" He motioned with his hand in my direction. "Why do none of you like her? What has she done to deserve your ire? Your wrath?"

My stomach flopped and nausea washed over me as they all turned to look. I didn't like being the center of their attention, but I pushed those thoughts away. Now was not the time to allow my emotions to take over my body. Vomiting in the middle of Thorn's interrogation would only make matters worse. Although, maybe he could've done this without me. Maybe I didn't need to be present for this.

No one said anything, and they all averted their eyes. No one wanted to answer Thorn's question. And why would they? If no one took responsibility, no one admitting what they'd done and why they'd done it, they could keep harassing me and getting their kicks from my humiliation with no real repercussions.

"The only person willing to be within arm's reach of Willow is Ronan. I have to wonder why that is." Thorn pointed to the man who had saved me the night before from the tower. I was grateful to him, more so because now they were all looking at him and not me.

Thorn let his gaze roam the crowd before he spoke again. "This woman has been beaten and most recently was left on top of the tower with no way to get down." He shook his head and paced to the center of the training ring. "There's something wrong within the ranks of the Royal Guard, and I want to know what it is."

"It's because she's screwing you," some brave soul at the back of the crowd yelled.

Thorn stood taller, prouder and snarled in the direction of the voice. Lucky for whichever guard had dared speak, his identity was hidden behind the sea of faces.

Coward. They were all cowards who hid behind their armor and shields.

My palms were sweaty, and my heart raced. I appreciated the intention behind this charade, but all it would serve to do was to make them isolate me even more. Although he was trying to get to the bottom of the issue, I couldn't fathom what Thorn was thinking. Also, a bit of fair warning that he was going to put me on display and force them all to play defense would've been nice.

"Alright. I see how it is." He crossed his arms, still gripping the training sword tightly. "Any man who can best me in battle, no, who can stay on their feet for more than sixty seconds against me, may continue to be hostile to Willow. If you can't make it the full sixty seconds, then I will have won our contest and you will stop treating her as if she has the plague." This was a man confident in his abilities.

He glanced at me and my heart leapt into my throat. I more than liked his confidence in himself, and I was grateful that he was standing up for me, putting his reputation on the line. I just wished it wasn't so public... or going to make me the target of their wrath once this was done.

"She's a valuable asset to the King's Guard and was requested by the King himself." Thorn tapped the wooden sword against his leg.

"Is she fucking the King, too?" Someone yelled from the crowd. A few chuckles went up, but some of them were decidedly more nervous ones.

Thorn pointed the sword in the direction of the voice, his voice going icy cold. "Are you seriously willing to commit treason just to insult one of the other guards? Must I remind you that it's forbidden to talk about the King in such a way?"

It was touching of Thorn to defend me and try to make my situation better, and it wasn't as if I needed more reason to like him. Another voice called out from the crowd, "Would you do this if it wasn't someone you were fucking?"

My heart sank. This was exactly what I was worried about.

"The fact that you're asking shows that you don't understand me as your leader at all. Let me make this very clear to you. Anyone being treated like this would have my attention because I'd want to know what was going on. Any one of you could bring your problems to me, and I'd be happy to hear them and help if I could. Willow never came to me with these issues. I discovered them on my own, when Ronan brought them to my attention."

"She's probably fucking both of them," someone else called out.

"Enough!" Thorn roared. "From this day forward, behavior like this will not be tolerated. You have an issue with another guard, you report it to your commander or me. If you continue in this manner, with any guard, then you will be dismissed from the King's Guard and sent to the front lines. Those of you who trained for this specific position will not get any different treatment, and I don't care if you only just came from there or if it takes replacing all of you.

"We will be a cohesive unit, and we will protect our king, which is not something that's been happening since you've all been so concerned with who Willow is fucking. Now, fight me and continue to be cruel if you can stand against me, but if you can't, you *will* shut up. Or by the stars, I will have you gone from the guard!"

Thorn threw the practice sword to the ground and kicked it away before leaving the ring. After a very short time where everyone waited and no one spoke, but they all glared at me, he returned, carrying two longswords from the weapon's rack. "Stand against me for more than a minute, or draw my blood, and speak as you wish. But if you cannot, then anyone caught slandering another guard will be sent to the front lines or the city walls, *if* I'm feeling generous that day. Anyone caught using physical violence against another guard outside of training will be dismissed from the military completely."

Now it made sense. The outer walls must have been where the guards who attacked me were sent.

His words were full of controlled rage, which made the fire that burned for him within me blaze even brighter. It did leave me with one question, though. How would Thorn protect the castle if he had to send all of the guards out there?

# CHAPTER
# THIRTY-ONE

S enara

I crossed my arms over my chest. The last thing I needed was one of the guards who remained standing and watching our comrades go down like trees in a forest seeing my heart beating so wildly I couldn't control it.

There was barely any sound other than the grunts and hisses of pain as Thorn took down guard after guard. He fought with sword and fist, spinning and twirling, putting one man down and then the next. And they kept coming at him, each one stepped forward confidently in hopes of earning the right to mistreat me, like they thought since they'd seen some of Thorn's moves it would be easier for them.

When another one moved into the ring, I let out a sigh that earned me a sidelong glance from Ronan. Why couldn't they just accept me and move on? Why fight for the right to insult me? With one quick move, Thorn knocked the guard to the ground.

I had to give him credit where credit was due. He hadn't taken it easy on anyone. Yet he hadn't broken a sweat, either, so I had to wonder if he was very well trained or if they were merely poorly trained.

These were the best of the best, the Royal Guards. Thorn made it look simple taking out the soldiers, not even giving them a chance to use the skills they'd learned while training at the castle. He dispensed with these men and women with speed and skill.

When I'd fought him, I lasted for a while—a lot longer than the guys he was fighting now. And he hadn't gone easy on me either. His strength was mind-blowing. His stamina... inspiring. And memorable.

Allynna stepped into the ring, and Thorn's lip curled. I wondered if that was because of what she did to me or just because he didn't like her for some reason. She came at him with more speed than some of the other guards had. For a moment, she actually held her own, enough to the point that I was impressed, but he had her on the ground before she was even close to succeeding.

Everyone had faced off against Thorn. Only Ronan and I were left.

I didn't think for one moment that Ronan would actually be mean to me. After all, he had saved my life, but it seemed that Thorn wanted everyone to fight him. He had a point to make, and he wasn't backing down. He was the Blade of the King for a reason, and he wanted there to be no doubt what that reason was.

Now it was my turn to give Ronan a sidelong glance, and he returned it with a roguish smile, as if he knew what I was thinking. He was Thorn's friend off the field of battle, but on it, they were combatants.

Thorn gestured for Ronan to come forward, and Ronan obeyed without hesitation. He stepped into the center of the sparring circle with a cocky strut that I'd never seen from him before. Only Thorn himself had displayed that level of confidence until then.

Ronan moved gracefully and swiftly, avoiding Thorn's blows with ease. He punched and faded to avoid the returns. When he slashed with his sword, Ronan brushed the blows away, but Thorn was toying with him. I could see it. I could see the slight smile. He was playing with Ronan, and Ronan played back, though not quite as recklessly as Thorn.

It was then that I realized the two of them were the most evenly matched out of all of the guards. From the way they moved, it was easy to see that they were the only ones who really seemed to want to challenge each other, not only having fun but getting better while fighting each other. Sure, the other guards trained, but they did so because they were told to. Because they had to for their job.

Thorn didn't. And if I had to guess, neither did Ronan.

I'd seen them fighting and sparring a few times before. The two of them seemed to use it as a physical and mental exercise to keep themselves sharp and hone their skills. Just when I thought they might call it a draw, the real fight started in earnest. Ronan attacked with a slash of his sword and a knee to the abdomen, getting in closer than I expected. Thorn countered, deflecting the blade and capturing Ronan's leg. Thorn attacked then, smacking the hilt of his own sword into Ronan's knee, which made me wince. Ronan countered the second blow, twisting and kicking to free himself of Thorn's hold.

They continued to fight, each one trying to outsmart the other, but neither giving in.

Ronan held his own for a few minutes, but eventually, Thorn went for the kill shot—not a real one but one that drove the point home, and Ronan finally succumbed to Thorn's unmatched abilities. It was as intoxicating to watch as the castle's ale was to drink.

It was enough though. Ronan had earned the right to mistreat me by staying on his feet long enough. I doubted he actually would, but I'd been wrong about people before, so I'd reserve my judgment until he proved otherwise.

Finally, there was no one left for Thorn to spar against, so he turned to face the crowd. And they all watched him. "Now, I would like you all to watch Willow as she spars with me."

Blood drained from my face. I couldn't believe what he was suggesting. Had I not been on display long enough already? I silently pleaded with Thorn, staring into his eyes and hoping he'd change his mind. Hoping he could read my look and know that I would rather die than fight in front of all these people who hated me and wanted me to lose, wanted to see me fall.

Instead, he motioned for me to come to the center of the ring.

With no other choice but to follow his commands, I picked up the sword that Ronan handed off to me and swung it around a few times, testing its weight and balance before I met Thorn in the center of the circle. The guards wrapped around the outside, watching and waiting, probably wondering what the fuss was all about, or just hating me for taking time out of their day. Whatever.

Thorn gave me a quick smile and then turned his attention back to the crowd of guards. And if I'd known what he was going to say, I would've stopped him. "I want you to observe how fluid and instinctual her motions are." Which was almost a guarantee I would be jerky and stilted. "Try to compare her movements with your own. Where did you go wrong when you fought against me?" He walked in front of each man as he spoke, made the full circle then came back to stand beside me. "And what can you take from Willow's display that could help you in future battles?"

"Of course, she'll hold her own. You'll go easy on her,"

someone shouted from the back of the crowd. No one was brave enough to come forward, though.

I couldn't believe that anyone would question him after he'd just fought them all into the ground. But I underestimated the guts of these men.

"No. That's not true." Thorn pointed his sword in the direction of the heckler and laughed. "As a matter of fact, I'll go harder on her than the rest of you." He shook his head and looked at me. "And she'll stand up longer than any one of you."

He nodded at me like I had any control over it. I'd learned to fight because I didn't have a choice. I had to survive, and I had to protect Wyn. Learning to fight was my only choice. A necessity. But I didn't say it now, not while they were all staring at me.

Instead, I let Thorn continue, uninterrupted. "And, if you think I'm taking it too easy on her, call me on it. You can take my place to fight Willow. You'll quickly see that her strength and skills far surpass that of your own."

Thorn turned to face me. My heart jumped into my throat. What if I didn't fight as well as the last time we sparred? What if he was disappointed in me? I pushed those thoughts aside. I knew what was going to happen next. It was time.

Well, if this was what he wanted, then fine. We could fight. Again.

I stepped forward and raised my sword. The battle began with us circling one another. He was a patient fighter, although in the heat of battle, I thought he would be different—more fierce, more frenzied, and probably more ferocious. But now, he was waiting, sizing me up and watching my moves to see if I had a tell, a move that would indicate when I was on the attack. But I'd worked hard for years to make sure I was unpredictable and dangerous.

He slashed at me with his sword, albeit half-heartedly. I

responded in kind and we parried blows back and forth for a moment before he actually tried to strike. With a step in the opposite direction I dodged out of the way, which made him grin.

Finally, I lashed out, going on the offensive instead of just defending myself. The sound of metal on metal filled my ears as our swords clashed, the vibration traveling up my arm familiar and exhilarating, as the fight began in earnest. At first, it was a mere test of strength between us but soon quickened to an exchange of attacks and counterattacks. I could feel my muscles strain with every parry and thrust, but I didn't give up even for a moment. I was tired and stiff but holding my own.

The crowd around us was silent, watching intently as we clashed our swords in perfect time, back and forth across the clearing.

I was sweaty with exertion, but I was also elated to be stretching my body rather than patrolling the castle grounds. This was what I was trained for, and *this* was what I'd experienced so many times on the front lines.

To the crowd of guards, this was just a jovial practice session. To me, it was my chance to show them that I was more than they assumed. I was a warrior, and I wanted them to know it, to acknowledge it.

Someone shouted something I couldn't make out from a balcony above. Only a few people heard, but they gasped in response. Whatever it was, I couldn't take my eyes off Thorn. Not for a second, but then they called again and the words hit me like a ton of bricks.

A *Magic Touched* had been found within the castle.

A ball of fear formed in the pit of my stomach. Being Magic Touched, like Moon Marked, was criminal.

Without thinking I turned to the speaker, desperate to see that it was some kind of prank, while knowing that there was only one person they could be talking about.

Wyn.

My mind went blank, and Thorn took his opportunity to strike, hitting me with such a vicious strike that it ripped through my shirt, undergarments, and belt, splitting my skin as well as baring my own mark to the crowd.

I fell to the ground from the sheer force of the hit as well as the pain that lanced through me. My entire being froze, shock making my brain feel like it was freezing over.

All of it had been for nothing. Everything I'd done. Everything I'd fought for. Everything I'd sacrificed. None of it mattered.

It was all over.

I was exposed.

The thought made me want to curl up into a ball but I knew any slight movement would result in agony from the slash across my back. It would also draw the attention of the surrounding guards. Dread churned in my stomach as I tried to think of a way out of this.

Before I could do anything a hush fell over the crowd. Without needing to look up, I knew that it could only mean one thing. They were all staring at my back. Something that was confirmed when someone close by shouted, "Magic Touched!"

As soon as the words hit my ears, I knew I was as good as dead.

"Moon Marked!" another shouted.

The words were like a whip that lashed across my soul and suddenly I was the little girl abandoned by her parents again.

"Traitor!" someone else spat.

The word was another metaphorical strike of the whip against my soul. Each time someone shouted an insult it hurt. I would have thought I'd developed tougher skin by now, but apparently not when it came to my damn mark.

The gasps were like thunder, or that was what it sounded like in my head.

Before I could protest or try to explain myself to Thorn, several of the guards that had been watching landed on me, pinning me down. They put extra force on my arms and legs, as though I could do magic with my toes.

I didn't fight them. Couldn't. What would be the point? There was no way I could fight through all of them. Even if I could, I would never be able to get past Thorn.

Another set of guards appeared, clustering around me. They'd come from wherever they'd been on duty, from the tower and the ramparts most likely. All armed and all on the attack.

One of them shoved his knee in my back as another stood on my sword hand so that my fingers were pinched between the hilt and the ground. It was as though they thought I would erupt with magic at any moment and kill them all.

The joke was on them, though. I was only marked. I had been blessed—or cursed—with absolutely no magical abilities.

Not that it mattered to the King. I was dead either way.

# THIRTY-TWO

S enara

After being shackled and dragged through the corridors of the castle while onlookers gasped and pointed to the Moon Mark on my back, I was tossed into the cold, damp dungeon. Water dripped somewhere close by, but I couldn't see any puddles or spots where it could be coming from. Of course, I couldn't really see anything since it was terribly dark and the only window was at the ceiling of the cell.

Once my eyes had a moment to adjust to the darkness, I focused on a small figure in the corner of the stone-walled prison next to mine. She was curled into a tight little ball that was mostly skirts and loose, long red hair. She wasn't moving, and my heart stopped for a moment as I recognized her.

It was Wyn.

I ran to the edge of my cell and called her name. She stirred but didn't wake. She moaned, and I tried to reach through the bars to touch her, but my arms weren't long enough. "Wyn? Wyn! Wyn, wake up!"

As I called out, I could see that her fingers were darker

than they had been last time, before she'd made her magical potion. If we were called before the King today, the evidence would be undeniable. There was nothing that could be done to save us now. I had to think of a way out, but first, I needed information. All of the information.

Slowly, she pushed up into a sitting position. Even in the dim light, I could tell that her eyes were puffy and her face tear-streaked. She didn't seem surprised to see me there, which was concerning.

"Do you know who turned you in?" I asked, trying not to stare at her hands that were so dark they looked to be charred. The King would know as soon as he saw them that she'd been practicing magic. Everyone knew the Magic Touched had issues with hiding the tell-tale signs. It didn't wipe off, and it was too late to restore the glamour now, even if I could somehow figure out how to get her the herbs and plants from the garden.

She nodded. "It was Tower. He saw us that night and has been stalking me ever since, trying to catch me in the act." Wyn paused and wiped a tear from her cheek. "I thought he was my friend, and I tried to reason with him, but he—he—" She hiccuped a sob. "He hates magic users. He even snuck into my room and trashed it so I couldn't make any more potions before he turned me in."

Wyn was so trusting, so naïve. I hadn't done enough to protect her. I covered my mouth to keep from screaming with anger. Of course it was Tower. That guy had given me bad vibes from the beginning, and now he'd turned poor Wyn in? If I could get my hands on him, I would kill him.

She shoved her hands under her legs as if ashamed of their discoloration. "My glamour has faded, and there's no way to hide it now."

"Why didn't you tell me you were in trouble?" Maybe I could've headed Tower off. Maybe I could've directed him another way. Maybe if he was so problematic, I could have taken him out of the equation completely. "We could've figured something out. Together."

She sighed. "I was working on getting a note to you when the guards came and took me from my room."

"Oh, Wyn." My emotions ran away with me as tears spilled over my eyes and landed on the dirt floor.

We fell silent for a while, and I couldn't help but investigate my wound. I reached for my Moon Mark that should've been covered. Instead, I felt the torn fabric from Thorn's blow and my bumpy skin out in the open for the world to see. There was also the skin that was caked with now drying blood, and the wound itself, which stung but wasn't the worst I'd ever had.

If I wasn't so sure I was going to die, I might have been worried about getting an infection while in the dungeon. Between the dirty straw, the bucket for me to use as a bathroom, the rats skittering about in the darkness, and who knew what on the walls and floor, it was pretty much a guarantee. But there was no doubt that it was also a guarantee that the King would make an example out of us by executing us.

His hatred of magic and the magic marked was legendary. If this had happened during his father's reign, we probably would have been drawn and quartered. So in some ways, we were lucky that our current king preferred faster executions.

For the most part.

"I don't want to die," Wyn whispered as though she could hear my thoughts. "There's so much more out there, in the library, to read and learn. I just found a treasure trove of instructions and recipes, and now it's all being taken from me."

I wished there was something I could say to make it better, but all I could say was, "I know. I don't want you to either."

There wasn't anything I could do from here, and that was

the most frustrating part. I'd always been able to help Wyn before, even helped with getting her a job after joining the army, but this was different.

I remembered the day she'd gotten the job and how excited she'd been. Wyn was a woman who loved knowledge more than pretty much anything else. She strived to learn and thrived around books.

The job at the castle's library was her dream come true. And now we were stuck in her nightmare. Mine, too.

I shook my head. Now wasn't the time for self-recriminations or regret. Right now, we had to think. Of course she was more upset about losing the chance to learn more magic than the fact that we were going to be sentenced to death any minute, that was how she'd always been. In some ways, her parents abandoning her because of the magic only made her want to learn more about it. She was determined to embrace the thing that had made her life so difficult.

Still, the thought of us losing our lives over my inability to protect Wyn made me sick, made my stomach churn and roll. I'd never been one for romance, and neither one of us had family. All we really had was each other.

We'd grown up together. We were all we had, and without her, I would've been lost. If Wyn was the only one sentenced to death since she was the one *practicing* magic, I knew I would do whatever I had to do to earn the same sentence from the king. I would rather die with her than live my life without her.

We were left to languish in the dungeon for a few days, and my thoughts grew darker and darker. Each day we were denied light and were given only enough food and water to survive.

No one spoke to us or told us what to expect. Instead, in the afternoons, one of the guards was assigned to throw small and usually molded chunks of bread at us and a bucket of water was placed just outside the door of our cells. I doubted they assigned him to spit at us, but he did it anyway.

Obviously, we couldn't be housed together. No one wanted to risk us formulating some strange magical alliance. Little did they know, our bond was stronger than magic could ever make it. And only one of us had the power of magic anyway.

It was a dark afternoon a few days later when we were finally pulled from our cells. It had been days since we'd bathed or been allowed to care for ourselves, and we both stank and were filthy. With a guard on each side of us, we were dragged up several flights of stairs and down multiple corridors until we were brought to the throne room and shoved onto the floor in front of the King. We were shackled for good measure, as though either of us was in any condition to pose a real threat to the king.

It wasn't just his royal highness that stared at our disgusting bodies. It felt like the entire kingdom had come to the castle, likely invited by royal decree to watch the Magic Touched be punished. High born and low born had all come together in their finest clothes—some in gowns with jewels sewn into the rich fabrics, some in tattered and resewn breeches that were well used and worn in. There were even those who normally stayed at the castle doors, begging for alms and food, who were, for this special occasion, invited to join with everyone else.

There was color and riches, poverty and excitement all in one room, and after being so long in the darkness, it was all enough to make me sick. My senses were overloaded, not just with the color and sound as voices layered on top of one another, but with the smell as well. Perfumes, body odor, fish, salt water, even the smokey notes of the chantry members, all mingled together and made my head spin.

I couldn't control what I breathed in, but I could control what I listened to and looked at, so I averted my eyes. I stared at the King's shoes—also bejeweled and sparkling under the hundreds of flickering candles that lit the room—and focused on Wyn's breathing next to me. Her breath sawed in and out, as though she was moments away from a panic attack.

The guard who had unceremoniously thrown me onto the floor stepped away only to be replaced by the commander, the man who had been my direct supervisor. He shoved my face into the stone floor and yanked my ripped shirt wide open to display my Moon Mark for the King to see, kicking me in the stomach as he straightened. I hadn't realized that my chemise had plastered itself to my body until it tore away from my skin. I bit the inside of my cheek to prevent myself from screaming aloud. As I lay there I became aware of the sudden oozing of what I assumed, or rather, hoped, was blood going down my back.

"This guard is Moon Marked," the commander announced loudly enough for all to hear. A collective gasp waved from one side of the room to the other.

He released me and moved to Wyn, pulling her manacled hands up for the crowd to observe. They were still black, even though it had been quite a while since she'd touched or been touched by any kind of magic. "And this one, who works in the Royal Library, is Magic Touched." The onlookers gasped some more as they stared at Wyn's darkened fingertips.

Thorn suddenly stepped away from the crowd, and for a moment, I hoped that he was there to help us. Maybe he could speak for me, say something, anything, to make the King see that we weren't a threat to the Crown... or anyone, for that matter. I couldn't do magic, and Wyn would never use it against anyone else.

Instead, he looked down at me with disgust, his lip curling before he spat on the floor close to where I was pinned by the commander's boot, and bowed deeply before the King. "I must apologize for having let such filth into the castle and for allowing them—both of them—" He sneered at me. "To be so close to you, Your Majesty."

Thorn straightened after some movement from the King and continued speaking loudly for all to hear. "I advise that any new employee be strip searched before they are allowed within the castle walls."

I glanced up at the King. The portraits and statues I'd seen of him around the castle were overly flattering.

He was chubby and had probably never seen a day of work in his entire life. He had a softly curved chin that blended all too easily with his neck and only a smattering of hair under the crown that seemed too big for his head. It continued to slip down when he moved his forehead, and the man next to him had to continue adjusting it.

I had no real sympathy for him, especially when I took into consideration how many lives had been lost thanks to his greed and prejudice. He was a small-witted man who let his fear justify the evils of murder to him.

The King shifted his gaze to me and realized that I was watching him. His lips curled, and he flicked his wrist, signaling to his commander.

The commander acted quickly, stomping my head back into the ground, almost hard enough to break the bones of my cheek and nose. The terror that rushed through me in that moment was overwhelming. I swallowed back the bile that rose with the pain that exploded through my face so I didn't make matters worse by vomiting on the king's bejeweled shoes.

When I looked up again, it was just a quick glance, but long enough to see the King smirking. He was not a handsome man, by any means, but the sneer he wore made him uglier. Someday, I hoped he came across someone who was brave enough to tell him that for all his money and power, he would still die unloved and alone. The death of a poor man rather than a king, and he would deserve it.

He looked out at his royal subjects, all of them waiting expectantly for his decision. The King pretended to mull it over for a few moments, shifting in his seat and scratching his fat chin. But I already knew his decision had been made as soon as he heard the words *Moon Marked* and *Magic Touched.*

With a grin, he stood. "I have given this matter great consideration." In the three minutes we'd been in his presence? I doubted it, but I wasn't in a position to call him a liar. "I sentence both of these women to death by the Veil for their treachery to the great kingdom of Eaorin."

Well, fuck. It wasn't unexpected, but still, I had no idea how I was going to get us out of this. Or if it was even possible.

# THIRTY-THREE

S enara

Before Wyn and I could be escorted back to the dungeons, Thorn stepped forward once more, putting himself closer to the King than was appropriate. "Please, Your Majesty, as your humble servant, I beg for your forgiveness one more time." He spoke sincerely, in the same tone that I'd come to enjoy in the time I'd known him.

But now, instead of swooning for his attention, I watched in shock as Thorn pleaded with the King. The Blade of the King was practically on his knees in front of the entire kingdom, and that wasn't something that happened every day.

As much as I wanted to focus on what was happening around me, to hear and see, the pain from my nose had radiated to the back of my head, throbbing there. When I tried to watch what was happening, there were little black voids obscuring my vision.

"Please, Your Majesty, allow me to make it up to you for the graveness of my error in allowing these two into the castle." Thorn dropped to his knees in front of the throne. I could see the soles of his boots and only his boots from my vantage point, but I heard his knees hit the stone. "Please, allow me to personally escort the prisoners to the Veil. It is my duty and my honor to make sure they're put to death under your order and your hand."

I must have blinked because suddenly he was next to me, his cedar and spice scent filling my nose even through all of the other perfumes. He yanked me up by the back of my shirt and paused as he glanced in my direction. If hate was a sickness, it would have oozed from every part of his body. His lip curled, and he sneered as he continued. "I want to watch them burn as the Veil consumes their wretched souls."

He wasn't a man who minced his words.

The King tilted his head as he looked at Thorn, visibly moved by Thorn's words. He grasped his chest and looked to the Blade of the King as if he'd just offered his firstborn as sacrifice to the throne. "Yes, I agree. You need to do something to atone for the mistakes you've made. A twenty day ride through the cold winds and rains would be adequate punishment, but I'm not comfortable having you away for too long. I'll give you ten days total to get to the Veil and back."

That was half the time required for a comfortable journey. We would be riding at breakneck speed, or we would be unable to stop for rests or food. Surely we would die before we ever got to the Veil. And maybe that was Thorn's plan.

But he stood and nodded his head reverently before his king. The bastard.

The King continued, "I hope you realize that means you only have a few days to get there. And, since the Veil is more than a week away under the best of circumstances, you will have to rush, as well as hope that there are no bandits on your route."

I hadn't even thought to consider the bandits. And

certainly a king's entourage would draw a crowd of them. It spoke volumes that the King knew about them but still let them persist, ambushing people who had no choice but to travel the main road.

But Thorn was undaunted. He smiled, and I hated him for it. Where he'd once been my champion, he was now my executioner. And I couldn't forgive that.

"Yes, Your Majesty." Thorn bowed again. "Thank you for the opportunity to make amends for my sins against the Crown." He couldn't have been more regretful than he was. More agreeable to the King. He couldn't even have bowed lower, unless he went down to his knees once more.

The commander and two of the guards I'd watched Thorn humiliate in the practice ring that last day snatched Wyn and me up from the stone floor and dragged us back to our cells. We were thrown in without ceremony or another word spoken. I had to bite my tongue to stop from screaming in pain, not just at my face hitting the floor since I couldn't catch myself with my hands, but from my back as well.

The skin wasn't healing right, and I thought it might be hot to the touch. But I couldn't reach it, the cut jagged and awkwardly placed. As I laid in the muck, the guard came in and took off my shackles before slamming the iron bars closed behind him. His buddy was doing a similar set of activities with Wyn, who had been completely silent through everything.

I spent the night silently considering what I had experienced and seen. The King's decision hadn't shocked me, but Thorn's reaction did.

He'd been inside me more than once. Why couldn't he see past a marking on my back and realize that I had done nothing wrong?

Each time I drifted off to sleep, Wyn's quiet crying and sniffling woke me. And there was nothing I could do.

Her tears had started some time after the guards left and hadn't stopped since. I wanted to comfort her and tell her that everything would be alright. But that was a lie, and we both knew it. So I kept my mouth shut and allowed myself to drift in and out of oblivion. Soon enough we would begin the journey to our certain deaths, and there wasn't a damned thing we could do about it.

We spent three more nights in the dungeon before we were dragged out again and brought to the stables where horses were saddled and waiting. It was time to leave for the Veil, but there weren't horses for Wyn and I. We would be on foot, for however long it took to get us to the Veil.

Thorn had somehow managed to convince the King to let Ronan come with him, along with a few other guards Thorn had sparred with on occasion before I was taken to the dungeons.

We were escorted through the city in irons, and I was tied to Thorn's horse. Wyn was tied to Ronan's. This gave the townspeople the opportunity to throw food and other less savory items at us as we passed through. I recognized some of the people hurling insults, some I didn't know.

When we passed The Red Kraken, I forced myself to make eye contact with some of the people who had treated me so badly as a child. Though I tried not to, I looked for Grimsby, but he was nowhere to be seen. Probably still behind the bar getting the food ready for the day or something. I was both glad he wasn't there to see us being taken to our deaths and sad because I could use a boost of encouragement to get through the next few days. Whether it was true or not, I had to believe that he wouldn't hate me or Wyn for what we were more than he would just be confused.

I wasn't sure anyone would have predicted how my life would have gone. Living on the streets, serving the King, and now being escorted to my death by the King's most trusted ally.

As soon as we were out of the city, Thorn stopped and pointed in the direction of the river. "Go bathe."

Apparently, we were going to be sent into the Veil clean.

One of the guards raised an eyebrow at Thorn. "I don't think the King would approve of such kindness being bestowed on these prisoners."

Thorn sighed. He wasn't a man who took well to others questioning his orders. "Do you really want to be stuck smelling that for the next few days?" Thorn asked, pointing to me.

With not more than a shrug, the guard shook his head and conceded to Thorn's point, moving to the side so I could pass to the river's edge.

Thorn and Ronan met us on the bank. I hoped it was to unlock the irons that bound my hands and made walking harder than it had to be, but they stood back instead. I sighed as Thorn nodded to the water, telling me to go ahead.

I stepped into the cold, rushing water, a gasp escaping me at just how frigid it was. Before I could move forward any further, Thorn came toward me and laid his hand on my shoulder, stopping me. When I turned to look, he pulled away and laid his hand on the hilt of his sword.

He cocked an eyebrow, and I could've sworn he smiled. When I looked again, he was scowling deeper than when we'd been standing in front of the king. "Take your clothes off," he instructed. "They smell like shit."

Wyn eyed me suspiciously, but I shrugged and did as I was told. He had all the power, and what was a little more humiliation? It didn't matter at that point. Nothing did.

We struggled to remove our clothing, but since we were both still shackled, it was slow going. Finally, Thorn huffed out a loud breath. He pulled a dagger from his belt, and I shifted back. There was nothing to stop him from killing us here. The King would never know if he delivered us to the Veil or not. But instead, he cut our clothes loose, leaving us completely exposed. Wyn squeaked with shame and immediately tried to cover herself.

I moved to shield her with my own body, not caring who saw what anymore. Thorn's gaze tracked my every movement making it feel like ants were crawling all over my skin.

He and Ronan stood guard—likely from the other guards who weren't so honorable as to leave us alone—as Wyn and I quickly bathed in the icy water. The fresh, clean scent of the water was a relief after being in the disgusting dungeons for the last several days. I'd lost track of just how long we were down there since there was never really any light and the feeding times weren't regular.

Thorn stood, watching me as I attempted to clean my filthy body. There was nothing of the molten heat that I was used to in his gaze now. Just a cold analysis—his hard gaze probably driven by his disgust that he'd put his hands on my marked body and not known. I couldn't blame him. I was pretty disgusted that he hadn't known, too.

The only time I noticed any kind of emotion flit across his face was when he saw my back, which told me exactly what kind of state I was in, or maybe it was just because he could see my Moon Mark there. I couldn't tell, and it wasn't like I was going to ask or he was going to share, so I pushed the thought from my mind and focused on the task at hand, trying to clean myself off as best as I could.

When we emerged from the river, shivering and soaking wet, Thorn threw us clean clothes. The pants were thick, woolen material and the tops were made in such a way that we could pull them on around our chained hands. I tied Wyn's sleeves and she tied mine. Simple slip-on boots were tossed by our feet, and then we were given cloaks to cover.

Once we were dressed, Thorn turned to the other guards. "Having women on foot will be too slow for the deadline the King has given us. I'm going to push hard to get back within the week, if possible."

The guards nodded, apparently understanding Thorn's point.

Before I could object, Thorn lifted me into his saddle while Ronan did the same thing with Wyn. Then they slid onto the horses behind each of us.

I had a long moment of panic as Thorn tied the rope from the horse to the shackles around my wrists once more, the same as it had been when we were walking through the city. If we fell from the horses, we'd just be dragged along to our death.

Unless a small part of Thorn cared enough to stop his horse. I couldn't decide what was better. Hoping he cared, or accepting that he didn't.

What he felt was irrelevant as he nudged the sides of his horse and led the group through the forest, in the direction of the Veil. Being so close to Thorn was torture. I felt the hard ridges of his body, his arms tight around me as he held the reins, his legs tight against my ass, and his body pressed against my back. Every inch of my body was balancing on a sharp edge at the sensation of his breath tickling the back of my neck.

I hadn't expected to experience any kind of attraction to him on this trip, but with every step the horse took, another sensation rippled through me. I wasn't sure I could make it to the Veil without completely going crazy. There was nothing I could do to block out the feelings entirely other than ignoring everything except the rhythmic motion of the horse's stride.

Soon, it lulled me to a dozing state, and as I started to tip forward, Thorn's arm wrapped around me, holding me in place. With the slightest nudge he moved me so I was leaning back against him. I wanted to wake up, to hold myself away from this man who was so disgusted with me, but I couldn't.

I'd barely slept while we were in the dungeons, and apparently my body and brain now felt safe enough to completely shut down. It was just my heart that was suffering. How could I fall asleep on the person who was escorting me to my death?

# THIRTY-FOUR

Senara

The first day was long, and when we finally stopped for the night, I was relieved. I needed the break from Thorn and the constant assault of my senses to him. He was everywhere and everything. The motion of the horse, his thighs against my own, and his arms around my waist had led me to fantasize as I recalled what he could do to my body if he so chose.

Not that he would ever consider it again. He had looked at me with pure disgust, and that left no room for debate. His hatred for me was as visible as it was undeniable.

I shook my head as I realized, once again, that I had been lusting over someone who was escorting me to my death. Never had I been in a more ridiculous situation than that. Of course, this *was* the first time anyone had sent me to my death.

My legs ached as Thorn lifted me off the horse and set me on the ground, my inner thighs screaming at the sudden change. Both Thorn and Ronan quickly moved away from us, and I found myself standing alone. I could have made a run for it if I really wanted to, not that I would leave Wyn, but I didn't think that would be wise.

I was sure that this was some kind of test, that all of them were listening intently or at least noting where we were in case we decided to try and escape. At least the horse didn't hate me. What had Thorn called it? Strider, I thought.

"Thank you for the smooth ride today, Strider," I said as I patted the side of the stallion's neck. I was surprised that the horse wasn't gelded, most horses owned by nobles or that served in battle were in order to make them easier to handle. Not Strider, though.

I had to wonder if that was why he and the other horses always had some space between them. Still, he was pleasant enough to ride, even if my thighs were complaining.

Wyn had been silent all day, though mostly crying as she rode in front of Ronan. Every time I snuck a peak behind me, her head hung low and she refused to make eye contact with me. I didn't know if I was allowed to comfort my friend, but they weren't going to stop me. Once the guards were occupied setting up camp and Thorn and Ronan seemed to be in a deep discussion, I made my way to Wyn's side.

She looked at me with dark circles under her eyes. The circles weren't from being Magic Touched, she was exhausted. Crying for hours was hard on the body and the soul. I wasn't sure how Ronan had been able to stand it and not offer her solace.

I held out my hands and she laid hers over mine, just like we'd always done as children when we were scared and needed each other's comfort. We held onto each other. If the guards saw us they might think our behavior was suspicious, but in reality, we were just trying to comfort one another.

I squeezed her hands gently. "At least we're together, huh?" If I was going to go, there were worse ways.

Her lips barely curled as she tried to give me a small grin. "Yeah. Not so bad."

"This is just another misadventure, like the good old days." I nodded my head. I had to convince her to perk up, to pay attention at least. We needed to be on alert at all times. Maybe there was a chance we could break away, but if we allowed our depression to take over, we didn't stand a chance.

We had survival skills, and I needed Wyn to tap into hers. We'd learned a lot as orphaned children, fighting to survive each and every day. And maybe something we picked up in that time could help us see an opportunity to escape.

"Remember how you tricked old man Robins into following you so I could take the loaf of bread?" She nodded, but there was no smile accompanying it. "We feasted that night."

The loaf of bread I'd stolen was more than we'd had to eat for days, and we stuffed ourselves, unable to keep from trying to satiate the hunger that had grown within us. That was when we'd first met, when we were both desperate enough that we trusted each other even though we both had secrets. I needed her to remember that, to pull on the strength that was within her once more. Because if she broke, I wasn't sure I'd be able to hold myself together either.

"Hey! Stop that." One of the guards quickly made it to our side and jerked me away from Wyn. The big oaf probably thought we were trying to do some sort of magic.

We weren't allowed to touch, but I still stayed close to Wyn. We watched silently as the guards busied themselves setting up tents, building fires, and cooking dinner. I hoped to discern some small mistake, some breach in their vigilance that they might make. It would only take one slip-up to allow us an opportunity to outwit them. But if we weren't paying attention, we wouldn't see it, wouldn't recognize the opportunity when it presented itself.

Just as the sun set, Thorn stepped out of his tent. "Bring me the two women, as well as two bowls of food." It seemed as if he planned to feed us, which meant we would at least go to the Veil without being starved half to death on the way.

The guards shoved us into Thorn's tent so hard that we both almost tripped. Fortunately, I was able to catch myself first and caught Wyn in turn.

Immediately, I noticed that it was much nicer than I'd expected. It reminded me of the tents the commanders used at the front line, which, if someone asked me, I would have said was a little excessive for a trip to the Veil. But then again, Thorn was the Blade of the King, so maybe I shouldn't have been surprised. Especially after the way he groveled at the King's feet.

The scent of smoke and herbs wafted throughout the tent, and there was a woven rug on the floor. His bedroll was thick, with enough pillows that it probably took up half the horse that our supplies had been on. If I had counted right, there were three horses that were transporting things for us including the tents, bedrolls, food, and who knows what else. Clearly Thorn liked to travel in style, which was very different from what I'd come to expect of the man I met at The Red Kraken.

I didn't comment or ask. There was no reason to point out that his traveling accommodations were better than most places I'd slept in my entire life. Thorn wasn't the kind of man who would let me play on his sympathy. Not that I would try.

After we were brought to him along with the food, Thorn handed us each a bowl of stew and a spoon. "Eat," he instructed as he took a seat at a table that must have been able to fold up to a much smaller size since I felt like I would have remembered a horse carrying a table. He sat on the floor next to it, and Wyn and I awkwardly sat down on the floor opposite him. We were barely on the rug that covered the floor, but I was thankful for the small amount of protection that it offered from the cold ground.

He turned away as we shoveled the food into our mouths. It was the best food we'd had in over a week, maybe more, and definitely beat the stale, moldy bread the guards had thrown to us in the dark dungeon.

The warmth of the stew filled my body, and for the first time since we were arrested, I was relieved that Thorn and I had some kind of relationship. I wasn't convinced he'd be so nice if we were strangers. It didn't bother me that he didn't unchain us or even look at us, all that mattered was that we were given time to eat our meals in peace and not have to worry about someone attacking us at any moment. Even if Thorn hated me, he was still treating us with a little bit of respect and some kindness, which was probably more than I was entitled to ask for.

I wished I could've told him about the markings on me, the reason I had them—not that I knew—but maybe if I had shown it to him, let him run his hand over the spot, he wouldn't have been so angry when he saw it. Maybe he wouldn't have been so disgusted by *what* I was that he forgot *who* I was. Maybe he wouldn't have ignored the fact that I was the same person he'd fallen into bed with, that he'd respected and, hopefully in his own way, admired.

Once we finished our meals, Thorn called for Ronan. "Escort Wyn to her sleeping quarters and guard her. Make sure none of the other guards take advantage of the situation." He nodded to Wyn.

The thought hadn't even occurred to me, but now that Thorn mentioned it, the idea made the stew I'd just eaten feel like a rock sitting in my stomach. It wasn't that Wyn had never been exposed to that kind of thing before, after all there was only so much I could protect her from when we were growing up, but that didn't mean that I liked the idea of her being out there alone. If I was with her, at least there was someone to fight them off.

These guards were ruthless and without any compassion or good graces, I had seen that first hand. Through the dark of night, with only the moon to witness their bad behavior, they would have a prime opportunity to take advantage of us. Especially since they were away from the castle and out in the wilderness. It would be easy for them to slip from their tents in the middle of the night to have their way with Wyn or me.

The thought made my heart race and the food churn.

Ronan took Wyn's arm and refused to make eye contact with me. He was the Blade's friend, a trusted confidant. There was no way he would hurt Wyn. I knew he was a good man, and if Thorn trusted him to keep Wyn safe, that was good enough for me. It had to be.

As soon as they left the tent, Thorn stared at me, propping his elbows on the table and steepling his fingers in front of his chin, eyes unreadable but focused. I assumed he'd dismiss me, but he didn't, which made me even more nervous. I didn't know what to expect, but it couldn't be good. I braced myself for a long, drawn out speech in which he cursed my name and reminded me of how much he hated me. At this point, it was as likely as anything and wouldn't have surprised me.

Instead, he watched me for a long time before finally speaking. "Did you like riding with me today, or would you prefer to ride with someone else? If we had time, I would let you walk, but I'm afraid that's not an option."

I opened my mouth to respond, but Thorn held a hand up to stop me. "Take some time to think about it. I won't make a change again since the other guards are already on edge." His voice was firm, but not sharp. And I tried not to be offended. Maybe he wanted me to choose someone else so he didn't have to touch me at all, didn't have to be so repulsed by the thought of me riding in front of him.

As he stood and walked away, I cleared my throat. "I don't need to think about it."

Thorn turned to face me.

"I'd rather be with you than a stranger." I paused, wondering if I should continue. "Even if you're disgusted by me."

Thorn flinched at my words, but he said nothing else.

# CHAPTER
# THIRTY-FIVE

Senara

The guards kept to their tents and allowed Wyn and I to get a little bit of sleep. I let her take the tiny tent and took my bedroll, which was about a quarter the size of Thorn's, out so I could sleep in front of it. Ronan gave me a strange look but didn't say anything.

Truthfully, I wanted Wyn to get the rest, she needed it. Besides, I knew if I was out here, I could stop anyone from going into the tent before it even became an issue. The night was uneventful, much to my relief.

We rode most of the next day, but the closer we got to the Veil, the more distraught Wyn became. Each time I'd turn to check on her, her entire body was slumped over, her shoulders heaving with deep sobs. My heart ached for my friend, but I couldn't do anything except sit still while Thorn led us to our deaths.

That night, once we set up camp, Thorn called us back into his tent to eat. I knew I needed to talk to him about Wyn, so I waited until Wyn and Ronan had left. He hadn't explicitly dismissed me, so I didn't feel bad staying behind, and it wasn't as if Ronan had waited for me.

Taking a deep breath, I pushed to my feet and made my way over to Thorn, who was stripping out of the platemail he'd been wearing. My mouth went dry at the sight of him taking it off, leaving me wishing that he'd remove more. I pushed that thought to the back of my mind, though.

That wasn't why I was here. Nor was it a good idea for me to be fantasizing about a man who found me disgusting.

I didn't want the other guards outside to overhear, so I kept my voice low and soft. "Please, Thorn. I'm begging you. Let Wyn go."

Thorn spun to face me, his eye burning as he searched my own, as though he was trying to figure out what was prompting this. A slight pursing of his lips and a minute twitch at the corner of his eye told me he was frustrated at my request, but he didn't stop me.

"I'm happy to go to the Veil. I'll give my life. But Wyn has never done anything bad other than steal a few items to survive when she was a child." A tear drifted down my cheek even though I was doing everything I could to keep my emotions in check. "She's innocent. She's just fascinated by knowledge. Please, let her go."

Thorn looked at me with what seemed to be pity in his eye. His brows lowered, and he seemed to be steeling himself to respond to me, as though I'd have an outburst or meltdown of some kind at his response.

I could tell his answer would be no, butI needed to convince him somehow. So out of desperation, I spoke back up, offering him the only thing I could. "I'll do whatever you want. I know you enjoyed being with me before."

Thorn's gaze turned from sympathetic to heated in a moment. "Drop to your knees and suck my cock." He blurted the words, which was unlike him.

I was shocked that he'd agreed to my pleading.

As though sensing my thoughts, he added to his instructions, his tone more cool and calculating than before. "I haven't agreed to anything, but I'll think about it if you please me."

Without hesitation, I dropped to my knees and looked up. Moving my bound hands up his legs, I reached to undo his pants.

Thorn shook his head and turned to the side so I couldn't do as he asked. "Will you let me fuck you over that table?" He pointed to the small table he used for eating his meals.

I shook my head. "Yes. I'll do whatever you want if you'll free Wyn."

Thorn thought for a moment. "Does that offer extend to the other members of the camp?"

My body turned cold.

When I didn't immediately respond, Thorn seemed to latch onto my hesitancy. "Would you please Ronan?" he asked, eyebrows raised.

After thinking for a few moments, I nodded my head hesitantly. "None of the other guards, though. They'd be cruel and you know it." As soon as the words left my mouth, I felt Wyn's freedom slipping through my fingers, so I backtracked. "If you want me to be with the other guards, you'd have to let Wyn go free first." Hearing the words fall from my mouth made me nauseous.

I knew Thorn probably hated me, at the very least, he was disgusted by me. He could make this as unpleasant as possible, and yet I trusted him not to. Was that foolish of me? Most likely, but the heat that was in Thorn's gaze as he watched me kneel before him was just as intense as it had been before he knew I was marked. And for some insane reason, that gave me hope.

Thorn reached out and pulled at one of the ties keeping my

shirt closed. He didn't do anything once it was open, as though he was testing my resolve. When I didn't flinch or shy away, he undid another, then another, until the piece of material was barely hanging on to me. My breasts were bared to him, but I didn't shy away, didn't try to hide myself as he took in the view. Eventually he said, "You must be quiet unless you want an audience. Pull your pants down and bend over." The rough tone of his voice sent a shiver of need through me.

I did as he instructed, crawling over to the short table and pulling my pants down once there. A gasp almost escaped me when he pulled the shirt off my body as I bent over. My entire back was completely exposed to him, which was both thrilling and horrifying.

Having been with him before made this easier. My body still wanted him, still desired him, even like this. I was sick at the thought, but it was there. Besides that, I knew I had to make sure I pleased him for Wyn's sake. I'd do anything if it meant that she survived.

"You still get wet for me, I see." His voice was full of barely contained need, and I wondered if he was disgusted with himself for still wanting me like this.

The sound of the laces as he undid his pants and the rustling of the rest of his clothes echoed inside the tent. He took his time as I took stock of my surroundings, honing in on them. Anybody could walk in, and Thorn wouldn't stop them from watching, I knew that somehow. It wasn't like the times before, where he would have hurt anyone who dared watch me.

"Move your legs apart. Let me see all of you."

I slid my knees wider apart, allowing him to do what he wished. My skin rippled with the knowledge of his eyes roaming over me, as if he were licking his way up and down my back and over my Moon Mark—the mark that I'd managed to keep hidden from almost everyone for my whole life. The mark that had made it impossible to have a relationship, to have friends, stars, to even have a family. It was the reason my parents abandoned me, and now it was the reason I was being hauled toward my death.

A quick snap stung my ass as his palm spanked me. I grunted and fell forward.

"Quiet, Senara. Remember."

I nodded and bit the inside of my cheek. Not watching him and seeing what he was doing had my heart thundering in my chest—anticipation coiled inside me, ready to snap.

A single finger swiped down my slit, and a sucking noise penetrated the tent a second later. "Mmmm, you still taste so good."

My belly spasmed, and heat flooded my core, causing me to drip a little more down my inner thigh.

"You like that, do you? You enjoy that I still find you tasty?"

His hand on my hip was the only warning I had before I was filled instantly, and I let out a yelp. I bit my bottom lip halfway through and was able to muffle my sound. An instant ache formed as the tip of his cock hit the deepest part of me. Not one inch of me wasn't stretched and pulled from his quick and sudden invasion, and I knew he wasn't even completely sheathed within me.

Thorn didn't waste time. He was taking exactly what I offered him. He began thrusting his hips hard and fast, working himself deeper until his hips finally connected with my own. His balls smacked my clit and my ass slapped against his lower abs with every thrust.

Gritting my teeth, I used my shackled hands to hold myself in place on the table, his movements making me and the small table unsteady. I had to bite down on the fleshy part of my arm to hold in the noises I wanted to shout. His cock pleasured every inch of me, made me acutely aware of my body in a way I'd never experienced before I'd been with him.

Even though this was rough and hard, it was mind-blowing. He stretched me and stimulated my clit with each bottomed-out thrust, even if he didn't intend to.

I could also sense his penetrating gaze zeroed in on my Moon Mark. It made me pause for a split moment in thought. How would everything have played out between us if the mark didn't matter? If it wasn't on me?

His solid hands grabbed my hips and pulled me hard against his forceful thrust. He smacked that line of thought right out of me. Nothing could be different and to wish it so was a waste of time, especially when I could just be enjoying the last time I was going to have sex.

I groaned and buried my head against my shoulder as I worked to shut myself up.

Without warning, and taken by complete surprise, something bubbled and swelled in the pit of my stomach and burst into a kaleidoscope of stars as I came hard. My body tightened and tensed as convulsive shocks wracked through my body.

Thorn growled as he leaned over my back and, with gritted teeth, growled in my ear, "Did I give you permission to come?"

Shocks spasmed throughout my body, the earth moved under my feet, and white light faded my vision. I could barely remember my own name at that moment, and his words didn't seem to make sense.

"Did." Thrust. "I." Thrust. "Tell." Thrust. "You." Thrust. "That." Thrust. "You." Thrust. "Could." Thrust. "Come?" Thrust.

Slowly falling back into my body, I finally registered his words. I shook my head. Stars help me if his words didn't turn me on all the more, though.

Grabbing a fistful of my hair, he leaned back and brought my back into an arch. "That's right. I didn't." He growled and tugged on my hair as he continued to slam into me.

With the force with which he moved and with the pleasure-pain of the feeling of him tugging my hair, another release started to build inside me. I panicked. How could I stop it?

"Thorn?" I panted between thrusts.

He growled and must've shifted his position because his thrusts started angling me to lift off my knees, one leg coming entirely off the ground. The change in position stalled the build of my orgasm but not for long.

"Thorn?"

Faster and harder, he pushed and tugged. My body was completely bent to his will, and I loved it.

"Thorn! I'm going to come," I rasped.

A beastly snarl ripped from him. "Fuck no, you're not. You're going to wait for me."

He let go of my hip with his left hand and braced it on my shoulder. My hair was still tugged in his other hand. He pushed me down to lie directly on the table once more, and my cheek smashed into it. I had a white-knuckled grip around the opposite side of the table, as if I'd be launched into the stars.

"Thorn!"

"Wait."

His voice was barely audible. He was huffing like there was hardly anything left in him. The release had to be on the rise, but he was holding out and prolonging the inevitable.

Squinting my eyes shut, I tried to hold off. It was building faster and faster. I couldn't fathom having another intense orgasm after the one I just had, but the way he was forcing me to delay it was making it so it would be life-altering.

With no warning, hot liquid burst inside of me.

"Now," Thorn demanded with a growl.

I let go, and my body clamped down on him. His cock jerked and seemed to swell inside me, stretching me more than I ever thought possible as he filled me to the brink. The pressure of his release only made mine even more intense as the shudders still worked through me.

Panting, sweaty, and boneless, Thorn pulled himself out of me once the little quakes subsided. Fluid rushed from me, dripping and pooling on the floor between my legs, thankfully missing my pants.

Lifting my head to look over my shoulder at Thorn, I saw Ronan watching from the doorway.

Thorn lifted his pants and tied them together. "Did you enjoy the show?"

My heart cracked, and a piece broke off at the loss of possessiveness I used to hear in his voice. I'd grown to like it, and now I was nothing more than a means to get him off.

I could handle it. I would. Especially if it meant he would free Wyn. Still, I couldn't help but mourn what I'd lost and what could have been. Thorn seemed to have no such regrets or hopes.

# THIRTY-SIX

S enara

As we rode in a group toward the Veil the next day, the sun beat down hard as the horses kicked up dust that coated my skin as we rode. Thorn slowly hung back, waiting for the other riders to pass us by.

Once we were alone, he sighed. "What do you think of the Veil?"

I stared at him, his question catching me off guard. The Veil was too vast, too... something to provide a single answer to his complicated question.

Thorn must have sensed my confusion, maybe because I looked as perplexed as I felt. In any case, he clarified, "Do you think it's evil?"

Evil? What an odd description for something that didn't have a personality or mind or ability to behave in a malicious way. "No, I don't." I pushed my hair over my shoulder and looked ahead at the other riders. I didn't want Wyn to move out of my line of sight or too far ahead that I couldn't catch up quickly if she needed me.

When I was certain she was safe enough for the moment, I

shook my head at Thorn. "Nature isn't evil, so how could the Veil be a bad thing? Is the wind evil when it blows over a tree?"

People used nature for their own nefarious purposes at times, like the soldier sent into the dark of night and the fierce cold to patrol as punishment.

The cold was always the cold, and the dark was always the dark. They each served their purpose but weren't evil until someone used them as such. Or a woman who was burned by the heat of the sun when she put the washing out to dry. Nature wasn't evil, but deserved respect. While not evil, it could be dangerous. And that was how people used it against one another.

"So you consider it to be a part of nature and not a separate, magical entity?" he asked. I looked over my shoulder at him to see his head cocked and eyes slightly narrowed, as if he was trying to understand my thoughts on the matter. I hadn't given the words much thought, but as I'd spoken them, I meant them. The Veil was the king's weapon, and it illustrated my point.

Again, the Veil was a part of nature, and there was nothing evil about that.

"Yes, I see it as a part of this world. It's natural, and therefore it *can* be destructive." I didn't know if I had the words to make him understand. "But there's nothing inherently evil or bad about it."

It would take a person to figure out how to make it such, to figure out how to weaponize it against others. Since the Veil was older than I was, probably a lot older than that too, someone had probably already figured out how to use the Veil to their benefit.

"Hmm." He cocked an eyebrow as he considered my explanation.

"Plus, the Veil helps keep people alive," I added. To me there was nothing evil about that. As a matter of fact, it was admirable. Like all other parts of nature, the Veil needed respect.

"Please explain. How so?" He looked at me, eyes serious and face without much expression other than a squinched brow.

The Veil had saved my life, provided for me in times when no one else had wanted the job. Although I wasn't sure he would appreciate the story, because of what it meant about who I was and what had shaped me into the person I'd become, I started it anyway. If I was going to die, I may as well get the truth out there. "When Wyn and I were young, we would steal the items that people left by the Veil to charge with magic. We'd take the items to the nearest town and sell them."

A smile spread across my face as I remembered the excitement we'd felt when we found something worth a decent amount. People left all sorts of things—coins and jewels, talismans—and some of those things brought us enough money for hot meals and places to stay. I'd never thought of the Veil as anything but a part of nature until the king weaponized it and Thorn had asked his questions.

Back then, when we were orphans, we had nothing and no way to get anything. We were too young to be useful except in ways we didn't want. We were too old to be cute, and so we needed the money to survive. We did what was necessary.

I couldn't see his face as we rode because I'd stopped turning to look, but if he couldn't understand it, he could deal with me as he saw fit.

Instead of a reprimand, though, he snorted in what was most likely disbelief. Of course he'd scoff at the mention of magic. Based on the way he reacted to my Moon Mark—called me filth in front of the court and the King—he was disgusted by it and probably had no real understanding of the power behind the mark. Or in my case, the lack of magic.

Ignorance of magic and the celestial powers was wide-spread in the kingdom. He was the Blade of the King, so it didn't surprise me that he was misinformed.

But I wasn't here to inform him of the error of his thoughts. I wasn't even here to answer his questions. Pathetically, I did offer more explanation because I wanted him to understand, to not think of me as beneath him. "You know, there's a healthy underground market for magical items. There was a raid on it the day I arrived in Veilhelm, so it shouldn't be a surprise to you."

He grunted, but I had no idea what it meant. "Believe it or not, I don't know everything that my commanders do. Apparently, they thought I didn't need to know about that."

Of course, they had, probably wanted to keep the glory, or the kills, for themselves. People loved the idea of magic, even if the King had outlawed it. Over the years, they'd just learned how to hide it. Certainly the King and his soldiers couldn't be so naïve as to think that just because it was outlawed that the mention and use of magic had completely ceased. If anything, it made the use and practice of magic more attractive.

Other people hated magic and believed it was the source of all our problems. As such they punished anyone they thought had anything to do with it. Guards that were taught that magic users were evil and needed to be expunged from society probably wanted that glory for themselves.

I looked back at him once more and shrugged. "This may come as a shock to you, but the practice of magic is alive and well in the kingdom." I wouldn't go out of my way to tell him where—he still worked for the Crown after all—but telling him it was true wouldn't hurt.

"Why not use that information? You could have leveraged it to try and get out of this execution," he said quietly, the curiosity in his voice plain for anyone to hear.

I snorted this time. "And sentence people who were just

trying to survive to death? No, thank you. I caused enough death on the battlefield, I don't need to cause it in Veilhelm as well." I paused, bracing for the next bit because it was hard to say aloud. "Besides, the King would have never stayed my execution. Once he had the names or locations I knew, he would have just added me to the list of problems that needed to be taken care of. I knew as soon as anyone saw my mark that my life was over."

"And yet you managed to hide it for so many years." He spoke more to himself than to me, so all I offered was a noise of agreement. He was silent after that, and I liked that he was giving honest consideration to what I explained.

Against my better judgment, I decided to continue talking about magic. He could draw any conclusion he wanted, but he should at least have true information. "Magic is still strong, and it's the center of so many people's lives." They used it for everything from cooking to healing. "Although, it has changed slightly from what it used to be."

Slightly was an inadequate description since magic was fluid and always changing, but I didn't want to overwhelm him with details. Then again, maybe I'd been hasty in saying it wasn't my job to inform him. Maybe that was precisely what I was meant to do. Maybe if I helped him understand, he would change his mind about leading me to my death.

He was quiet for so long that I thought the conversation about magic was over, but I couldn't help asking one more question. "Do you believe me about seeing a fae in the castle?"

Thorn tensed ever so slightly before murmuring, "I do."

I turned to face him. "They have returned?"

He made a noncommittal noise. "Some believe they never fully left, and some believe they can move through the Veil whenever they like, that it's only our ban on magic that keeps them at bay and makes the land unappealing to them. Others believe that they are tiny creatures that we overlook most of the time and can use magic to hide in shadows and moonlight. Still others believe that they are monstrous looking men who are as savage and wild as they are magical."

He was quiet for a long time after that, but I could sense that there was more going on in his mind than he was saying aloud, so I left him to his thoughts. Eventually, he added, "Who knows what is real and what is an old wives' tale?" He didn't sound like he believed the last part. No, he sounded like he knew exactly which parts were true and which weren't, and I knew it had to be some high-level knowledge that only people like himself and the King possessed.

I waited for him to say more, but after a while, I realized that was all I was going to get. I shifted in the saddle, trying to find a more comfortable position. Or maybe I shifted because I wanted to feel the warmth from between Thorn's legs against my back. Or maybe it was because I wanted to be closer to him because that was the actual end result.

Even though he'd been hurtful to me, being closer to him didn't upset me. I didn't necessarily want to examine why, but it was the truth. It made me feel more alive, and if this was supposed to be the last of my days, being alive wasn't a bad way to feel.

"Stop squirming," he growled.

I wasn't sure if it was my imagination or not, but I could have sworn I felt his hips roll toward me, pressing himself against me and making me aware that our riding together didn't just affect me but him as well. Unable to help myself, I shifted again. We'd already been on horseback for most of the day, only stopping once for a quick snack and to give the horses a water break. My ass was starting to go numb, so I couldn't help it. At least that's what I was telling myself.

"Senara, I'm warning you."

I couldn't stop the little flame of hope that sprang to life in my heart. Maybe he wasn't immune to my charms after all.

"Sorry, I'm just not used to being on horseback for so long," I replied as an excuse.

"You've been tormenting me a lot longer than we've been on the horse."

His words made my face heat. "It's never been my intention."

"You don't have to intend something like that, it just is."

I wanted to provoke him further, to tease him to the point that he would be going out of his mind with need like I had been around him for the last few weeks. Before we could continue our conversation, I felt Thorn tense behind me, his legs tightening around me as a rider—one of ours—came against the flow and toward us.

This was one of the guards from the front of our group, Tailor was his name. He was one of the better ones. "Sir, there's a downed tree up ahead." A ball of worry formed in my stomach. "It's covering the trail, blocking it completely." There was a note of apprehension in his tone. I understood because this wasn't a rare occurrence. But common or not, a downed tree like this wasn't a good thing, and fear joined the foreboding in my belly.

My breath caught somewhere between my chest and in my throat. A downed tree positioned perfectly over the trail could only mean one thing.

Bandits.

S enara

Thorn moved forward slowly but with resolve. As Blade of the King, he'd surely encountered bandits in the past. Since I was tied up, there was nothing I could do but allow Thorn to lead us into danger. There was no way around the downed tree if we wanted to reach the Veil within the time limit given to us by the King.

The bandits had to be nearby. Healthy looking hundred year old trees didn't fall on their own, blocking trails and sealing off the way to the Veil. Part of me was thankful for the blockage, yet part of me was terrified. There were tales of those who had encountered bandits and been left to die by the side of the road. Slowly bleeding out or being injured and going septic was not on my list of preferred ways to die.

Of course, none of those people had been traveling with the King's Guard and the Blade of the King himself.

I was more than a little worried since I knew there was no chance I'd be trusted to fight, but Thorn refused to show any fear as he commanded the group that we should ride directly toward the obstacle.

The tree was huge and laid across the road, its top laying in the nearby lake. It would take hours to detour around it, too. I couldn't see where the lake began or where it ended. As soon as we were within sight of the root end of the tree, the bandits scrambled out into the open and attacked.

Thorn slid off his horse, somehow taking me with him, while Ronan did the same with Wyn. The two of them were in an attack stance as soon as they shoved me and Wyn off to the side. Within moments, Thorn and the other guards were attacking the closest bandits.

He shouted orders, directing his men to take defensive positions.

"Stay back here, out of the way," he growled at us before he moved forward once more to fight off more of the attackers.

I watched in awe as Thorn parried blows with a grace that reminded me of one of his swordsmanship drills. The bandits were fierce, but Thorn remained calm and collected as he deflected their attacks.

It pissed me off to helplessly stand by as the battle took place. I was a seasoned warrior and should have been helping, should've been fighting and taking the bandits down as well. If only I had a weapon.

Of course, if ever they gave me one, no way would I give it back once we overtook the bandits. I'd keep it and turn on the guards, freeing us from our death by the Veil. And that was exactly why they didn't—wouldn't—give me a weapon, even if I was one of the best fighters there.

We watched as Thorn and Ronan led the other guards against the bandits. This type of fighting was much different than the training they'd received back at the castle. These were seasoned King's Guards, but I hadn't seen them practicing their hand-to-hand fighting since I arrived in Veilhelm. They only ever spent their time swinging swords and spears around. This wasn't an even match with weapons, this was a scrap and the bandits were more than willing to do whatever it took to win and use what the trainers back at the castle would call underhanded tactics. They weren't prepared for how dirty the bandits fought. These guys spat in the guards' faces, bit their shoulders, and knocked their feet out from under them with quick, low-to-the-ground sweeping kicks. They jabbed at exposed pressure points and were more than happy to break bones and go for the guards' eyes if given the opportunity.

Just as one bandit was handled, several more would appear, seemingly out of nowhere.

The metallic tang of blood hung heavily on the air, and I tried my best to protect Wyn, to shield her not only from the danger but from the sight of the fighting and the bloodshed as she shook violently while the battle unfolded before us. She wasn't a woman who was accustomed to these types of fights —some back alley dealings, some rough housing, sure, but nothing like this. And I couldn't blame her for reacting so strongly. I'd been engaged many times in battle and still didn't like the sight of things like this. But the fact was, men fought and men died. Just because it was a fact didn't make it any easier to watch what people did to one another when it was a fight for survival.

The scene was gruesome. Bloody. And she shrieked when a man lost his arm and it landed near us.

One of the bandits noticed that Wyn and I were shackled and elbowed his friend, gesturing in our direction. I held my breath as I stood to block the bandit's view of Wyn. Part of me wished that she could use her magic and make all of this stop, but not only would that require a massive amount of energy on her part, but it would be extremely painful given the iron manacles we wore. Iron was one of the only things that could counteract magic, and there wasn't a lot of it in the kingdom, so it was usually saved for things like bars in dungeons or metal cuffs to keep prisoners in line.

Knowing Wyn, she probably already had an incantation memorized that would be useful in this exact situation, only she'd never counted on herself being chained and sentenced to death. That kind of thing messes with a woman's head.

The leader of the group stood on the branch of a tall tree and cupped his hands around his mouth. "Leave your gold armor behind," he bellowed. "And for your gracious generosity, we'll allow you to leave with your lives." He laughed because no one here was naïve enough to think that a bandit would let members of the King's Guard or their prisoners walk away with their lives.

The bandit who'd spotted us gestured in our direction, and the leader amended his offer. Well, he proved my point, anyway. "Leave the gold *and* the women."

Thorn snarled viciously and threw a dagger that seemed to appear from nowhere. It was small and gold-handled and flew end over end. It pierced the bandit leader's neck. Both hands instinctively moved to the wound, and he fell to his death at the feet of his followers.

The group of remaining bandits, which outnumbered the remaining guards, was thrown into a fit of rage. They doubled their efforts, jumping onto the backs of the guards, strangling them, poking their eyes, and any other tactic they could think of to take down the group that had killed their leader.

The guards fought valiantly, but there were so many bandits, and the skirmish wasn't looking favorable for Thorn. While the guards were occupied, fighting for their lives, four or five of the bandits seized their opportunity to rush toward Wyn and me. Thorn and Ronan jumped into their path, fighting them off as best they could, but there were too many of them. Two continued to battle, but the others and more behind them, surged toward us.

As the bandits reached our side, I tried my best to fight them off. Since I was in irons, the only thing I could do was use my chains to protect us. As I twisted and turned, I used the chains to deflect blows and knife slashes as best as I could. I yelped as one sliced down my arm leaving a long slash in its wake. I wasn't sure if the man was trying to kill me or subdue me. Either way, blood dripped down my arm as I continued to fight off the bandits as best I could.

The bandits yanked and pulled, jerking us to and fro, and when one caught a hold of Wyn, he ran his hands up and down her torso. Wyn screamed in terror as I kicked and clawed, pushing them away, but again, where one left off, another appeared. And then, pain burned in my abdomen, and I couldn't focus on anything more than the agony of it. I'd been cut. Badly.

And then Thorn was there, beating away the men with his sword and brutal force. He took the bandits down, one by one, until they were all sprawled out on the forest floor.

Once there was no one left to challenge him, Thorn turned his attention to me. He tore a piece of fabric from his jacket and gently bound the cut on my arm.

"Why are we wasting so much time defending them?" One of the guards stepped forward as he pressed his hand to a head wound.

"Yeah." Another guard spoke up. "You should just let her bleed, Thorn."

The other guards nodded their heads in agreement, some muttering under their breath that no one should save a Magic Touched or Moon Marked.

Thorn spun around and lunged toward the guard. "Are you questioning the King's orders?" He took the man by the throat and backed him into a tree. "Your king commands that we deliver them to the Veil. Is your plan better than your king's?"

His voice was as sharp as his blade. He was a man who was following orders and he expected nothing less from his men.

"No." When Thorn let him go, the guard lowered his head, averting eye contact with Thorn. "But how is the King going to know if they die at the Veil or if they die in a bandit attack?" Of course he wouldn't. I'd said as much, or at least thought it, and it shamed me that I'd had the same idea as one of these guards.

This time, Ronan stepped forward, his shoulders squared and his eyes set on the guard who continued to eye Thorn. "Are you comfortable lying to your King?"

The guard stared at Ronan as defiantly as he'd stared at Thorn. Lying to the King was as illegal as using magic and could certainly result in their own trips to the Veil if anyone caught them, regardless of their positions.

Thorn punched his hands onto his hips, and turned in a circle, observing the mass slaughter. "I want to move to a safer area. Then we'll set up camp."

It wasn't just bandits that went down but some of the guards as well. The horses had spooked and a couple had made a break for it, so we were all around worse for wear, just not as bad off as the bandits.

"Get your horses and let's go," Ronan commanded.

"What about the bodies?" Tailor, the guard who had warned us about the fallen tree, asked.

"We have no choice but to leave them. We'll pick our guards up on the way back to Castle Roth. Hopefully we find the horses along the way, or we're all likely to be riding with a fallen soldier behind us." Thorn sounded tired, world weary at the sight of so much death.

I couldn't blame him, it took a lot to get used to scenes like the one that had just unfolded. After time away from it, that tolerance lessened, making the viewer vulnerable to it all over again. I had no idea when Thorn had last seen a real battle, but he definitely seemed irritated by what had occurred.

"You want us to just leave Myers and Greenleaf here? After everything they've done for the Crown?" The guard who questioned him earlier demanded.

It surprised me when Ronan was the one who exploded. "Did you forget how to count? We're going to be riding with multiple people on most of the horses and one with some of the supplies ran off as well. We don't have room or energy to carry them right now. I'm angry that they are gone, that their lives were lost like this."

He slashed a hand through the air, and I couldn't tell if he meant that he was upset their lives were lost to bandits, protecting me and Wyn, or both. "We need to get moving and get somewhere safe before nightfall in case more bandits come looking. We don't know if these are all there are. There could easily be more, and I don't know about you, but I'm exhausted and just want to get some rest and some food." He ran a hand through his hair, like he couldn't believe that he had to have this conversation.

"We'll move them to the side of the road, cover them with what blankets we have to spare, and pick them up on the way back when there will be more room," Thorn commanded.

"All this for that?" the first guard demanded as he gestured again to me and Wyn.

"We are not having this conversation again, Kobal, now either get them moved, or leave and go back to Veilhelm. You are no longer needed on this trip."

The unspoken part of Thorns' words hit me like a ton of bricks. He wasn't needed because we were almost at the Veil, which meant my time was almost up.

# CHAPTER
# THIRTY-EIGHT

Senara

The remaining guards passed on the forest side of the tree, picking their way among the roots and cutting a path for the horses. We then continued along the path we'd been on for a few more hours until Thorn found an area he felt would be safe enough to camp for the night.

The spot he chose was a small clearing surrounded by a thick wall of trees. The ground was soft and blanketed with moss, providing us with a clear place to rest. The trees to the north created a barrier of shelter from the bitter winds that accompanied the night air while also providing enough camouflage to avoid any more bandits. It was like the place had been made for people to stop in, and I wondered how many before us had taken advantage of such a tactical spot.

Although night had fallen, the moonlight through the trees provided plenty of light for the guards to build a fire and cook our dinner.

Poor Wyn was weak and continued to avoid eye contact with me. I couldn't help but feel that she had completely checked out, accepting her fate to die at the Veil. Even though

I'd encouraged her to look for a way out, I wasn't sure she ever had.

Once dinner was ready, Thorn called us into his tent to eat. The guards led us to the opening of the tent and shoved us in, with a little more force than usual. Clearly, they were still unhappy over the fact that we were still alive and not dead by a bandit's hand when their peers were.

I supposed they had a point to make. They weren't happy that Thorn had gone out of his way to save us from the bandits. And even though they'd agreed to not lie to the King about our death by the Veil, they'd all silently agreed to make our next day or two a living nightmare. Or maybe not so silently. Maybe they'd huddled together, drawn straws to see who got to be mean first, and in which order they got to play their part in my demise.

Thorn sat in front of his small table, the same one he'd fucked me over, and motioned for us to take seats across from him. The rug was down once more, and I had to wonder again at what the point was of making the tent so homey when it was just being packed up the next day. At least on the front lines, the tents were up for a week or more before we moved on.

"Do you need anything else?" A guard stood at the opening of the tent, eyeing Wyn and me with a stare cold enough to send chills down my spine. I almost couldn't wait for all of this to be over. Being hated was tiresome, and I was at my limit.

"No, that will be all for now." Thorn waved his hand in the air, dismissing the guard. And then he looked at me. There were words that needed to be spoken, but I was too fearful and in too much pain, so they remained unsaid.

Instead, I carefully brought a spoonful of stew to my lips, wincing from the pain of my wounds. Even the smallest move sent shooting stabs through me, and I didn't want to gasp, or wince, or show anyone that I wasn't tough enough to survive the wounds just so Thorn could shove me through the Veil. Unfortunately, the wincing was out of my control.

Although Thorn had bound them tightly, they continued to ooze blood, and the pain was excruciating. In the grand scheme of things, I was going to die soon anyway, so I tried not to give the wounds too much thought. They probably hurt far less than the Veil was going to.

When we were little, we watched as someone was pushed into it. The scream haunted me for years after, and I knew it had done the same to Wyn. I just hoped that she'd forgotten it at some point and that wasn't what was on repeat in her mind right now.

The annoying man must have noticed I was still in pain because he said, "Lift your shirt."

I did as he asked, exposing the bandage to the room. He immediately moved from where he'd been seated eating his food to come and kneel next to me.

"Why didn't you tell me it was still bleeding?" he demanded. His scowl was almost terrifying. Maybe it would have been if I wasn't struggling just to breathe.

After taking a strangled breath, I braced myself for the pain that I knew would come from talking. "What does it matter? We're going to die anyway."

Anger and what was possibly regret flashed in his eyes. He ignored my question, which frustrated me.

"Wyn," Thorn whispered as he leaned closer to her, but not so close or so quietly that I couldn't hear despite the ringing in my ears from the pain. "Can you heal Senara? If we don't stop the bleeding, she won't make it through the night."

Wyn looked up from her meal, possibly shocked that Thorn was directly addressing her but probably more shocked that he'd asked her the question he had. "Oh, umm, I think so. But why would you want to?" It seemed as though she hadn't been listening to us at all until that moment.

I leaned forward, just as interested to hear the answer as Wyn.

Thorn seemed to debate saying anything at all. After a moment, he crossed his arms over his chest and looked every inch the Blade of the King as he whispered softly, "It's my job to get you to the Veil. I'm just doing what I was ordered to do."

Wyn and I stared at one another. I cocked a brow, and she tilted her head. He was lying to us or maybe just keeping a secret. It probably didn't matter, and both of us knew it, but I wondered what it was. That curiosity didn't mean that either of us was brave enough to ask, though.

Wyn pushed her bowl back onto the small table and carefully turned to face me, and for what was probably the hundredth time, I was thankful that all she'd suffered were some bruises and scrapes. "I'm not sure if I can heal her with the irons on, but I'll do my best." It was well-known that iron deterred magic.

"I'm not removing them. You'll have to figure out a way to work around them. All you have to do is stop the bleeding, anything else is unnecessary." Thorn pushed to his feet and moved to the other side of the table, still not settling. I wondered if it was because he didn't know what to expect from Wyn's magic or if there was something more to it.

She knelt over me as I lay back on the ground, partly because the pain was too much and partly because I wanted to give her better access to the wound. She hovered over me, raising her shackled hands. Just as she'd done before in the castle, she chanted words that made no sense to me.

I closed my eyes, waiting for the warmth I'd felt before.

When nothing happened, I opened my eyes to find Wyn wincing in pain. She was exhausted, and she was bound by iron chains. It wasn't a good combination for someone attempting magical healing.

"You don't have to do this," I murmured to Wyn so only she could hear. "I'm okay. I'll survive just like I always have."

Her eyes popped open, and she stared at me before shaking her head. "No, you won't. Don't lie to me, Senara. Not now."

We stared each other down for a long moment, but I nodded and let my own eyes close as she worked, knowing that if I had to watch her wince and struggle, I wouldn't be able to let her finish.

It took much longer than before, but eventually I felt the warming sensation in my arm and abdomen. After a few long minutes, the sensation subsided, and I was mostly healed. I lifted my shirt to find the skin on my stomach somewhat knitted together, a red, still slightly bloody mark meeting my eyes where just a moment ago there had been a deep knife wound.

Wyn collapsed into the chair, exhausted from the extra effort and energy she'd used.

"Eat, Wyn." I pushed the bowl of stew in her direction, encouraging her to rebuild her strength. I needed Wyn to eat it, though, and was more than willing to give her my portion to help her build herself back up.

She did as she was told and when she'd finished her meal, Thorn dismissed her. "On your way out, tell Ronan that Senara's bleeding has stopped." Why Ronan needed to know, I couldn't begin to guess, but I didn't understand very much of what was happening these days.

Wyn nodded her head, warily glancing at me before exiting the tent. I didn't know what she thought happened when she left the tent, but she was probably too exhausted to care, too worn out by fighting the iron to use her magic. Plus, her fingers and now most of her hands were black. There were even tendrils of it snaking along her wrists.

If any of the guards were actually observant, I might have

worried that they realized what happened. I could only imagine what their reaction would be to that. Not only had Thorn saved us from the bandits, but he'd let Wyn use magic right in front of him to heal me. They would be outraged.

Now that Wyn was off to bed, I focused all of my attention on Thorn. He hadn't kept his end of the bargain. After he'd fucked me, there was no mention of releasing Wyn. And if the stipulation of the agreement was pleasing him, I'd say that I fulfilled my end of the bargain.

"Now will you let Wyn go?" I asked, keeping my voice steady and my eyes straight ahead.

Thorn didn't respond, and I suddenly realized that he'd just witnessed her performing magic. That certainly wouldn't help her case.

"Healing is primarily all she's done with magic." I chose to keep the fact that I was unaware of what type of magic Wyn had been performing since she arrived at the castle to myself. There were things he didn't know and things I didn't know to tell him. Wyn had her own secrets like I had mine, and it was probably for the best that she didn't divulge them to me. What I didn't know I couldn't tell, and what she didn't tell me couldn't be overheard.

Thorn sat and stared at me for a few seconds before answering. "We should get to the Veil tomorrow. I'll make my decision tomorrow night." When he was done speaking, he looked back to his food before going back to eating. It wasn't quite a dismissal, but I got the feeling that whatever was going on between us was done for the night, which I wasn't okay with.

I wanted to demand a decision now, but if I knew anything about Thorn, it was that he only did things when *he* wanted to. Instead of saying what I wanted, I found myself uttering, "Do you want me to please you again? Would that help sway your decision?"

His gaze snapped up from his food, heat pooling in the amber depths of his eye. "Senara, you're on death's doorstep. Even I have some standards. As much as I want to feel you one last time, I won't risk undoing Wyn's work. You still need to make the trip tomorrow, and you're no good to me if you bleed to death out here."

My heart shriveled and burned inside my chest. All I could do was nod before I shakily pushed to my feet and walked out of his tent. We were done, and that was that. His only concern now was getting me to the Veil so he could kill me and move on. I tried to understand it from his point of view and thought about the number of times at the front when we were told that we'd be moving camp the next day. It was the same as the enemies I'd killed in that situation—I didn't think about them as people anymore, and I had a feeling that the same thing had happened to me in his mind.

To Thorn, I was nothing more than a task that needed to be checked off of a list. All I could hope was that he'd see reason and let Wyn go, even if he killed me.

# CHAPTER
# THIRTY-NINE

Senara

All that night and the following day, the only thing I could focus on was the Veil. I still remembered what it looked like—a sheer wall of magic. It could almost be mistaken for a cloud if it wasn't for the colors that danced over the surface. Purples, blues, and greens all shone from within somewhere. Occasionally, it looked like there were silhouettes of trees on the other side, but that was rare, and what could be seen mainly looked like branches or twigs, as though whatever was there was long dead. Life sucked out of it by the Veil itself.

It stretched as far as the eye could see, cutting the peninsula that was the bulk of the kingdom off from the land on the other side. Eaorin was essentially an island, or it had been until the King became unhappy with the idea and forced us to expand, crossing the Storm Strait and bringing war to the Qaennarian Empire.

Once upon a time, seeing the Veil and the gifts left at the base gave me great comfort. It was a reminder of the freedom I had fought for from the Chantry and the hope for my survival.

It also reminded me of Wyn and the first time we met under the shadow of the Veil.

When I closed my eyes, I longed for those days. But now, knowing how the King and his guards were going to use it, the impending sense of doom covered me as if I'd been buried alive, all of my enemies scooping shovels full of dirt onto my body.

When I was a very young child, the Veil had been a place of great mystery and intrigue for Wyn and me. Later, it became a honey pot of income for two street urchins. Once we no longer needed to steal the magically-charged items, we never returned to the Veil. It was probably for the best. What happened back then was best forgotten.

One of the last times we went was when we saw the man being pushed into the Veil in retaliation for something. We'd only seen the results of the argument, which was the push and subsequent death. The shimmery surface of the Veil had almost seemed to reach out and take what was offered, and screams erupted from the man that it consumed until there was nothing left but a wisp of white smoke marking the spot where he'd been standing.

Watching him go into it changed how we looked at it. Not only was it the source of magic in our world, not only had it saved our lives, but it was more than happy to take lives as well. That was how I'd arrived at the conclusion that it wasn't good or evil. It just was.

As we rode, my mind continued to drift back, and I wondered if the Veil had changed in any way or if it had become more powerful. My thoughts slowly drifted from seeing the Veil to being fearful of it.

I wondered what it would feel like to be thrown directly into the Veil. How much would we suffer? How long would we scream? I never heard of anyone who had ever just touched the

Veil or had a partial encounter with it and lived to tell about it. There was a reason the King had been able to weaponize it.

Even though my gaze was unfocused as we continued along the trail, my mind saw things that I distinctly recalled from coming here as a child. A once small tree now towered alone on a hill in the distance. A flowering vine that hung over the trail stretching from the trees on one side to the trees on the other that had once been thin now formed an entire canopy. The whole time, the shimmer of the Veil peeked through the trees in the distance as though it was both warning and welcoming me.

It was all familiar and suddenly terrifying. I didn't have the heart to tell Wyn that we were almost there. If she knew, she would wallow in her torment just as I was doing. Our fates were sealed.

As we traveled closer and closer to the Veil, I could feel the magic radiating off of it. The hairs on my arm stood at attention, and a soft buzzing rang through my head. It always had whenever I got close to it. The couple of times I asked Wyn about it, she looked at me like I was losing my mind, so I never mentioned it again.

It took all day to reach our destination, and once we were just at the edge of the area that had been abandoned to the Veil, Thorn motioned for the unit to stop. "I'm tired."

He dismounted his horse and lifted me to the ground. Ronan did the same with Wyn, and we stared at each other with tears in our eyes. This was it. Every heartache, trial, and battle we'd experienced in our lives had all led up to this moment, and I didn't want to die.

Living hadn't been easy, but it was better than dying. I didn't know that for sure, but I was fairly certain.

Thorn turned to face me. "Would you all like one last meal before you're given to the Veil?"

Last meal? I expected him to drag me by the hair and toss

me directly into the Veil without a moment's hesitation. I expected that he wouldn't be able to resist considering—even though he'd asked Wyn to use her magic to save me—since he found me so repulsive. Yet he offered us food.

Before I could respond, the other guards protested.

"We're here. The Veil is just at the top of that hill." One of the guards pointed toward the location of the Veil as if we didn't know, as if we couldn't see it already. By now, even Wyn was aware of how close we were. "The prisoners should be given to the Veil, and then we can have a celebratory dinner before turning around in the morning."

Another guard stepped forward, his hands on his hips. "Why waste the rations on dead women?" I couldn't deny that I was wondering the same thing.

Thorn stared at the ground for a moment. For being the commander, he'd taken a lot of unnecessary questioning of his authority, something my old commander at the front lines wouldn't have put up with. But he breathed in deep and looked up at the man who'd asked. "I'll hunt, and if I don't find anything, then we can give them to the Veil tonight. But if I find food, then the women are welcome to eat a last meal."

With that, Thorn turned and stalked off into the woods.

For a moment, I expected the guards to push the issue, to drag us to the Veil and force us in while Thorn was away, but Ronan stepped in front of Wyn and me, clearly protecting us before the guards could try anything. If I hadn't seen all of them fight recently, I might have been worried about them ganging up on Ronan, but he was a better fighter than all of them put together, and they knew that.

When they stood down, I sighed with relief. It looked like we might get a last meal after all. I wondered what it would be and if I would have enough time to savor the flavors before being given to the Veil. I tried not to get my hopes up, even though Thorn had implied that if he did catch something and we ate, we might not be given to the Veil until the morning.

While we all waited for Thorn's return, the camp was tense. The guards alternated between pacing and standing glaring at us while Ronan marched back and forth, not allowing anyone to get close enough to us to pose a threat.

None of the guards dared to speak or move forward, but I could see the wheels in their minds turning. They weren't happy with the most recent turn of events, let alone of anything that had happened since I'd arrived at the castle. I had been quite the bad luck charm for a lot of them.

Thorn returned after a handful of minutes with several small mammals, or maybe it was a type of large rodent, in his clutch, which was impressive. I couldn't see clearly around Ronan, who still stood with his arms crossed, refusing to move from in front of us so that the guards could get to us.

Once he held his bounty up for the other guards to see, Thorn pulled his dagger from his belt and set to work cleaning, skinning, and preparing each animal. When he was finished, he put them on sticks over the fire. This was a man who'd seen battle at the front lines, who had cooked in the rough, who was as familiar with eating in the wilderness as he was with dining in the King's hall. I had yet to find anything that Thorn couldn't do well. Other than having enough sympathy for two magic marked women to spare their lives.

My stomach growled in response to the smell of the cooking meat. We hadn't eaten since the night before in Thorn's tent, but I hadn't given my hunger much thought. Now, with the option to eat one more time, I couldn't wait, especially since it was fresh. The rations were good, but the idea of something fresh as my last meal made my mouth water.

Wyn leaned over and whispered in my ear. "I don't think I can eat." I looked into her eyes and saw the scared little girl I'd once known. I hoped to the gods that Thorn chose to release her. Night was falling, and I anxiously awaited his decision.

"Don't worry about it, Wyn." I leaned my forehead against her own. "Just enjoy what you can."

Once the meat was fully cooked, Thorn put some of it into the stew that he'd made from whatever rations he found in the supply pack, and the rest he sectioned off. Thorn invited everyone, including us, to sit around the fire. He served us all a bowl of stew and a hunk of meat, and I ate, doing my best to savor each mouthful. I still wasn't sure what type of animal I was eating, but I didn't care. Thorn had cooked it perfectly, crispy on the outside with tender meat within.

As I bit into the meat the juices dribbled down my chin, and I wiped the liquid away with the back of my hand. I no longer cared about manners or attempting to be ladylike in the presence of the Blade of the King. None of that mattered anymore.

Once everyone had eaten, the guards drifted to their tents, and Thorn disappeared into his own. I couldn't help but hope that he would summon me and tell me that he was going to let Wyn go, but it never happened. With Ronan on guard, Wyn and I curled up together near the fire. I was surprised when no one tried to separate us, but I figured that Thorn had left Ronan with instructions to keep the other guards at bay.

Wyn fell asleep as soon as the guards moved away, her exhaustion and lack of nourishment catching up with her, forcing her body to shut down in order to protect itself. In some ways, I was glad. I didn't want her to be up all night crying and fretting about what was going to happen in the morning.

For myself, I didn't think that sleep would even be possible. The tension over the last few days had been more than I was used to anymore, and I was left feeling drained. The warmth of the fire and Wyn's rhythmic breathing relaxed me enough that as I stared up at the twinkling stars and watched the moon emerge from the clouds, I fell into a deep, dreamless sleep.

The only thought that held on as I drifted off was that being so close to the Veil made me feel strange.

# CHAPTER
# FORTY

S enara
A loud crash of metal on metal—not like swords, though; the sound was more hollow—woke me from a deep sleep. It took a moment for me to remember where I was, but then the reality of my situation jolted me into an upright position. I looked around, wishing and hoping that it wasn't true, but in my guts I knew.

This was the end for me. For Wyn.

If the lack of communication from Thorn was anything to go by, he had decided not to release her, which meant he'd just used me. For that, I hated him a little. He had given me hope when he never should have.

The guards were up early, moving throughout the camp, tearing down tents, putting supplies in packs, and loading the horses. There was a lot of bustle and noise, and for the moment, no one was paying attention to us. When I looked out at the vastness of the land, I considered the possibility that we could run. Maybe we could get away and never look back.

But the soldiers were almost completely packed up–ready

to get on with our death sentence and head back to the castle, back to their patrols and marches, their ale and wenches.

It didn't help that Wyn and I were both weak. We'd been living on half the rations the guards got, and I was fairly certain that if I tried to make Wyn run, her body would give out long before we gained our freedom. Most likely, mine would as well.

Wyn stirred next to me, like she was coming from a deeper, darker part of sleep, and I rubbed her back helping her wake without startling her. "I think it's almost time to go." We were marching toward death, and nothing was going to stop our progress. The thought, morbid as it was, gave me a small measure of comfort. It would be finished soon. No more dragging it out.

Wyn sat up and gasped, her face pinched with sadness and grief, with realization and fear. "I thought it was all a bad dream."

The guards walked toward us and, as much as my pride didn't want me to, I shifted away from them. But they were strong, and we were shackled. The ringleader grabbed the chain between my wrists and jerked me to my feet before doing the same thing to Wyn.

Each second, we were closer to death. Closer to dying for something we'd neither asked for or, speaking for myself, particularly wanted.

I scanned the camp for Thorn and Ronan. They were near enough that I could make out their facial expressions but not their words. I could only tell that they were in the middle of a heated discussion, obviously not worried about protecting us from the roughness of the guards anymore. And the guards seemed to know it as well. They jerked us around, me especially, moving me this way and that, chuckling when I stumbled and spitting at me when they knew Ronan and Thorn weren't looking. One of the guards jerked me to the left hard enough it felt as though he pulled my arm out of my shoulder, a searing pain shot through me, and I had to bite my cheek to prevent myself from crying out.

"Ready?" one of the guards called to Thorn as he pushed Wyn toward me. Her shoulder bumped into my back, and we both stumbled forward. The ground was soft, and I slid a step before I caught my balance. I shot him a glare he deftly ignored.

He nodded his head and motioned for the guards to walk us to the Veil. I didn't want to believe that after everything we'd shared, he was so indifferent. Indifference would have been better than the fresh anger that seemed to be written all over his features, this desire to see me die. Unable to look at him any longer, I turned away. I stopped fighting the guards and let them push me forward toward my death.

Thorn and Ronan followed closely behind but didn't attempt to speak to us or even make eye contact. This was a sad ending in more ways than one.

The closer we got to the Veil, the more it felt like we were walking through mud, each step becoming harder than the last. It was as if my body was giving up, refusing to go further because it knew that obliteration awaited it. Whether they killed me themselves on this side of the Veil or they forced me into the unforgiving wall of magic to do away with me, the result would be the same.

With each step we took, the less certain I grew about anything. I wasn't sure if it was because of the magic radiating from the Veil—I could feel it as though it was washing over me in waves—or the fact that I didn't want to die. Maybe my body was responding to the fear against my will.

Wyn and I shared a knowing glance, both of us knowing that it was pointless to beg for our lives at this point. If the man I'd slept with–the man who had fought every other guard to get them to stop being cruel to me, the man who had been so enraged to see his friend touching me that I thought they were going to come to blows—couldn't be troubled to save me, if he was so disgusted by magic and that I was Moon Marked, then there was nothing I could do.

But before we could take so much as a single step closer to the Veil, I dug my heels in, pushing hard against the guards trying to urge me forward.

I turned and glanced over my shoulder at Thorn. I hadn't asked him for anything since I asked him to release Wyn, not until now. Hopefully, that carried some weight. "Please, allow us to hold hands so we can go to our deaths together." If I had to die, dying with my best friend in the world wasn't the worst way to go.

He looked at me, then at Wyn, and then back again without a word. For a second, he didn't move, then Thorn nodded in agreement.

As he reached for the key that was attached to his belt, one of the guards spoke up. "They'll use magic and get away! She could kill us all with the blink of an eye!"

"I'm not that powerful," Wyn mumbled.

Another guard sputtered as he realized that Thorn was seriously considering my request. "You would say anything to gain your freedom! She's probably got magic ready to go right now, and as soon as you release those shackles, we'll all be dead."

"Don't you know anything?" Ronan demanded from where he stood just behind Wyn. "Iron depletes magic, and it takes a while for it to build back up. In the time it takes for us to get the shackles off and get them into the Veil, she won't regain any useful amount of power."

That was a bold-faced lie, but he said it with so much confidence that I almost believed it, and it definitely shook the guards' belief in what would happen. Maybe if I hadn't seen Wyn use her magic while the cuffs were on, I'd be more apt to believe him, but she'd healed me; and while she couldn't perform great feats of magic without severe pain, it didn't sap her magic for any length of time.

Thorn cocked his head to the side as though considering the guard's point as well as Ronan's. After a few tense moments, he said, "Iron is too rare to waste by just throwing it into the Veil. I'm willing to risk it since it is as Ronan says and her magic won't regenerate for a while once I remove them."

Noises of outrage came from the guards, but Thorn just ignored it and unlocked the shackles that bound us. Even the ones who hadn't vocalized their opinions looked as though they couldn't believe what they were seeing.

His fingers brushed against my own, and the sensation of his hands against my skin was overwhelming—took my breath away—but he wouldn't even look at me. Any feelings we'd had for one another were long gone. Well, that wasn't entirely true. Not on my part anyway. I understood his duty. That he felt as honor bound to serve his king as he was repulsed by me. This was a mission he'd been chosen to lead, and I was the target. Anything I'd meant to him was gone. He lost all respect for me once he saw my Moon Mark.

Wyn and I held onto one another's hands, tightly because we were bound together in life much as we would be in death. Flashes of every time we'd clutched tightly to one another out of fear or using each other for strength ran through my mind. The thoughts would be comforting if I wasn't standing directly in front of the Veil. We'd had each other then, and we had each other now.

Neither of us were willing to let go as we were edged closer and closer to the Veil, the magic powerful and staggering. The scent of the air just before a storm filled my nostrils, and for a moment, it felt like the air around us was charging with some-thing I couldn't explain.

"Whatever is coming, we'll face it like the sisters that we

are." I squeezed Wyn's hand and forced a smile even though tears were rolling down both of our cheeks.

One of the guards scoffed while his friends jeered. "The only thing coming for you is death, one not even your souls will survive." The stories of the Veil were horrific, and they alone would have been enough to terrify me even if I hadn't seen it first hand.

Another guard spat on the ground near my foot. I scooted it inward toward Wyn's, but he wasn't to be deterred. "Death by the Veil means that you'll become nothing. Your souls won't move on to the next world."

If the next world was anything like this one, I wasn't sure that was much of a threat. Wyn sobbed harder, unable to keep her eyes open as her whole body shook.

Wyn and I squeezed one another's hands, holding tightly. Neither of us was willing to let go as we were edged closer and closer to the Veil.

"We'll never let the other go again." I reached out and wiped the tears from Wyn's face with my free hand. "It's okay, at least we're together." I hoped she found some comfort in that. I did.

"Just hurry up and die." One of the guards pushed me forward. "We don't have any more time to waste on you scum."

They were all there watching us, moving closer, and pushing us toward the Veil. I wanted to scream, to cry out at the unfairness of it. In all of our time, in all the ways we could've used magic to get them, we hadn't. Moreover, she hadn't. She didn't deserve to die.

Before the guards could object any further, Thorn nodded at Ronan, daggers suddenly appearing in their hands. I watched in stunned silence as they slit the throats of the guards closest to us before they drew their swords and attacked the remaining guards that we had traveled with to the Veil.

Thorn attacked his own men.

I didn't know what it meant, but I knew that no one was watching Wyn or me as we moved away from the Veil and closer to safety.

After that, everything happened so fast that we didn't have time to react. One after another, the soldiers fell. I watched in shock as each of the guards met a swift death at the tip of Ronan's and Thorn's swords. Blood darkened the grass, and the metallic tang of it coated the air. Ronan tried to wipe another man's blood from his face, but all it did was smear a red streak over his cheek. Thorn stood and looked at me, breathing hard.

Wyn stared at me, too. We were both stunned, frozen in shock.

Had Thorn decided to let us go after all? I couldn't read his expression, but his actions said a whole lot more than words would. I didn't need a miracle anymore. I just needed to understand what was going on. And I wouldn't drop my guard until I knew I wasn't going to end up skewered on the tip of his sword.

# CHAPTER
# FORTY-ONE

Senara

Just when I thought the coast was clear and I was about to go to Thorn to demand that he explain what he'd just done and why, another guard stepped out of the woods. He hadn't traveled with us, but he looked familiar to me. I certainly knew him from somewhere.

He had long dark hair that was braided back–though even the braid couldn't hide the curls that hid in his locks–and a strong jawline. He was about four or five inches shorter than Thorn, not as built, but clearly a soldier armed with sword, dagger, and shield.

"Hello, old friend." The newcomer greeted Thorn. He continued walking toward Thorn with neither sword or dagger drawn. I didn't know if the rumbling in my stomach was just the fear subsiding or the relief of escaping death, if only for a few more moments, but I stayed on guard.

"Good to see you." Thorn continued walking toward him until he met the man in the center of the clearing. They gripped each others' forearms and shook, a smile spreading over the stranger's face.

It came to me as I watched them that I had seen him around the castle, but I had no idea what his name was. And of course, neither Thorn nor Ronan addressed him by name, but I was certain I'd seen him before. My curiosity left me wanting to ask who he was, but faint music drew my attention away from the men who were speaking a few steps away.

I listened closely before realizing that I'd heard the music before. It was coming from the Veil or maybe beyond it. Soft and melodic, the music drew me toward it just like it had done when I heard it as a child.

Once, when I had first started coming to the Veil, I'd almost stepped into the wall of magic trying to get to the music. That day, it was lucky Wyn was with me. She'd saved me by pulling me backward. If she hadn't, I would've met an untimely death. The music was a lure—a smart one for whoever across the Veil needed deaths from this side.

There was something about the music that seemed to be calling for me. I tried to ignore it, tried to listen to what was going on with Thorn, Ronan, and the mystery man. But no matter how hard I tried, I couldn't block out the tune.

I glanced at Wyn. "Do you hear that?"

Wyn raised her eyebrows and shook her head, looking at me with worried eyes. I couldn't stand worrying her again after we'd been through so much in the last couple days. The music was unrelenting in its call, though, and I moved toward the Veil of my own free will. She must have recognized my reaction because she reached for my arm, but I shook her off.

I needed to find someone else who could hear it. Or maybe I was just going crazy.

When I turned around to call for Thorn and Ronan to ask if they could hear the music, I was surprised to find them both standing nearer than I had expected. Ronan was just in front of Wyn and Thorn was so close I could feel the warmth of his body radiating into mine, could see the flecks of gold in his eye, feel the intensity with which he was staring down at me. It was only when I made eye contact with him that the music softened and faded, reducing the draw I felt.

He looked down at me, and warmth surged through my stomach, but his face was blanker than I'd ever seen it before, making it impossible to read him. "Do you believe that there's life beyond the Veil?" His voice was soft, but not curious as much as there was something I couldn't quite place hiding in the depths of it. It felt as if he wasn't waiting for an answer, but as if he was waiting for me to realize the truth of whatever my answer was. It was like he wanted me to see something he was trying to show me without actually showing me.

Before I could respond, he laid his hands heavily on my shoulders and gave a slight squeeze.

He saved me, at the risk of his own career in the guard. It wasn't unrealistic for me to expect him to pull me back away from the Veil, away from the lure of the music, and into the safety of his arms. But instead, he pushed me directly into the Veil's glow. I cried out, screamed, flailed, and then there was nothing I could do.

I screamed again just as I heard Wyn screaming next to me.

He'd lied, and I was a fool–the grandest, worst, most naïve kind. This whole time I thought maybe I meant enough for him to save me, or that I'd at least done enough for him to let Wyn go free.

As the shimmer enveloped me, I watched as Thorn removed his eye patch, the scar seeming to come alive and the damaged eye behind it beginning to glow. Finally, the heat of the Veil touched my skin, and the pain I'd already felt doubled. I knew without a doubt that my life was over.

. . .

Don't miss the next part of Senara's story! Pre-order your copy of Cursed by the Veil today!

# Also by Helen Scott

Don't forget to check out Helen's other series!

Bound by the Veil

Marked by the Moon

Cursed by the Veil - Coming Soon

Blood Vow University

Vampire's Nest

Vampire's Fledgling

Vampire's Bite - Coming Soon

Sweetest Sacrifice (Contemporary) Cowritten with Zoey Shelby

Dark Knight - Coming Soon

Sinners' Secrets (Contemporary) Cowritten with Zoey Shelby

Cruel Kiss

Sweetest Revenge (Contemporary) Cowritten with Zoey Shelby

Bloody Princess

Hateful Regent

Cruel Reign

Broken Heir

Ruined Dynasty

Of Demons and Dragons

Elemental Awakened

Elemental Shadowed

Elemental Taken

Elemental Bound

Elemental Evolved


House of Wolves and Magic

Her Dark Moon

Her Fated Mates

Her Shadowed Wolves

Her Hidden Pack

Her Shifter Kingdom


Magical Midlife in Mystic Hollow

(Cowritten with Lacey Carter Andersen and L.A. Boruff)

Karma's Spell

Karma's Shift

Karma's Spirit

Karma's Stake


Immortal Hunters MC

(Cowritten with Lacey Carter Andersen)

Van Helsing Rising

Van Helsing Damned

Van Helsing Saved


Prisoners of Nightstone

(Cowritten with May Dawson)

Potions and Punishments

Incantations and Inmates

Curses and Convicts

Legends Unleashed

(Cowritten with Lacey Carter Andersen)

Don't Say My Name

Don't Cross My Path

Don't Touch My Men

Twisted Fae

(Cowritten with Lucinda Dark)

Court of Crimson

Court of Frost

Court of Midnight

The Hollow

(Cowritten with Ellabee Andrews)

<u>Survival</u>

<u>Seduction</u>

<u>Surrender</u>

Salsang Chronicles

(Cowritten with Serena Akeroyd)

Stained Egos

Stained Hearts

Stained Minds

Stained Bonds

Stained Souls

Salsang Chronicles Box Set

The Wild Hunt

Daughter of the Hunt

<u>Challenger of the Hunt</u>

Champion of the Hunt – Coming Soon

Cerberus

Daughter of Persephone

Daughter of Hades

Queen of the Underworld

Cerberus Series Box Set

Hera's Gift (A Cerberus Series Novella)

Wardens of Midnight

Woman of Midnight (A Wardens of Midnight Novella)

Sanctuary at Midnight

The Siren Legacy

The Oracle (A Siren Legacy Novella)

The Siren's Son

The Siren's Eyes

The Siren's Code

The Siren's Heart

The Banshee (A Siren Legacy Novella)

The Siren's Bride

Fury's Valentine (A Siren Legacy Novella)

Standalones, Shared Worlds, and Box Sets

The Sex Tape (Cowritten with Serena Akeroyd)

Spin My Gold (Cowritten with Lacey Carter Andersen)

Buttercup

Neve

# Acknowledgments

The biggest thank you goes to my husband for encouraging me to stretch my wings and try new things.

A huge thank you to you, the reader, for taking a chance on this book and allowing me the opportunity to entertain you. I hope you have enjoyed the first part of Thorn and Senara's story, as well as your first look into this world. I promise it's an epic one, and I hope you stay with me for the rest of the adventure!

Thank you to Bianca for an amazing cover and to my editor, Christine, for helping me get the best possible version of this book out there.

Finally, thank you to all my amazing author friends who listened to me go on and on about this book before I ever even wrote the first word. You guys rock!

# About the Author

*USA Today* bestselling author Helen Scott spends her time alternating between fantasy and reality. She likes to think she'd be sorted into Hufflepuff and would have been a Physical Kid from Brakebills. Her days are fueled by tea and cuddles from her four-legged kids and amazing husband in their home in the Chicago suburbs.

When not reading or writing, Helen can be found baking, enjoying a walk in the woods, crafting, or playing video games. She's a lover of sushi and K-Dramas and is convinced there is magic in the world if you know where to look. Whether paranormal or contemporary, Helen loves writing sassy, kick-butt heroines and drool-worthy love interests. She's the author of the House of Wolves and Magic series, the Cerberus series, and the Of Demons and Dragons series.

Thank you for reading!
You can also come and hang out in my reader group, Helen's Hellraisers, where you can find out all about what I'm working on, sneak peeks, and even exclusive giveaways!
Come and join the fun here!
Don't want to join the group but want to know what's going on?
Follow me on social media:
Website: http://www.helenscottauthor.com
Facebook: http://www.facebook.com/helenscottauthor/
Twitter: http://twitter.com/HelenM459

Instagram: http://www.instagram.com/helenscottauthor/
Don't forget to sign up for my newsletter for new release alerts, giveaways, and other fun stuff!

Printed in Great Britain
by Amazon

21857105R00179